Dear Mystery Lover,

With *Final Arrangements*, Donna Huston Murray returns us to the Main Line investigations of her charming amateur sleuth, Ginger Struve Barnes.

Even the most elite of neighborhoods has its malicious side. At the prestigious Philadelphia Flower Show, Ginger uses her green thumb and eye for red herrings to weed her way through another puzzling death. There are a lot of ways to hide a crime at the world's largest indoor horticultural competition.

Ginger's unmistakeably authentic voice has earned this series all sorts of praise, from the likes of Nancy Pickard, Gillian Roberts, and Jeremiah Healy, to name a few. If you like John Katz's Kit Deleeuw series, you'll love this look at the tony suburbs of Philadelphia.

Each Main Line mystery brings a great new addition to the cozy scene. If you haven't read the first Ginger Barnes mystery, pick up *The Main Line Is Murder*. And look for more to come from Donna Huston Murray in the near future.

Keep your eye out for DEAD LETTER—and build yourself a library of paperback mysteries to die for.

Yours in crime,

Shawn Coyne
Senior Editor
St. Martin's DEAD LETTER Paperback Mysteries

Titles now available from St. Martin's Dead Letter Mysteries

THE LADY CHAPEL by Candace M. Robb
NINE LIVES TO MURDER by Marian Babson
THE BRIDLED GROOM by J.S. Borthwick
THE FAMOUS DAR MURDER MYSTERY by Graham Landrum
NO ONE DIES IN BRANSON by Kathryn Buckstaff
SOMETHING TO KILL FOR by Susan Holtzer
CHINA TRADE by S.J. Rozan
THE SCOLD'S BRIDLE by Minette Walters
THE MAIN LINE IS MURDER by Donna Huston Murray
CUTTER by Laura Crum
MURDER IN THE EXECUTIVE MANSION by Elliott Roosevelt
NEVERMORE by William Hjortsberg
A VOW OF PENANCE by Veronica Black
ICEWATER MANSIONS by Doug Allyn
FINAL ARRANGEMENTS by Donna Huston Murray

"With Ginger Barnes, the headmaster's wife who can do-it-herself—fix a drain o[r]
out a murderer—Donn[a]
treat for all lovers of d[e]
   —Gillian Robert[s]

"A welcome new serie[s]
   —Jeremiah Heal[y]

"A new star rises in t[he]
love the mysteries of [?]
Diane Mott Davidson, y[ou]
series to your library."
   —Nancy Pick[?]

"Intelligent, wise, wit[?]
Barnes is the sleuth an[d]
   —Camilla Crespi[?]

St. Martin's Paperbacks titles
by Donna Huston Murray

THE MAIN LINE IS MURDER
FINAL ARRANGEMENTS

To Hench,

. . . tell you the rest at home.

Acknowledgments

My immense gratitude to the following experts and friends who contributed either to the background of this book or to its publication: Carolyn Bach, Barbara Bates, Susan Chapin, Joan Lindley, Harold Masur, and especially Kay Thomas. Also, Robert Tabian for interesting Shawn Coyne, and long-time friend Dianne Solomon for not being the least bit surprised by my good luck. Thanks, guys. I owe you all.

—Donna Huston Murray

❈ *Chapter 1* ❈

A bump in the road bounced Mother's chin off her chest and opened her eyes. She grimaced at the light thrown by my elderly Nissan station wagon.

"Good morning," I said.

"Umph," she replied.

When she seemed alert enough, I said, "Tell me again. Why are we doing this?"

She sighed. "You know Sylvia planned Alfie's retirement party months ago. I couldn't very well let her down."

I downshifted for a curve.

"That part I understand." For an early start, ordinarily Mother would have stayed overnight with Rip and me. The party meant I had to be at Mother's at 5:30 a.m., drive to Bryn Mawr to pick up her friend Winifred "Iffy" Bigelow, then hurry along to the Civic Center so Iffy could do an entry in the Philadelphia Flower Show. Apparently competition went on all week.

"What I'd really like to know is why your friend Iffy offered us maintenance passes."

"Because I don't drive, and I was sure you'd love to go."

I shook my head. "No, Mom . . ."

"I beg your pardon, you practically jumped at the chance."

I wagged my head. "What I actually said was, 'If you need me to drive, I'll take you.'"

Mother stiffened. "Well, I'm terribly sorry to put you out. I thought you'd be delighted to avoid the crowds."

I spread my hand in a mollifying gesture. "Yes. Yes, you're absolutely right. I hate seeing the flower show an inch at a time. But what I'm trying to find out here is exactly why we were offered not one but two maintenance passes. People who belong there have trouble getting them. Why did this 'Iffy' person offer them to you?"

"What do you mean, why?"

"Why? W-H-Y. Why?"

"Her car is in the shop."

I braked a little hard for a red light. "Let me put this another way. Who the hell is Iffy Bigelow?"

Mother blinked. "She came to the funeral." I understood her to mean my father's funeral since it was the only one we had attended together in the last decade.

"Mom, nobody said more than a sentence to us that day. Sometimes less."

"You'll remember," she told me confidently. She recalled details with ease. Since she considered me to be the new-improved product of Cynthia and Donald Struve, naturally I would retain whatever she had and more. "Iffy Bigelow," she prompted. "We were in high school together."

Surely I wasn't expected to remember that! I stretched to make some connection, if only to finish the conversation.

"Is her husband named Arthur, by any chance?" A few years back I took an investment course from a dry stick named Arthur Bigelow, until I caught on that you needed *money* to make money. Discerning my frustration, Arthur had invited me for coffee and suggested a couple ways to start a college fund for the kids. I thanked him, and we parted company. Nice enough guy, but stiff as starch.

"That's right." Mother gloated.

I tempered my astonishment. "Small world," I said, "but I still don't remember Iffy."

"You will," Mother assured me. "You will."

While my car coughed itself out in the driveway of the Bigelow's hulking brick Tudor, I squinted at the two women silhouetted by the front door light. Mother's friend had to be the short lump with the hat, but all I recognized was the set of her shoulders and the way her purse hung from her fist. She was loaded for bear.

"Oh, good," Mother remarked. "I thought we might have to pick up Julia."

"Julia who?"

"Iffy's niece. We'll be looking after the girl while Iffy's busy with her entries."

Before I could press for more, Mother began relocating to the back seat, leaving the amenities to me. I rolled my eyes and climbed out into the chilled March air.

Iffy Bigelow shouted, "You're late," with a voice that could singe paint.

I glanced at my watch. Five fifty-five a.m. According to Mother's schedule, we were early. When I got close enough to speak normally, I tried to correct the injustice.

"We're okay by me. Should we have synchronized watches?"

"Don't get flip with me, young woman." Mrs. Bigelow ignored my outstretched hand, so I swung it toward the younger woman cowering behind her.

"Ginger Struve Barnes," I said, maintaining my friendly expression. Not really the "girl" mother described, like me Iffy's niece was at least thirty, yet her ingenuous expression spoke of a sheltered life.

"Julia Stone," she mumbled, hesitantly accepting my handshake. Little puffs of breath condensed and dispersed around us.

I willed a little extra kindness onto my own face; adults just don't look that uncomplicated without a reason. Lord knows there were complications and undertones written all over her aunt.

Winifred Bigelow tapped a foot, and Julia jumped to retrieve a cardboard box from the stoop.

"Julia, give that to her," Iffy snapped, efficiently insulting Julia and reducing me to a flunky with one succinct phrase.

I accepted the carton with a sympathetic smile.

Meanwhile, Iffy collected a bulky potted plant off the step. Its leaves were a fistful of splayed green belts. From the center rose a tall stalk sporting a pompon of orange trumpets.

"It's a clivia," Iffy announced protectively, adding, "in perfect condition," as she cringed away from her niece.

Julia clutched her coat closed at the throat. We all paraded toward Mother, who wiggled her fingers hello through the rear window.

"Julia! Open that back door," Iffy barked.

I practiced projecting saintly patience as I slid the open carton of arrangement equipment and carefully wrapped plant materials into the rear of the car.

Julia leaned close. "I'm just out of the hospital," she confided with pride. "My psychiatrist said I was ready for an outing."

My eyes widened, and my smile went stiff. Clinical depression? Paranoia? Schizophrenia? You can't help wondering, but you don't dare ask.

"Congratulations," I said, hanging onto that smile.

We each climbed into the Nissan thinking our own thoughts.

"No expressways," commanded Mrs. Winifred Bigelow. A clue perhaps to why she felt we were late and I thought we were early?

I risked a questioning glance. No wink, no joke. She actually wanted a whistle-stop tour of the Main Line. This was developing into quite a morning.

"You're the boss," I said.

I heard a rustling in the back seat as I backed the car into the street. Since Julia was quietly staring out the window, I surmised that Mother sensed the tension between Iffy and me and was itching to diffuse it.

"All set, are we?" she asked, sounding ominously like a kindergarten teacher.

Fortunately, Iffy's mind was elsewhere. "Cynthia. Have you seen a paper yet?" she asked my mother. "Ours didn't come."

"Sorry, dear."

A raised eyebrow queried me.

I turned onto Lancaster aiming for the city fifteen miles away. "Not yet," I answered. At 4:30 when my alarm went off, not even the birds were up.

"Coverage has been deplorable," Iffy complained. "They had a few photos last Saturday, a minimal spread for Sunday's official opening, and then scarcely anything the rest of the week. The largest indoor show in the world, not to mention the most prestigious, and they treat it like, like it was nothing."

"Well, it's Friday, dear. Maybe they ran out of things to say," Mother suggested.

I might have added "years ago." The spreads I'd seen on the annual nine-day event reminded me of the desperate human interest pieces they did for a recent Olympics.

I steered around a van that was turning left into Dunkin' Donuts. "Did they ever interview you?" I asked Iffy.

Iffy bristled, so apparently not.

"Now that would be a good article," Mother enthused. "Did I tell you Iffy won the Pennsylvania Horticulture Society's Grand Sweepstakes trophy last year? She earned more points in more categories than anybody else. Isn't that right, dear?" Iffy didn't respond, so Mother just kept talking. "She's making a run at it again this year, too."

Under her breath Iffy muttered, "Watch out for that pothole."

"Tell Ginger about that day when what's-his-name approved your container," Mother urged her friend.

"She doesn't want to hear that." Iffy pressed her lips tight.

"Oh yes she does." Mother punched my sleeve.

"What happened?" I asked. Julia seemed to be asleep.

"It was years ago," Iffy said dismissively.

"Yes?" I prompted. Much more of this and I'd be asleep, too.

Winifred Bigelow sighed and gazed through the windshield as if viewing a film she'd seen once too often. "My garden club was doing a table arrangement that year—do you know anything about them?"

I did, from a friend involved with the show. They were simulated dining rooms with only a back wall, five or six spaced side by side of an aisle. Different decors, but always with a floral arrangement as the focal point. Because of the expense, I was under the impression that they were mostly prepared by garden clubs with about sixty members.

Iffy accepted my nod. "Well, I found a container that reflected the lines of a chair in the painting we had for our back wall. Miriam Snelling insisted that we use an atrocious antique vat. We argued—that is the five of us on the committee—until I noticed the chairman of the show walking by—"

"Gin," Mother interrupted. "You have to understand the power this guy had. His endorsement could make or break a career."

"—and I invited him over to give us his opinion." Iffy didn't care for the interruption, even if it did enhance her story.

"What a chance you took!" Mother exclaimed.

"Yes."

"He picked your container?" I asked.

"Yes."

"He raved about it, Gin," Mother interjected. " 'Look

how it reflects the lines of that chair,' he said. 'It's perfect.'
Made Iffy's reputation right on the spot. Isn't that right?''

"Yes. That's true."

"Really?"

Iffy still seemed disinclined to speak to me, so Mother
elaborated. "That's right, Gin. One minute she's the token
newcomer on the committee and the next minute she's an
authority."

"Your club win?" I asked.

Iffy snorted. "Miriam's gladiolus overpowered the
design. I told them how to fix it for Wednesday—tables are
judged Saturday and again Wednesday—but they botched
it." *I* found the container, but *they* botched it. Yay team.

"You still in a club?" The question was out of my mouth
before I realized it might not have been tactful.

Winifred Bigelow looked at me hard. Not only had she
caught my implied criticism of her people skills, my name
was now in her permanent ledger. "Not at the present," she
replied. Then she added, "Watch the road."

I gave her a glance. She returned a scowl, and I realized
this whole conversation had been meant to humor my
mother. Iffy still blamed me for being late and wanted me
to know I was not forgiven.

I spoke to Mother over my shoulder. "I had no idea
people take the show so seriously." This, at least, was quite
true. Naively, I always thought the perfection viewed by the
public was of the whimsical, "Oh, your azalea is lovely—
why don't you enter it?" variety. But apparently Iffy and
her ilk were not the dabblers I had imagined. Rather they
were deadly serious competitors clawing their way up a
social lattice I never knew existed.

My token display of interest delighted Mother. Leaning
enthusiastically toward my ear, she told me, "One time
Arthur wanted to take a little vacation a whole six months
before the show, but Iffy refused to leave her plants. Isn't
that right, dear?" Poor Arthur.

Iffy snorted. "Lots of people stay home to get ready."

"And spend any amount it takes to win," Mother added.

Iffy sighed impatiently. "Of course. There aren't any limits. You can hire an army of professionals, or you can do it yourself. The judges only care about the final result."

Mother was into it. "Once they drove some flowers four hundred miles across Africa on top of a bus at night just to fly them to Philadelphia for an exhibit. And they've hand-carried specimens down from the volcanoes of Hawaii, too. I saw it in the paper."

"Not this year," Iffy muttered.

Minutes later, with dawn's early light defining the hotels and apartment buildings, we arrived at the western border of Philadelphia. Mostly for the sake of the clivia, I bumped across City Line Avenue on yellow rather than stopping short. Julia woke up, and Mrs. Bigelow responded with a tight-lipped glower.

Naturally, Mother felt it necessary to draw Julia out of her fog and into her circle of imagined warmth. "You're probably wondering why Ginger is driving instead of me," she said. Iffy's chin jerked.

"The simple truth is I lost my license." Dramatic pause.

"Lost it?" Julia repeated.

"Can't find it anywhere."

The young woman's self-conscious giggle was just what I needed to hear. Mother, too, because I glimpsed her smug grin in my mirror.

The street soon ducked under an overpass and set us onto the tree-lined West River Drive. To our left across a brief swath of dead grass lay the Schuylkill River, black and swollen from last night's heavy rain.

While we waited for a traffic light, a trash truck lumbered across a deep brick gutter to turn left in front of us. For a moment the top-heavy vehicle wobbled precariously over my tiny car.

"Why did you stop so far into the intersection?" Iffy

snapped. "Honestly, if I wanted to ride with someone this reckless, I could have taken a cab."

Determined not to lose my composure, I inquired whether coffee would be available at the Civic Center so early or whether we'd have to wait.

Iffy snorted and showed me the back of her head, and Mother leaned forward to speak into my ear. "Stage nerves," she said.

The light changed. I shifted from first to second. My muffler blew. A scraping, dragging noise suggested a broken clamp. Iffy Bigelow grumbled under her breath.

I parked under the nearest street lamp on a grassy spot between two gnarled trees. When I turned off the ignition, the silence was extreme.

Instinctively, Mother filled the vacuum. "Need any help, dear?"

Declining politely, I scrambled out of the car, but not quite fast enough to escape her next line. "Ginger's so capable—she can fix anything."

With the aid of a flashlight and the duct tape I carry in the car, I did manage to wrap a crack in the burning hot pipe just in front of the muffler. After a censorious stare, Iffy consented to the use of her wire cutters and one of the two extension cords from her box of flower arranging equipment (I'd already borrowed some gloves without asking), and in about fifteen minutes I had the muffler tied off the ground. Nothing could be done about the roar, but at least we wouldn't be throwing off sparks.

Wet grass stuck to my hair, my lined raincoat needed dry cleaning, and sometime in the very near future I would have to pay for the privilege of spending an hour on a plastic chair smelling stale cigarettes and reading old magazines and car repair jokes Scotch-taped to a plywood counter. I didn't care if Iffy Bigelow was defending her title as Big Shot of the Big Shots of the Pennsylvania Horticulture Society or the world. I'd heard enough out of her. I turned on my radio—loud. To an oldies station.

Dumbstruck, Iffy stared at the horizon—presently pigeon-colored office buildings backlighted in pearl gray. On the opposite riverbank, dawn had dimmed the white lights that outline Boathouse Row.

Checking in my mirror, I saw Julia twisting a strand of hair around her finger. She looked bewildered and frail, and the thought of such an apparently sweet person incapacitated by a psychiatric disorder made me count my blessings, one of whom was petting Julia's hand and beaming motherly trust into the back of my head.

Figuring I had no Brownie points to lose, I turned up the radio. Julia added another notch to her forehead, Iffy squeezed another wrinkle into her collection, and Mother tapped in time with a free finger.

For us and all the passing parts of West Philadelphia, Jerry Lee Lewis belted out "Whole Lotta Shakin' Goin' On." Courageous programming for 6:15 on a Friday morning.

I probably should have listened to the words.

❈ *Chapter 2* ❈

The Philadelphia Civic Center looked like a sprawling stucco barn or maybe a warehouse. I drove down a ramp on the far right into the parking garage, a damp dungeon supported by thick posts. Enclosed by cement, my muffler roared like all the souls of Hell; we could scarcely hear the radio.

"I think this is the Beatles," I shouted as if conversation were possible. Yes, it seemed to be their version of "Twist and Shout," done in one take to spare John's tortured vocal chords. Easing down an aisle of parked cars, I wondered once again how the British managed to sound so American the minute they opened their mouths to sing.

Abruptly, Iffy punched off the music and threatened me with her face. I turned back to my driving just in time to brake for an obstruction. A creamy beige BMW containing a white-haired, wild-eyed driver squatted sideways across our path.

"You idiot!" Iffy shouted. "You went the wrong way. You almost got us killed! You are the worst driver I have ever encountered." She hugged her houseplant and huffed.

Judging by insurance rates, my driving was about average

for Philadelphia. Plus I was almost positive there had been
no directional sign. Maintenance passes or no, next time the
old grouch could take that cab.

"Just pull over there," she commanded.

There happened to be thirty yards ahead, a large, lighted
doorway labeled with 11 written on white cardboard.

The guard underscored his disapproval of me and my
muffler problem by pointedly heaping courtesies upon Iffy
and my mother: opening doors, supporting elbows, grinning
encouragement. Before I had a chance to become useful, he
lifted the hatch, extracted Iffy's cardboard box, and delivered
it into Julia's tentative arms.

She shot a desperate look toward her aunt, who hesitated
before grumbling, "Oh, all right, but for Heaven's sake be
careful."

"Shall we leave our coats in the car?" Mother suggested,
and we all agreed. Getting them back from the coat room
always meant standing in a long line.

A juggling of clivia and box and pocketbook ensued while
overcoats were removed, followed by a breather in which
the two older women pretended to be waiting for each other.
They were dressed like a pair of pink dumplings in tweed
suits and awful hats. Julia had become one with the carton—
a disheveled palette of brown hair, clay-colored dress, and
matching flat shoes.

Soon, Iffy proceeded headlong into Wonderland, the
clivia's pompon of bright orange trumpets pointing her
way.

Mother squeezed Julia's shoulder with a gloved hand,
then rummaged in her purse for the maintenance passes Iffy
must have entrusted to her earlier. She also crushed a dollar
bill into the guard's palm because I saw his jaw drop and
his face redden.

After parking and surrendering my own pass, my first
priority was to locate the other women; but once inside the
six-acre Civic Center I had to stop and stare.

To my left lay a living-room sized chunk of rain forest dripping with multi-colored orchids. Across the aisle a foot-bridge led to a pink-and-white carousel centered on a flower-bordered green. To the right, tall, twisted pines sheltered an idyllic log cabin nestled near a fern-lined stream complete with gurgling water. All were major exhibits designed by commercial enterprises. Most took a year to plan and repre-sented an entire year's advertising budget. Probably money well spent, particularly if the display took a prize.

Through the greenery I glimpsed Julia tripping along at a brisk pace. Other than a group of visitors in wheelchairs, we were the only people in the aisles, a privilege that made me even more skeptical of Iffy's generosity. This was a favor you bestowed upon your nearest and dearest. At best, she and Mother were on-again/off-again friends.

The smaller exhibits were just past the entrance escalators, and I dawdled past some exquisite miniature scenes scarcely larger than microwave ovens before locating the roped off "Sew What?" competition. It consisted of a dark gray wall with six recessed, eye-level boxes about a foot square. In front of them Iffy and five others worked from two lengthy tables.

Iffy Bigelow frowned at the wire cutters in her hand. To streamline movement, she had removed her lumpy magenta-and-blue tweed suit jacket, leaving a pale blue crepe blouse with a blue flowered scarf bowed at the throat. A silver hat pin shaped like a feather secured her blue felt hat. Shoes: black orthopedic. Either Iffy preferred to spend Arthur dar-ling's considerable earnings on plant food or this was the getup she wore when she won her first blue ribbon way back when.

Standing near her in the midst of everything was my mother. Fake cherries dangling from a black pillbox hat pelted her forehead. Her gray tweeds exuded an aura of camphor.

"Why don't you come out of there," I suggested. "You look as if you're in the way."

"Oh no, dear," she said without removing her gaze from her high school friend. "I'm helping Iffy."

"How's that?" I asked.

"The clivia, dear. I'm guarding it."

Sure enough, Iffy's precious clivia remained under the worktable, Mother's short legs protecting it like iron bars cemented into sensible shoes. "Later deadline?" I guessed.

Mother nodded without tearing her eyes from the work in progress.

I found myself a place to stand and watch, a slot against the opposite wall between a red-smocked woman with hair like yellow fur and a man who bit his thumb when he concentrated.

To Iffy's right worked an anxious woman wearing a camel hair blazer with a ribbon badge. Parked beside her was an odd yellow scooter with a tall, T-shaped handle for driving standing up. I assumed the woman was a highly ranked official of the show taking time out for a personal entry.

The big-boned competitor to Iffy's left had breasts the size of throw pillows. To accommodate them, she habitually spread her elbows like the front of an old locomotive. Mother stiffened and scowled every time the woman switched direction.

I expected the cowcatcher's design to be equally disproportionate and blunt, but in keeping with the sewing theme it featured a graceful spiral of safety pins stuck into a wooden spool sprouting pink blossoms.

Then there was a frump in a handwoven skirt and sandals working with a pincushion set on a blue draped cloth; an executive-type playing hookey from some downtown office (rock, scissors, paper, and leaves); a grimly serious Asian

woman (rough woven fabric, needle and thread with sun-
flower); and finally a cherub-faced man with thin curly hair
wearing khakis and canvas shoes. His miniature, hot pink
orchids gracefully spilled out of a small sewing basket.

As I watched, he dropped a flower stem into a cup, the
better to wring his hands. "Oh, damn damn damn," he
said. Then he had the courtesy to blush. "Sorry, ladies," he
amended, although the person nearest, the intense Asian
woman, appeared to hear neither the curse nor the apology.
"My best blossom just dropped a petal," he added, lifting
his chin in an effort to look brave.

The aide with the furry hair shook her head over the
wasted gentility. "Like petting a school of sharks," she
remarked.

"Gin-ger!" Mother was on tiptoe scanning the crowd.

"Duty calls," I told my fellow observer.

"Me, too," she said, for a voice had also trilled, "Aide.
Oh, aide . . ."

"The scooter lady?" I asked as we nudged our way toward
the table. I was still trying to figure out what all the smocks
and ribbon badges meant.

"Nah." My acquaintance jerked her head to indicate the
padded cowcatcher. She lowered her voice. "The Grande
Dame of Niches."

"Aide! Oh, yoo-hoo . . ."

She shot me a look. "Probably needs water. Sooner or
later they all do."

"Listen, darling," I heard the Grande Dame confide as
she splayed her elbows and lowered her chest. "Do you
know where there's any electrical tape?"

So now I knew that aides wearing red smocks were essen-
tially gophers. Privileged gophers who got to see the show
before the crowds arrived.

"Ginger!"

I rounded the thumb-biter and a twelve-year-old girl to meet my mother at the end of the table.

"Julia's wandered off, dear, and Iffy's quite concerned."

The back of Iffy's head didn't express much, but Mother's worried face certainly did.

"Please be a sweetheart and go find the girl?"

❀ *Chapter 3* ❀

"She's not a girl, Mom. She's thirty if she's a day."

"She's gone is the point, dear." Mother's panic supplied my imagination with enough horrible possibilities to get me moving.

Although it was only 8:30 and the Civic Center's population a scant hundred people, catching up with Julia still represented quite a chore. For thoroughness I made a quick search of the immediate area, which was not unlike scanning the aisles of a grocery store. Most of that section consisted of freestanding walls of "black boxes," aligned with the escalator. Beyond that spread an expanse I could check at a glance: the individual plants of the horticulture classes grouped together in lengthy pebble boxes on the floor, and the row of free standing windows adorned with houseplants. Julia was nowhere in sight.

Along the back wall were two large doorways labeled "FOOD." The concession booths beyond were closed, but I smelled coffee in the vicinity of the Tastee Freeze booth and decided to investigate.

Protected by an officious sign, the Pennsylvania Horticulture Society MEMBERS' LOUNGE was enclosed by flimsy lattice fencing backed by white drapes. Inside were rickety little patio tables and chairs and two women sipping coffee. Neither one was Julia. Neither one invited me in.

Out in the main room I hurried past the escalator and the splashy entrance spread (a floral rainbow), scarcely glanced at the corner of a stone mill complete with turning waterwheel, zipped past a yard of some sort—I was following Julia's earlier path now—glanced left across the heaps of beautified earth and strips of cement and tried to cancel out the color in search of Julia's bland brown.

A young woman with a long fuzzy braid gently planted a purple flower in the curved border around the carousel.

"Has a woman come by here?" I asked. "Brown dress. Brown shoes. Brown everything?"

"Sorry," she said with a shrug. "Didn't notice anybody."

I hurried on.

High above a simulated inner-city vegetable garden, a photographer was perched in one of those cherry-picker trucks used to fix things up on telephone poles. I shouted up to him, surprised by the anxiety in my voice.

"Did a woman in a brown dress go by?"

"What?"

"A woman. Brown dress. You see her?"

"Nope. Not me."

In short order I was at the far edge of the main attractions where a few wide openings enticed you into the market area. Back there narrow aisles were crammed with about a hundred and thirty stores offering thick leafy merchandise, and I had to cover the entire grid before I could be certain Julia was elsewhere. By then I was short on breath and patience, but I still had to check the side of the commercial exhibits where we had come in.

Passing Entrance # 11 reminded me that there was a whole city out there. I doubted that Julia would have ventured outdoors without her coat, which was locked inside my car; but if she was still inside—where? Six acres is a lot of space, with plenty of plant material blocking my view, plenty of enclosures if Julia wanted to hide.

My last hope was some competitors waiting around a table for their entries to be "passed," meaning they were insect-free and identified with the proper nomenclature. No one had seen Julia, but I wasn't surprised. She simply wasn't noticeable.

Rounding the final section of the tall, floral rainbow at a weary walk, I encountered a welcome sight—a coffee cart.

"Good morning," I said to the ill-humored grandmother guarding the pot.

"If you say so," she replied.

"Is it possible for me to get a cup of coffee?"

The woman grimaced her disapproval, took a cup off the stack and filled it.

"And one for my mother?"

Her eyes narrowed, but she gave me another cup.

I strolled back toward the "Sew What?" niches feeling that all was right with the world. Julia would be there. Iffy would thank me for my effort, Mother would thank me for the coffee . . .

Even at a distance I noticed a change in the crowd. Instead of casually interested individuals milling around, as one, the clutch of spectators craned to focus on something toward the right end. Iffy's end.

My pulse picked up as I joined the outer layer of gawkers.

"Yes you did," said an all-too-familiar voice.

"I did not, and I wish you'd mind your own business."

I threw the coffee into the nearest trash can.

"And furthermore you did it on purpose."

"Of all the . . ."

I wriggled myself through and even under the end rope until I could tap my mother on the arm. She shrugged me off belligerently.

"Mom," I mumbled discreetly. "What's going on here?"

She refocused her attention onto me. We might as well have been alone in a closed room.

"Iffy put me in charge, darling. And that vile woman over there bumped the wall and made Iffy's arrangement wiggle. They do that, you know, some of them. Cause accidents to happen to their opponents and pretend they didn't. Iffy told me all about it. That's why she wanted me to guard her niche while she—"

I interrupted to steer her in a more productive direction. "Where is Iffy, Mom?"

"I was just saying. Iffy took that plant she brought, that clivia thing, where it was supposed to go, and I must say it was your fault, dear. And then she probably went looking for Julia because she's been gone awfully long. So then this woman . . ."

Suddenly the spectators cringed back from the far end of the rope. Two people approached, one of them speaking in a loud, agitated voice. Even Mother paused to listen.

The crowd parted enough to reveal a woman leading a brown-uniformed guard by the arm. He had one thumb behind his belt in an attempt to appear confident.

The woman pointed toward us. "There she is. The one with the cherries." I was really sorry Mother wore that hat.

The small amount of murmuring around us hushed.

"Are you a friend of Mrs. Winifred Bigelow?" the guard asked.

"Yes." I felt her arms tremble inside the thick wool of her sleeves and realized I had surrounded her elbows with my hands.

"And you are . . .?" he asked.

I told him our names.

"May I see you both a moment?"

The pointer stood back, crossed her arms, and bit her lip. The guard used his right arm to shepherd Mother and me around the corner to relative privacy.

I can't remember his face at all, but his exact words were: "Something's happened to Mrs. Bigelow."

"What?" I prompted. The guard looked at me and blinked.

"I'm afraid she's . . . dead."

I gawked at him.

He nodded to confirm his words. "Strangled," he added, glancing quickly at Mother.

She gathered his lapels firmly in her fists and screamed.

❈ *Chapter 4* ❈

I saw now that the guard had narrow shoulders and a broad bottom, possibly from too many doughnuts in front of the old security monitor. He said, "Please come with me," steadily enough, but it seemed an effort.

As we walked, he muttered almost to himself, "I'm sorry, I really didn't mean to blurt that way. Will your mother . . . Is your mother . . .?"

"She'll be all right. It was going to be a shock any way you said it." The guard nodded doubtfully.

He gestured toward the concession area. Six other brown-uniformed security men stood sentinel across the three openings, sealing off the area until the Philadelphia police and their specialists could arrive.

We came to a halt back among the red-and-white striped concession booths. My mother's breathing was deep and ragged and her face highly colored. Yet she was under control. I was proud of her.

"Where is she?" she asked. Our man's eyes strayed past the PHS Lounge to a white curtain at the left rear of the Tastee Freeze booth. There two more private cops succeeded in looking stern.

"You'll need me to identify the body," Mother said, taking a step toward the curtain.

Our monitor-watcher put a gentle hand on her arm and said no.

"But I want . . ."

"No," he insisted. "Mrs. Bigelow has already been identified."

It made sense. Iffy would have been known by most of the exhibitors, if only because she won last year's Grand Sweepstakes.

"How was she found so quickly?" I asked.

The guard turned toward me. "Guy runs the booth needed something in back." He shrugged and opened his mouth to say more. However, Mother left him gaping. She bustled past us and through the curtain guarded by the brown bookends before anyone could stop her.

When I got there, she was wobbling with her knuckles against her teeth.

Iffy Bigelow lay with her feet toward us. The soles of her orthopedic shoes looked especially thick and new. Her tweed suit skirt was rucked up around her knees revealing a white slip edged with Chantilly.

I saw those details mainly trying to avoid Iffy's protruding purple-black tongue and the disproportionate narrowness of her throat where the scarf was knotted around it. Even when I took that in I focused instead on the whiteness of her nostrils and how they looked like a pair of keyholes. There was a foul odor, too, the unmentionable one that comes naturally with death. My stomach clenched and my mouth tasted sour. My head felt light and my feet very, very heavy.

Irrationally, it crossed my mind that if Iffy were alive she probably would have been mortified. Judging by her house and her consuming interest in flower arrangements, appearances meant a lot to her. But then none of the physical certainties are especially dignified. Not childbirth or death or much of anything in between.

I thought back over Iffy's last two hours and regretted giving her such a hard time. She'd had a lot on her mind, maybe more than just the competition, and I'd treated her . . . come to think of it, better than she had treated me.

So she was difficult to like, particularly under stress. I still couldn't imagine why someone had wanted her dead. But dead she was, and violently so. I had seen her and I knew, but my mind wanted to pretend that Iffy's passing was natural. Assimilating the concept of murder could wait. My mother needed me right now.

The three guards had given her a moment to deal with the shock of Iffy's appearance, but that grace period was up. I could feel their authority closing in, intending to secure the physical evidence range and confine us to the merely restricted area.

As I began to back Mother through the curtain, I remembered a certain problem of hers.

"I've got to take her to a rest room," I told our guard.

"I don't know . . ."

"Believe me, she really needs to go." I checked that the women's room was in the corner I remembered then hastened to point out that we couldn't go anywhere else without passing another guard.

"Well, I guess . . ."

"Thanks."

Mother's face was blank; she was unaware of her surroundings, even of her own propulsion. Inside the rest room I guided her into a stall and closed the door between us. The latch snicked and other familiar noises assured me that I'd done the right thing. "Lord, I just made it. Thank you, dear."

Washing my face with cold water, I paused to smile. My childhood memories consisted of unmade beds, burned peas and gummy candy apples, purple box kites that wouldn't fly, and quilts draped over the dining room table to make a rainy-day playhouse. On my tenth birthday duMaurier's pirate book *Frenchman's Creek* was handed to me along with a flashlight. "Only way it should be read," Mother insisted, and she was right. I loved that daffy woman fiercely, and it infuriated me to think that one of the foundations of my life could be kicked from under me without warning. One minute I might be running around on a fool's errand or drinking a cup of coffee, and the next minute my world might be irrevocably changed.

Suddenly it occurred to me that Iffy Bigelow had a husband, a man who had been kind and considerate to me.

"Be right outside," I told Mother. As usual, a pay phone hung on the wall that angled away from the lavatory door.

Information gave me the number of Bigelow and Associates' Ardmore office, but no one answered after ten rings. Arthur Bigelow would probably have to hear it from a stranger after all. My impulse had been a foolish one anyway, since I wasn't much more than a stranger myself.

Suddenly I remembered Julia. What would her reaction be to Iffy's death? Horrible loss? Fear? Relief? Nothing at all? Was she tuned in enough to assimilate the information? For that matter, was she insane enough to have done it? Whatever the case, Mother and I were responsible for her, at least until someone more appropriate could be summoned. Probably Arthur Bigelow, but I didn't know where he was.

For that matter—where was Julia?

Five uniformed cops bustled about stringing plastic yellow tape across the wide center entrance arch and the two smaller doorways right and left. Enough flower show people had caught onto the commotion to form a row of spectators three deep beyond the barrier. Civic Center guards attempted to bully them away.

Mother and I returned to our monitor-watching escort.

"Friends of the deceased," he said, waving us toward a perplexed cop with wire-rimmed glasses.

He interrupted his hand-rubbing to indicate a row of five sculpted plastic chairs joined at the hip. "Please . . . have a seat over here," he said. Once white, the chairs were now somewhere between yellow and gray. Mother sunk onto the nearest end with an exhausted sigh. Joining her, I took her hand in my lap. It was nearing ten o'clock.

Wire Rims remarked, "Homicide will be here shortly. They'll need to speak with you."

"What about the public?" a woman on the other end of the seats addressed the cop. She had a stranglehold on the handle of a yellow scooter—the show official who arranged the niche next to Iffy's. "Will they be allowed in on time?"

Minutes from now.

"Not my decision, ma'am," Wire Rims replied curtly.

Scooter Lady whimpered with frustration. Her now inter-locked hands levitated off her lap and dropped, lifted and dropped.

Suddenly I realized the staggering scope of the problems caused by Iffy's murder. Already thousands of people would be outside clamoring to get into the Civic Center to see the biggest event of the year. If recent statistics held up, thirty-two thousand would demand entrance today alone. I pictured each one of them trampling on a clue.

I was curious, so I asked the cop now discreetly keeping an eye on us whether the public would be admitted at all. "Not my decision," he repeated, but I could tell the question intrigued him, too.

I shrugged. "It's not as if you have to search for a weapon."

The cop raised an eyebrow, so I mentioned that we had seen the body.

It occurred to me how lucky it was for the authorities that she hadn't been stabbed with clippers or any of the other tools in plentiful supply. Something like that could have been hidden anywhere for later disposal—in someone's toolbox, buried in a mound of dirt . . . then the show would have been closed for sure.

Scooter Lady was rubbing her earlobe, crossing and uncrossing her legs. Swishy, medium brown hair enclosed her cheeks. To distract her from her worries, I asked if she'd had time to finish her niche.

"What? Oh, that. Penny asked me to do one at the last minute because one of the entrants had to drop out."

"You mean you got that together overnight?" I was remembering a bunch of blue bachelor buttons on a tuxedo lapel and a needle and thread poked through the coat button.

"Well, yes, sort of. I mean I had ideas, materials . . . it won't be judged, of course. We just needed to fill the niche."

The scooter at her side reminded me of her larger responsibilities. "It must be hectic running an event of this magnitude."

She slid back on her chair and rolled her head. "Unbelievable. So much work. And now this . . ." Her eyes strayed over my shoulder toward the guarded curtain.

I wagged my head, thinking how high-stakes competition always seemed to expose the underside of human nature. "The problems must be staggering," I sympathized.

My companion threw up her hands. "It's the little things that get to me. Like a judge calling from California to ask if its cold enough for her fur coat. Then worrying whether there's any security in the coat check room. We do get some theft. Cameras, wallets, stuff like that.

"One time we had a banner up high you could see when you first came in? Just a greeting with that year's theme written on it. Some con artist said she was reading it and twisted her ankle at the bottom of the escalator. Sued us, sued the Civic Center, sued everybody."

"She win?"

Scooter suddenly looked suspicious. "Why? You think you've got a case here?"

"Oh no. No. Mrs. Bigelow wasn't . . . I just drove her here as a favor." That didn't begin to cover the situation, but Scooter seemed satisfied.

Mother suddenly jerked to attention. "Julia!" she said to no one and anyone. She turned to me. "Did you find Julia?"

I admitted I had not.

Mother shot upright and confronted Wire Rims. "One of our party is missing," she informed him. "A young woman named Julia Stone. She was wearing a brown dress . . ." The officer shrugged.

Mother clucked with disgust and began canvassing all the uniformed people in the area, which was everyone except Scooter and me. As she spoke her left hand did a pleading "have you seen her?" ballet. By the time the homicide men walked in the hand was up to tarantella speed. A gray-suited man with an authoritative air paused to get her drift. He stilled the dancing arm at the shoulder and poured some soothing phrase onto Mother's upturned face. Mother slunk back to her seat, and I put my arm around her.

The suited homicide man parted the curtain to view Iffy's body, stroked his chin, wheeled on his heel and began barking orders. Momentum brought him into the center of the aisle near our chairs. Behind him a camera commenced flashing and a couple laboratory types waited like vultures eager to invade Iffy's personal space.

I meant to watch the man in charge but instead noticed one of his sidekicks, a muscular fellow in a black, brown, and white tweed sportcoat smiling at me non-committally. His close-cropped black hair receded into a widow's peak. A trimmed moustache made up for the lost hair above, permitting the speculation that a patch simply slipped. But balance was achieved and he probably knew he was handsome. Certainly the jacket and the sharply creased black slacks, bright white shirt, and patterned black-and-brown tie pulled the package together. This was a man who took himself seriously. The smile flicked up on one corner as I watched.

The homicide captain was thinking out loud, his thoughts becoming commands even as they were uttered. "So the last place we know she was seen was the roped-off area where she was working on her flower arrangement. So we have to find out who was with her, whether anybody else left the vicinity when she did. You know the drill."

I lifted my hand and the sidekick gave me an expectant look.

I said, "Maybe the aide who worked there could help."

Sidekick tapped his boss on the arm and gestured toward me.

"And you are?" the boss asked.

"Ginger Barnes. I drove Mrs. Bigelow here today. She and my mother were friends." Sidekick rolled his head; and if his hands weren't stuffed into his pants pockets, he'd have slapped his forehead. When he was over this peculiar attack, he resumed staring with a bemused smile bordering on rude. It was difficult to finish what I was saying.

"I overheard you say you wanted to check the movements of the people working near Mrs. Bigelow, and I suggested you ask the aide who was assigned to help them. She's wearing a red smock and has very short yellow hair . . ."

"Sally Metz," Scooter volunteered. "She'll be around the hort section now."

"Charlie." The homicide chief jerked his chin. Charlie pivoted on his heel and aimed for the barricade.

"Straight through. You can't miss it," Scooter called after him. Charlie didn't break stride, but his neck lit up.

The man in charge addressed me. "Thank you, Mrs . . ."

"Barnes," I repeated, but the man's back was already turned.

His sidekick crooked a finger at me and began to back up. I patted my mother and followed him a few paces out of his boss's hearing.

"The lady you're with wouldn't be a Mrs. Struve by any chance?"

I widened my eyes. "Cynthia Struve, yes. How did you . . .?"

He extended his hand for me to shake. "George Masterson Mills."

The name sounded familiar, a little formal, but . . .

"General Motors Mills? My God, George. It's been what? At least fifteen years. How on earth did you guess it was me?"

"For one thing, I'm a police detective, and for another—how many strawberry blondes you know named Ginger?"

"I'm not a strawberry blonde."

"Whatever. How you been?"

"Fine. Good. Great, until this morning." His face closed around my thought, so I shifted away from business for another moment. "So this is where you moved when you left Ludwig Elementary." At the time our acquaintance had been somewhat of a novelty for us both, a blonde girl and a black boy teaming up for playground games, laughing easily together but never quite connecting. Already our rapport seemed more genuine, as if our earlier try at friendship carried considerable weight now.

"Philadelphia, yeah. When my dad died, my uncle took us in."

"Wow." Twelve or fifteen miles can be a very long distance when you're eight, especially when the move is from a predominantly white suburb to a rough inner-city neighborhood. Easy to imagine how a boy who squawked if you cheated at hopscotch decided to become a cop.

"So what you doin' now?" he asked.

I raised my palm apologetically. "My husband's a headmaster." I never knew how to answer that question.

"No. I mean what do you do?"

After the school day has pulled my husband apart for nearly twelve hours, I put him back together; e.g., listen, offer a second perspective, compliment his judgment, sympathize, laugh, rub his shoulders, or possibly change the subject. I also clear time for our two kids and our friends outside of education and relieve Rip of everything domestic except lifting and hauling. Most of my recipes were for hors d'oeuvres. I could change oil and install a chandelier, and I never sent out a shirt. Yet I was hard pressed to say what I'd accomplished on any given day.

I told George, "I guess I fix things."

"Same old Tink," he observed, and I marveled at his perception. My dad had nicknamed me Tink because I loved to watch him make household repairs. Tink for Tinker, but the kids picked up on it and teased me with Tinkerbell, or some variation of tinkle, so the nickname was not one I favored. My best and oldest friend Didi had dispensation to use it, as did my mother when she felt fragile, but it was "Gin" now or just plain "Ginger."

"Okay," George said, going back to business. "Tell me something about the woman who's missing."

Briefly, I described Julia, adding that I last saw her after my own arrival. I also mentioned that this was her first outing after hospitalization for some unspecified psychiatric problem.

"Will you find her?" I asked, but his mind was elsewhere.

"Listen," he said. "More later." He was getting quizzical eyebrows from his boss.

So I sat down with Mother and waited, practically dozing until some shouting and scuffling woke me up but good.

"Guard! Stop her! She stole that flower."

"Let me go!"

By the time I turned to look a guard held Julia by the arm across the tape barrier. Behind her a man in a white shirt and menacing expression shook his fist as if he wanted to thump her in the head.

"Julia!" Mother shouted. "That's Julia." I hurried along behind as she rushed toward our bewildered charge.

The homicide chief intercepted us. "Please," he said. "I'll handle this." Then to the guard: "What seems to be the problem?"

White Shirt blurted, "She stole my lily. Right in front of my eyes. Couldn't goddamn believe it." His accent was very Philly, that sort of thuggy slur that makes "Eagles" sound like "Iggles" and "water" a dead giveaway.

The cop in charge studied Julia's stunned face, glanced at the limp flower clutched to her breast, nodded to the guard to let her in, then put his left arm around the white-shirted man to shepherd him safely out of Julia's range.

"Hey, you a cop or what?" the man asked and pointed over his shoulder. "Why'nt you arrest her . . ." and other words I couldn't catch. The homicide man waved for George to take over, and he proceeded to counsel with the man in quiet tones until he became wide-eyed and contrite. While George wrote something in a notebook, I noticed the complainant throw Julia that disdainful little head shake supposedly sane people use to write off all the supposedly crazy people of our world.

Meanwhile, the captain was allowing a tableau to run its course. With a forceful stop signal he had frozen us all in place. All except Julia, who sleepwalked her lily toward the guarded curtain like a macabre bride. Then, when she was approximately four feet away, the captain changed the stop to go, and the two nearest guards swooped in.

Julia gave off a terrified yelp. Her body began to vibrate and crumble, and soon she was sitting on the floor. While she sobbed miserably, the two cops who had tried to detain her directed helpless expressions toward their boss.

My mother was cradling Julia and pushing away policemen and cooing and offering a tissue before anyone else could begin to move. When the captain eventually secured Mother's attention, he made a circling motion with one of his long fingers and somehow conveyed that Mother and Julia might prefer the plastic Siamese chairs to the cement floor.

Mother nodded gratefully, accepted one of the hands she

had so recently swatted, straightened the straw pillbox until the cherries were back over her left eye, then devoted herself once again to comforting Julia.

Cynthia Struve, the woman who can't cook, clean, or balance a checkbook. At what she does do, she's splendid.

❈ *Chapter 5* ❈

"Sad," George murmured at my side. Arms crossed, philo-sophical expression.

We were watching Julia as she rocked back and forth on the plastic chair. Since he didn't seem to refer to the murder, I said, "What's sad?"

"That the niece makes such a good suspect."

"What!"

George offered up his palm. "You saw her. She went straight to that curtain. And how about that flower she brought? She's a suspect all right. No doubt about it."

I wanted to refute his reasoning but could not. While we didn't really know what prompted Julia to bring an Easter lily to the exact location of Iffy's body, clearly she already knew her aunt was dead.

"So maybe she just found the body. It's possible, isn't it? Mrs. Bigelow had been looking for Julia, but we don't know whether they got together or not. Maybe Julia only saw her aunt at a distance, watched her come back here. Eventually, she looked inside the curtain and got one hell of a shock. Her mind shut out everything but the idea of lilies for her aunt's funeral. Don't laugh at me, George."

"Sorry. I was just picturing you bullying off five big sixth graders while I wet my pants under the school steps." He wagged his head. "Unbelievable. Five of them, and you put up those pathetic little fists and yelled . . . all for some scrawny black kid you scarcely knew."

I was tempted to use one of my pathetic little fists to erase his grin. Cynthia was the starry-eyed idealist in our family, not me. I folded my fists under my arms and huffed. "You wouldn't have let them beat me up."

George laughed until something behind me caught his eye. "Yeah. Right. Anyhow, we'll know more about *her*," his chin indicated Julia, "after the boss talks to her."

That brought me up short.- "Surely he won't question her now. She's under psychiatric care. Shouldn't he wait for her doctor?"

"Maybe. It depends."

Across the food court the captain snapped his fingers and pointed to his watch for George's benefit. George nodded. "Got a phone call to make," he explained.

"Arthur Bigelow?"

His eyebrows stretched toward his widow's peak. "As a matter of fact . . ."

"He isn't in his office," I said.

"Oh?"

"At least he wasn't ten minutes ago."

George hooked my arm. "Let's find out if he's there now."

I glanced toward Mother and her charge. Julia had stopped rocking and had begun to stare.

"They're fine for now," George remarked. "Come with me."

When we were alone by the phones outside the women's room, he half penned me in the corner by leaning his left arm against the wall. "So. Who'd you talk to, and what'd you say?"

"When?"

His face hardened. "When you phoned Arthur Bigelow's office."

"I didn't say anything. Nobody answered."

George rubbed his chin for a second then nodded. "Good. That's good. Wouldn't want ol' Tink arrested for obstruction." His face clouded.

I picked up a phone receiver. "You want me to dial for you?" I asked.

He nodded gloomily, clearly dreading his task.

I punched numbers and a moment later a female voice droned, "Bigelow and Associates."

"Is Mr. Bigelow available?"

"Mr. Bigelow is out of town. Could I take a message?" Her words were right, but her heart was elsewhere.

"Just a moment." I handed the receiver to George and leaned in to listen.

"This is Lt. George Mills of the Philadelphia police. It's extremely important for us to reach Mr. Bigelow. Can you tell me where he is?"

It emerged that Iffy's husband was currently in transit to Los Angeles. His plane was supposed to have landed at 9:48 a.m., but the secretary had no idea when he would actually arrive at his destination.

"How about an educated guess," George suggested.

"Oh no. I couldn't begin to guess," she replied as if the accounting firm exacted a vow of accuracy when she signed on.

George stiffened inside his sportcoat and his voice took on an edge. "There has been an accident involving Mrs. Bigelow. It is imperative that we reach her husband. Perhaps you would be kind enough to leave a message for him at his hotel. Ask him to call you as soon as he arrives. He may wish to take a return flight."

I didn't hear the secretary's reply, but George hung up with a certain amount of satisfaction. "Officious secretaries. Where do they find them?" he asked rhetorically.

I'd been a secretary myself for a few years, so I said, "Same place they find traffic cops?"

George was gracious enough to smile.

Soon after that the head of homicide, finally introduced as Capt. Theodore Spahr, led Mother to a distant table for questioning.

I watched with growing concern until George reassured me she was not considered a suspect. Sally Metz, the blonde aide with the sense of humor, had already reported that, whenever she herself had been there, Mother had remained behind the "Sew What?" tables.

Iffy's competitors further confirmed Mother's presence with varying degrees of chagrin. Naturally, the most aggrieved was the Grande Dame with the elbows. She bitched about Mother's horrible accusations so convincingly that no one could fail to remember where either of them were at the time of the murder.

When it was my turn, Capt. Spahr asked my relationship to the victim: none; and my movements during the time in question: around. The only witness I could think of was the coffee cart lady.

The general public was admitted around eleven, approximately an hour late, and the yellow-taped crime scene immediately became a must-see. Those of us awaiting permission to leave the food enclosure were ogled by literally hundreds of people—sómber women of all ages and a smaller percentage of morbidly curious older men, more or less anyone with discretionary time on a Friday morning.

After a while, I turned my back on the doorways and allowed my darker thoughts to reign. The discrete removal of Iffy's body through a service door served to deepen the sense of finality and loss.

Meanwhile, Capt. Spahr's lengthy questioning of Julia nearly unglued my mother. When, after forty-five minutes, he unceremoniously deposited her back on the row of plastic chairs, Mother cut in front of him like a terrier guarding a mailbox.

"What do you mean by pestering this poor girl? Can't you see she's out of her mind with grief?"

Actually, Julia looked more dumbstruck than stricken and more exhausted than anything. She just sat there with wilted hands in her lap and empty eyes hypnotized by some internal test pattern.

"If you wanted to know Julia's whereabouts, why didn't you ask me?" Mother put her fists to her hips for emphasis.

Capt. Spahr blinked and shifted on his feet until he mentally broke through at the correct point. "You know?"

Mother compressed her lips. "Of course." Then she hooked his arm to steer him away from Julia. Intrigued, I drifted along to listen.

Mother glanced around, then confided, "She saw her aunt coming at a distance and made a point of keeping out of her reach. She'd been gone quite a while and was afraid Iffy would be angry. She said she hid behind a white curtain, probably that one around the Members' Lounge; and when she heard Iffy berating someone else, the darling was so relieved that she didn't really listen very carefully."

"You asked exactly what was said?"

Mother cocked back her head and narrowed her eyes. "Of course I asked. Aren't you paying attention? All Julia remembered was that Iffy said 'no' a lot."

"You're certain . . ."

"Push, push, push. Don't you people ever listen?"

Capt. Spahr drew in a deep breath. "Please, go on."

"That's better." Mother straightened her tweed suit jacket and her chin, causing the pair of cherries to bounce.

"Where was I? Oh yes. Then Iffy shouted an especially loud 'no,' and Julia ran into the ladies' room."

Evidently, that was all Mother planned to say.

"And then what happened, Mrs. Struve?"

Mother squinted at the captain again in a manner critical of his intelligence. "Then she came out and found the body."

"Yes . . . ?"

''And then she went to look for a lily.''

''But quite a lot of time elapsed before she came back here,'' Spahr pointed out. ''The body was discovered by the owner of the concession, identified by the woman who knew her. One of the guards summoned you and your daughter from the floor . . .''

''She was crying, no doubt, and she probably had difficulty finding a lily.'' Mother glared at the homicide captain until he acknowledged her implications with a nod. Iffy was already dead, so what did it matter how long Julia took to locate her flower? She could have taken two hours before wandering back to the crime scene, and it still would not have meant she killed her aunt—merely that she had seen the body. Point and game to Cynthia!

I looked around for Lt. George Masterson Mills, intending to gloat ever so slightly. After all, Mother had just led his boss right up to the theory I had outlined. My childhood acquaintance was nowhere in sight.

Capt. Spahr told my mother, ''You can go now, but stay available.'' I contemplated what further use the police could have for us until Mother led Julia toward me by the arm.

Then I started to wonder what we should be doing about her.

Chapter 6

I had forgotten about my muffler problem but Mother, Julia, and I were reminded for all of the forty painfully slow minutes it took to travel along Lancaster Avenue into Bryn Mawr. Although Lancaster draws a line through the commercial centers of most of the Main Line communities, even the business establishments possessed a tone that I was loathe to disturb. Still, it was better than shedding metal parts onto the expressway.

A right turn sent us wandering through rolling, twisted roads with hundred-year-old trees whispering above tiny creeks, all comprising people's yards. Viewed from a distance, you would see exactly what Natty Bumpo (or rather his author, James Fenimore Cooper) saw in his day: treetops.

Another turn led us past a huge, self-important heap of gray stone, the original mansion of this particular tract. Back before adequate sewer systems and central air, smart executives escaped the city (via the "main line" of the Pennsylvania railway) to the luxurious hundred and ten acre "farms" they called home. Your prototype commuters.

If by dogged determination or outstanding good fortune one of their estates remained intact long enough to sell today, it might be carved up for more custom-built homes; or it might become an exclusive retirement community, an increasingly popular alternative to the difficult problem of getting good help for dear old Mom.

And so it went around every corner. Considering the twenty-mile extent of the area, somebody had to be doing pretty well selling Fords or dry-cleaning clothes or maybe even styling hair. There are only so many CEO's of so many companies, so many top lawyers, doctors, university presidents. Even the granddaddys who invented hearing aids or manufactured steel during the war had to be numbered. Yet the Main Line endured, modified but intrinsically intact, old money augmented by lots of new.

As far as I knew, Arthur Bigelow's earning power was solely responsible for the splendor to which we had returned, a huge brick Tudor on two acres of well-serviced lawn. Since Iffy and my mother were high school friends, her folks probably didn't have beans, although they might have grown some. Ludwig was and still is small and insular. Even when I was growing up there, marrying right out of high school was the norm, attending college was not. Ball games were watched on TV with pretzels and beer, not at the stadium, not at those prices. After the oil scare in the seventies, firewood appeared on most front porches. Dad might be an auto mechanic, a meat packer, or perhaps a teacher like mine. Cynthia was queen of the volunteers, but my friend Didi's mother stacked the dinner dishes and rushed off to a night job at the Pepsi plant.

College got me away; marriage kept me from going back. Later, when Rip became headmaster of a small school on the Main Line, I learned just how far from Ludwig a person could get.

Anyone familiar with Iffy's background could understand the need to measure her talents with a more sophisticated yardstick, but this morning her attitude toward me bordered on being downright nasty. I couldn't help wondering if her two-faced behavior had something to do with her death.

"Do you have keys, darling?" Mother asked Julia as the three of us climbed out of the car.

When there was no response, Mother handed Julia's purse back to me. It was a leather envelope on a long strap containing only a few folded tissues, a comb, two keys on a ring, and fabric lining repeatedly stamped with a designer's logo. Not at all the indispensable catchall of a woman, this was the purse of a little girl pretending to be grownup. As Mother turned Julia toward the house, I glimpsed the young woman's equally empty expression; and my heart ached and eyes stung for her. Life should contain much more.

As I finished with borrowing one of Julia's tissues, Mother turned back to me. "I know, dear. Me, too." Her face winced and quivered. "But let's talk about it inside."

"Sure, Mom," I said. But she meant Iffy, and talking about the murder probably wouldn't be good for Julia just yet. I hoped Arthur Bigelow would come home soon so we could contact her doctor.

One of the keys worked the front door, and we entered a slate-floored foyer warmed by pale peach walls and a patterned area rug. An iron staircase with a polished brass rail and peach padded treads curved toward the second floor.

To the right, a coat closet, a closed door that led to an office, and at the right rear a formal dining room with an Oriental carpet, pecan furniture, and a refreshing ice blue on the walls.

To the left, a huge living room spanned the depth of the house. Its two sitting areas were clustered on two complementary Orientals in rich reds. The drapes were also deep red, their length emphasizing the tall, diamond-patterned, leaded-glass windows. A few landscapes in gold frames with their own discreet lighting adorned the inside wall and the mantel. Bookshelves filled the gap between the three side windows. A red cushioned, crescent-shaped window seat beneath the front bay offered a view of the lawn. For perfection, the room needed a sleepy gray cat, but there was no sign of life anywhere. No magazines carelessly tossed, no book turned face down, no junk mail, no cat.

Mother removed her coat and her suit coat with it, then helped Julia with hers and handed the pile to me. I dropped them all onto a chair. "Coffee? Lunch?" I asked.

"Tea, I think, dear," Mother replied, watching Julia drift toward the window seat.

I wound my way through the dining room, the pantry, and into the kitchen, and took my time fixing ham and watercress sandwiches and lemon-laced tea that could bend a spoon or jump-start your heart. It was either what we all needed most or least.

By the time I returned to the living room Julia was curled up on the window seat asleep and Mother droned daintily through her nose on the nearest sofa. I covered them with coats and sat down to the sandwiches. If food really medicates depression, I helped myself to quite a dose. Naturally, the ham made me thirsty, so I also drank most of the tea.

It is not easy to sit still and watch other people sleep, especially on a caffeine kick, so I began to explore Arthur and Iffy Bigelow's house. Mostly I admired with my hands in my pockets, not wishing to accidentally wiggle the bisque statuettes or smear fingerprints on the glowing mahogany.

It took no effort to imagine Iffy translating her exquisite taste into prize-winning flower arrangements, but her home's rigid perfection made me pity Arthur and their only son, whose growing-up and wedding pictures reposed in polished silver frames. I was reminded of a woman who wiped the football bleacher in front of me with a tissue before she sat down. She also made her husband wait while she wiped his section, then proceeded to clean a spot for her purse. I concluded that she must be mean and asexual, which of course I am not.

A broad window sill in the Bigelow's ice blue dining room displayed several unusual plants, each fascinating and perfect in its own way. I'd heard how horticulture buffs collected plants, and apparently Iffy was no exception. The greenhouse off the kitchen contained about forty or fifty more specimens, none quite perfect enough for the flower show or even the dining room display, but all interesting and beautiful. I didn't know any by name.

Since there were several significant gaps in the greenhouse rows, I assumed many were currently entered in the show. At the far end of a pebbled bench I even detected a muddy ring not yet washed clean by watering—where the clivia must have grown to its competitive form. I flicked a few pebbles with my finger and tried not to become maudlin. Emotions were primarily useful for determining action, so I'd been taught. I wandered back into the kitchen wondering what actions would be useful now, what could possibly make me feel better?

Surely the most immediate concern was to get some care for Julia. Below the wall phone in the kitchen desk I found a personal address book—page after page of meaningless names. Occasionally, a notation identified someone as the Bigelow's plumber or roofer or hairdresser, but no one marked "Julia's shrink."

I felt stymied and depressed, and I wanted to hear my husband's voice. He needed to hear where I was and why anyhow, so I phoned the school.

"My God!" Rip said when I told him what had happened. "That's awful." I could imagine him standing at his desk, steadying fingertips on a pile of papers, his mind already past the facts and their implications and arriving at his own bottom line: "Are you okay?" he asked.

"All things considered, yes," I said. "And Mother, too. You should have heard her with the homicide captain."

"I look forward to hearing about that." His voice had settled back into the reassuring tones so necessary to his job. "Any idea when you'll be home?"

"No clue. We should stay with Julia at least until Arthur returns."

"Okay, I'll get the kids' dinner, and we'll see you when-ever. Take care."

I hung up the kitchen phone with regret, promising myself to call Rip just once with good news, then realizing why I never did. The good stuff will usually hold, but bad things tend to need attention *now*. Rip would say that alone makes them bad, and he should know.

Off the kitchen was a short hall leading to the hunter green and leather office centered in the front of the house. The desk yielded no other address books, or none I could find without a set of keys. However, another temptation took the form of a blinking red light—an answering machine with one message on it, according to the display.

My conscience listened to reason. It could be Arthur Bigelow calling with information about his flight home. It could be important. I pressed the play button.

"Mrs. Bigelow, I need to talk to you . . . oh, never mind." Could mean anything. Nothing. I played it again.

"Mrs. Bigelow, I need to talk to you . . . oh, never mind."

A female voice, not a close friend, probably younger than Iffy or she would have used her first name. I played it again.

The voice sounded torn, not excited, but maybe resigned. Also the words backed up the tone of voice. The young woman wanted to tell Iffy something unpleasant, something she didn't have to tell her but felt she should. "Mrs. Bigelow, your check bounced." No. No reason to change her mind.

"Mrs. Bigelow, I stole your wallet out of your purse, and I'm sorry." No. Nothing to talk about there.

The house cleaner quitting? Better.

When did the call come? Not yesterday. Nobody can resist phone messages, and the Bigelows had both been home until early this morning. Even if Iffy missed seeing the blinking light, Arthur would have checked his office before going away, listened to any messages, reset the machine. So the call must have come after 5:45 this morning when I picked up Iffy and Julia to take them to the flower show. Hard to imagine it having anything to do with the murder. For all I knew, it might even have been placed during the murder.

I looked at my watch. Five before one, plenty of time before Arthur Bigelow would get home under the best of circumstances, even if he lucked into an immediate return flight. There was nothing more for me to do at the house, so I scribbled a note about getting my muffler fixed and set it on the coffee table for Mother to see as soon as she woke up.

I did not mention that I also planned to visit Arthur Bigelow's office. Mother would have misunderstood.

❃ *Chapter 7* ❃

*I*f I had told Mother I was stopping in at Bigelow and Associates, she would have thought, "Oh good, Ginger's getting involved."

The truth was, I hoped a little more personal information would cure my ambivalence toward Iffy. It's probably a character flaw with a long fancy name, but I like to get to know what makes a person tick. Don't give me the press-kit fodder you put over on most people, I want the stuff you keep from your mother and sometimes even yourself. No one can hide from somebody who is looking closely enough; and for me, reading people accurately has become both a bad habit and a necessity. Until I'm satisfied, I can't decide how I should feel or behave. Iffy just wasn't coming into focus, and I thought a little information from Arthur's secretary might help.

Also, I hoped the office files would contain the name of Julia's doctor.

Everything about the Bigelow and Associates office building indicated that serious business was conducted within. It was a brick-and-stucco cube a convenient half-block off Lancaster. The Ardmore address implied Main Line solidarity but not necessarily the inflated overhead natives automatically figured into their bill. At the entrance to a thirty-car parking lot a hanging burgundy sign in the gold-lettered Colonial style almost literally said, "Trust us, we've been here forever."

In the secretary-receptionist's area of the accounting firm's third floor suite a woman stood on a filing cabinet watering an enormous fern. A few smaller plants softened what was otherwise ordinary aluminum and formica, tweed chairs, and framed watercolors lighted from above by two generous skylights.

"Excuse me," I said.

The woman jerked and wobbled, and some water splashed from the blue watering can onto the phone books stored at her feet. Her fingers groped for the wall and some bracelets jangled on a thick wrist. She stared at me open-mouthed.

"Guess you didn't hear me come in." I threw in an apologetic shrug. She was thirty-something with sallow skin storing butterfat like a chipmunk anticipating winter. When she cut her wavy brown hair, I think she bunched it in her left hand as far up and back as her arm would go and hacked the excess onto the floor.

"Who are you?" she asked, forgetting her secretarial manners. Of course my flower show skirt and blouse had been through a muffler mess and a murder, so she was safe to guess I wasn't a client.

"Why don't you come down from there and I'll tell you." I was worried she would fall.

Also, I was tired of looking up people's noses. Maybe I was just touchy from viewing Iffy's remains, but I had formed a pretty strong preference for plumbing remaining out of sight under the sink.

The secretary turned and stepped off the file cabinet onto a chair, placing her ample rump at my eye level for a moment while she finished watering the plants. When she got to one with a Tuckahoe Nursery tag sticking out of the plastic pot, I ventured, "Nice shamrock. Get it at the flower show?"

Since St. Patrick's Day was two days away, little pots of shamrocks had been on sale throughout the trade section.

She smiled and nodded. "Mrs. Bigelow gave me a pass, and Mr. B was kind enough to give me a few hours off."

"I don't remember seeing pots of shamrocks that large." But this late in the week probably lots of items were sold out.

She lifted it fondly and smiled as if it were a pet. "Yes, it was a lucky find. But they're supposed to be lucky, aren't they? With moving and all I could use a little luck."

"Irish?" I asked.

"Cloris Huber? Probably not."

I extended my hand. "Nice to meet you, Cloris. I'm Ginger Barnes. I know the Bigelows through my mother."

Behind glasses framed in shades of gray, the woman's hazel eyes focused on an unpleasant inward picture.

"Of course you know about the tragic accident. The police . . ."

Her eyes flashed. "Don't call it an accident. Mrs. Bigelow is dead, and it wasn't an accident." Sounded as if George Masterson Mills had called again. He hadn't been so specific before.

"You're right. I'm sorry. Sometimes there's no way around the truth."

"The truth is usually best."

"Yes." Strong spine under that butterfat. "Have you spoken to Mr. Bigelow yet? Is he on his way back?"

She glanced at her watch with chagrin. "He should have called already. I keep picturing him circling, circling while his poor wife . . ." She nibbled a lip.

"Mind if I wait with you a few minutes? I need to get in touch with his niece's psychiatrist. You don't know who that is by any chance?"

Cloris said she did not. Nor did she appear to care. She offered me some coffee, which I declined, and poured some for herself.

Now or never. I took a deep breath and dove into my deceptions.

"Was it true the Bigelows weren't getting along too well?"

Cloris stared at me across the top of her coffee mug. "What have you heard?"

Nothing, but I shrugged and smiled vaguely. To ease the feeling of ghoulishness, I babbled on. "Mother was pretty upset by some of the talk. As you can imagine, the rumors were really flying." If that wasn't already true, it soon would be.

"They were friends, your mother and Mrs. Bigelow?"

"Old friends. Only saw each other off and on. That's why Mother didn't know what to believe. Some of the things she heard were quite distressing."

Cloris breathed again, a great deflation that lowered the shoulders of her pink chiffon blouse a good two inches. "They disagreed, of course," she said. "Everybody does."

"Recently?"

"Well, Mrs. B fussed quite a bit about her husband not going to see her 'Sew What?' arrangement. Actually, she was furious. It was sort of a big deal to her."

I nodded knowingly. The points for the niche would have gone far toward a second Grand Sweepstakes win for Iffy.

"Mr. B tried to change his plane reservation, but it was too late. Still, he did make an effort to stay." A token effort, from the sounds of it.

"That's it?" I prompted. "No other complaints?" I considered myself happily married, yet I could have come up with a list. On the other hand, it wouldn't have thrilled me to learn that Rip's secretary kept a record of his complaints about me.

Cloris lowered her eyelids conspiratorially. Her hair fluffed forward. "I shouldn't be saying this." But she was going to anyway. "Mr. B thought his wife seemed to need an awful lot of money." Her lips pursed with disapproval, whether her own or Arthur Bigelow's I couldn't tell.

In the silence my mind echoed Cloris's words, ". . . *needs* an awful lot of money." Odd. The phrase was usually, "my wife *spends* too much money."

I summoned what I imagined to be a reassuring voice. "Don't worry, honey. I won't repeat it to a soul."

The phone rang just then, and we both jumped. It was a business call, so I busied myself with a magazine off the visitor's end table while Cloris took a lengthy message. When she was again free, I asked her if I might flip through Mr. Bigelow's Rolodex.

"Why?" she asked.

"Neither Mother nor I feel right about leaving Julia alone at the Bigelows'," I explained, "and we don't know whether it's okay to take her home. We really need the advice of her psychiatrist."

Cloris pushed the metal file box across the desk.

I spent fifteen minutes reading every card from A to Z. Unfortunately, Cloris invariably identified all the doctors as clients, including the physician and dentist used by the Bigelows themselves. The obvious back-scratching compounded my disappointment, although I should have known better. Private schools are fueled by networking of every sort; even Bryn Derwyn Academy—the establishment that houses and feeds me and mine—uses the professional services of its parents whenever possible.

This time when the phone rang, it was Arthur Bigelow. Cloris backed her chair away from the desk, dipped her head and hid her panicked eyes behind the fluff of her hair.

"Mr. Bigelow," she said softly. "You've got to come right home. It's your wife. The police called . . . No, I'm afraid not," then a hushed, "Yes, I'm so sorry."

In a choked voice Cloris proceeded to sketch in details.

Where it happened. How it happened. A lump formed in my throat as I imagined Arthur's horrified and disbelieving responses. How could I have thought an acquaintance breaking the news would be a kindness? In the future I promised myself to think twice before . . . before doing anything.

So naturally I shouted, ''Wait!''

❈ Chapter 8 ❈

Despite my yelp, Cloris hung up the phone.

"What?" she asked, her expression pained. My outcry had startled her.

"Julia's psychiatrist," I reminded her, knowing even as I spoke it would have been inappropriate for her to ask Arthur the question.

"Sorry," she said. "It isn't every day I have to tell my boss his wife is dead."

I gathered my purse and backed out the door.

I proceeded to a muffler shop on Lancaster Avenue that I'd found in the Bigelows' phone book. It was every bit as filthy and smelly as predicted, and the desk man neglected to mention that my car's parts were not in stock. An assistant slipped out to buy them while I twiddled my thumbs in their waiting room. This detail emerged as I dotted the 'i' on the signature of my check. "Thanks," I said with open sarcasm as the manager and I exchanged paperwork.

First insensitive and now grouchy. For penance, I drove through a fast food joint and bought a bag of burgers and fries. Neither Julia nor my mother had eaten since breakfast and it was almost five p.m., confirmed by the density and aggressiveness of the traffic on Lancaster Avenue.

Twilight and its accompanying chill followed me into the Bigelow vestibule.

"Oh, darling. You're back," Mother greeted me.

I handed her the food, shed my coat, and gave her a kiss.

"Shall I light the fire?" I remembered logs were already laid on the glass-fronted brick hearth at the back of the living room. Maybe lighting it was a little presumptuous; but I felt we deserved the luxury, and it might be nice for Arthur to come home to.

"Oh do," Mother agreed.

Julia groggily emerged from under the coat I had used to cover her and silently gravitated from the window seat toward the warmth at the far end of the room.

Mother parked on the nearest sofa and unpacked our meal on the mahogany coffee table; she's not especially into worldly goods anymore, but it didn't seem right for me to worry more about the furniture than her feelings. We ate with gluttonous abandon and to hell with the carpet.

George Mills phoned just before six, for the third time apparently. We left it that if Arthur didn't return his call immediately, I would contact George myself to let him know Iffy's husband was back. Since Arthur wasn't a suspect, I supposed stationing a policeman at his home would have been a waste of time as well as money.

Between the side windows a television was hidden in a cabinet at the base of a bookcase. I put it on for a while. Cable offered a rerun station guaranteed not to disturb Julia with anything close to reality.

During the fifth car commercial Mother wandered off. When the show ended and she still wasn't back, I set out to find her.

She was upstairs in the middle of a walk-in closet holding the sleeve of a black sable coat. The fragrance of stale perfume made the small enclosure smell intimate, as if Iffy were close enough for us to touch.

I waited in the doorway, letting my presence gently draw Mother back from her thoughts.

"Iffy had it so tough," she said to me and to herself. Then just to me she said, "Winifred wasn't always strong, you know. Not in the beginning. She wasn't strong at all." She gazed upon the coat sleeve as if it contained Iffy's hand.

I reached out to pet the silky fur. "She learned," I said, guessing that was what Mother wanted to hear.

"Oh yes." She laughed a little and raised her chin. "Some people wish she hadn't learned so well. But yes, she learned."

I smiled back and glanced around at the plentiful display. "At least we know she didn't have to wear that godawful suit." The right hand wall, about six feet of it, was devoted to long-hanging dresses and coats. The facing wall held a double row of blouses and skirts. I noticed a fair amount of cashmere and silk and a few items with tags still dangling.

"Godawful? The blue Pendleton?" Mother's eyes widened with surprise. "That was her lucky suit!" Then suddenly the eyes widened even more, blinked sharply, and dissolved. Instead of luring Mother away from the pain, I had managed to walk her straight into it.

I held her against my shoulder until the little room became stuffy. Trying to kick the door open further, I unintentionally broke the pattern of my mother's sobs. She drew herself up and implored me with wet, red eyes.

"Do something, Gin."

I drew back, but she grabbed both my hands. "Please," she said.

"No, Mom. There's nothing. Really. The police . . ." She didn't just want me to change a light bulb; she wanted me to interfere in a murder case.

"It could have been one of her friends, one of *our* friends." She looked at me. "And what if it was Julia? What then?" She wagged her head and shrugged her short round shoulders. "I just can't stand not knowing, Gin."

"We're not supposed to interfere with the police, Mom. They really don't like it.

Mother's lips pressed shut, and her eyes tightened. "You solved that other one before the police even got started."

"That was different. Two years ago I had no choice. A murder was committed on the campus—I literally lived in the middle of the investigation."

"But you were brilliant."

"Terror is very motivating. Honestly, Mom. The police were not at all grateful."

"Rip was."

"He doesn't really know what I did."

"Want me to tell him?" My mother smiled naughtily, knowing full well that the part about me saving the school's delicate reputation should—and would—remain between us.

I couldn't help thinking about the part that Cynthia didn't know. Solving the murder on Bryn Derwyn's campus probably had been the most important thing I'd ever done in my life. Certainly being a wife and mother offered outstanding job satisfaction, but those accomplishments were in no way unique.

"You did it for a stranger. Do this for me."

I sighed. Originally, my intention had been to help my husband, but as Mother pointed out, the person my unofficial inquiries helped most, the man my information acquitted, had indeed been a stranger.

"Please?"

"Capt. Spahr would skewer and broil me if he thought I crossed the line into his territory."

On the other hand, George Mills, although he certainly wouldn't ask for help, might be receptive, maybe even grateful considering that I had an advantage over him. Much as I often felt like a tourist from the other side of the river, my years connected to a prep school had taught me how to blend into the affluent Main Line environment. I knew what to wear, and where to go, and most of the time what to say. I could appear harmless nearly to the point of invisibility. In other words, a female Bryn Mawr Wasp might talk to me while George, a black inner-city cop, would get nada.

Mother was waiting for my answer.

"Maybe I could ask a few questions, keep my eyes open." Surely, my face betrayed my lack of enthusiasm. "But I'm going straight to the police if I learn anything."

Mother ignored my face and addressed my words. "You're wonderful," she sighed heavily.

John Hancock may have signed the Declaration of Independence all by himself; but, trust me, the flamboyant loops and whorls were for his mother. "Now," he probably thought with the final flourish, "are you satisfied?"

Later, when Arthur Bigelow's key turned in the front door lock, I became acutely aware of how at home we intruders had made ourselves. Tilted against one of the sofas like a bloated ironing board, Mother watched an episode of "The Brady Bunch" with an expression of disbelief mixed with horror. Julia had drawn up stockinged feet and collected throw pillows around herself like so many stuffed animals. Primarily, she stared and plucked fringe. More from nerves than from hunger, I sat on the floor nibbling cold French fries from one greasy container among many.

With the arrival of the owner of the house I hastily wiped my hands on my skirt and, blushing, bounded into the hallway.

Arthur's face registered nothing. It seemed that at some point his receptors had overloaded and rendered his face unable to respond to input of any kind. Behind the gray stubble on his boxy jaw his skin looked undernourished and sickly. His eyes, too, seemed withdrawn behind rectangular, silver-rimmed glasses. He wore a wilted charcoal gray pin-striped suit and carried a lined London Fog. The black brief-case appeared to be a natural extension of his arm.

I gawked at him for a long agony-filled moment before he blinked and surprised me into speech. After I reminded him of my name and mother's, I babbled some relevant information, the gist of which was, "I'm sorry about your wife, I'm sorry we're here, just tell us what to do with Julia and Mother and I will be happy to leave."

"Julia? Julia's here?" he said, as his eyes slid into focus. I realized he had forgotten that his niece had accompanied us to the flower show and had no idea what condition she was in as a result.

"She's had quite a shock," I said, underscoring my understatement with my face. "We thought we should ask her doctor what to do."

"Yes, of course." He seemed relieved to have something easy and immediate to attend to, something within his present scope.

Phoning Julia's doctor wasn't it. He walked past me to hang his coat in the closet under the stairs.

"Mother and I didn't know who to call."

Bigelow blinked.

"Who is her doctor?" I prompted.

"Why, Willoby McDonald, of course." He remained stationary, gazing through narrowed eyes toward the back of Julia's head. Then, apropos of his thoughts, he said, "You know they didn't have anyone there who could tell me anything. Not a soul. Isn't that disgraceful?"

"They?"

"The police. I went straight there, to the—to the division in the message. But there was no one who could tell me anything." His flat gray eyes searched mine for some logical explanation.

Logistics, I could have told him. The men on the case were human beings who had to eat and sleep, and the human beings on duty now probably couldn't give out information without clearance.

I put my hand on Arthur's arm. "Have you eaten anything?"

He shook his head sadly. "No."

"I have the home number of the officer in charge. Why don't you phone him while I fix you some soup."

Half an hour later I called Dr. Willoby McDonald myself. He listened to my scenario with alarm; and to his credit, agreed to make a house call.

"Thank you. I'm sure Julia will be fine now if you'd like to take your mother home." Understandably, Arthur Bigelow wanted his privacy, the sooner the better.

Mother was so done in she didn't even squawk about missing Julia's diagnosis.

❈ *Chapter 9* ❈

Our house is the last on a quiet, woodsy cul de sac named Beech Tree Lane. After such a horrible day, the street lamp meant to keep strangers from accidentally barrelling across the lawn into our sprawling red rancher literally looked like the light at the end of a tunnel. Rip had remembered to put the porch light on.

In our small entrance hallway, he greeted my mother with an embrace and gave me a concerned, sympathetic smile over the top of her head. At our feet Barney, our enormous, aging Irish setter, wriggled with joy.

Being home and seeing Rip went a long way toward restoring my frazzled nerves. Most women would describe my husband as an attractive man, probably in the way that responsible, overworked adults who live right remain attractive all their lives. Lord knows I had more than enough competition for him when we met, but now I read so much into his face that I seldom viewed him dispassionately. He's got brown hair and greenish-brown eyes and a crooked smile. I knew, don't ask me how, that something bothered him that had nothing to do with Iffy's murder.

"Dad?" our daughter Chelsea pleaded from the direction of her ground floor bedroom. "Can I come see Mom?"

"Mom will come see you," he answered. "Later."

I raised my eyebrows. Rip rolled his eyes. Despite a lingering something, his face was smiling, so I assumed that the bedroom punishment was for a crime only thirteen-year-old girls might commit.

Mother kissed Rip on the cheek and proceeded down the hall on the right to Chelsea's room. The door closed gently behind her. As we all know, grandmothers are exempt from punishing their grandchildren; neither do they have to live with the results of their indulgences, having created their own monsters to do that.

From our remote family room located beyond the kids' bedrooms came the staccato dialogue of a gangster movie, one of the many in our eleven-year-old son Garry's collection. We like to think that means he's interested in law enforcement.

Rip took advantage of our relative privacy. He cupped my shoulders in his hands and asked again, "You okay?"

When any sort of problem came up, it was always his first question and I had long ago learned to accept the bottom-line way he meant it. Unless I was unconscious, my answer was supposed to be "yes."

"Oh sure," I replied, but before I had time to say, "How about you?" he pulled me into the darkness of our narrow kitchen and kissed me.

Then he held my head against his chest and stroked my back with his free hand. Death isn't something a couple often thinks about. Even when it touches you, you might not mention it. You might just hug in the quiet darkness of your own kitchen.

"You want to tell me about it?" Rip asked.

"Eventually," I sighed. "How about you?"

"Later."

I didn't like the sound of that and probably borrowed some of Rip's worry wrinkles for my own brow. If he stayed in the headmastering business for the duration, by retirement we'd both probably look like dried apricots.

I addressed the lesser problem. "So what did Chelsea do?"

Rip released me, crossed his arms. The porch light cast enough light through the windows for me to see his eyebrow rise with a wry smile. "Swore at her science experiment. Teacher happened to be right behind her."

I smiled and asked, "My department?"

Rip opened his palms. "You word things so well." Disciplining other people's children on a daily basis for anything from punching a teacher to having sex in a storage room does not dispose a man to scold his daughter for cursing out her science experiment.

"Shall we make up the sofa bed?" I suggested. Both Mother and I had been too tired to drive to her place, so I invited her to stay until morning or later. Luckily she had no pet waiting for her, not even a houseplant to water. Since Dad died, she preferred to travel light.

"Sure. Your mom can watch the end of Garry's movie while she falls asleep."

We headed in separate directions, but Rip turned back in mid-stride. "Actually, I forgot to ask a favor," he said, clasping his hands together and grimacing. Obviously he was reluctant to broach the subject but was compelled by some time constraint—probably the Open House the school had scheduled for Sunday. Preparations had been going on for weeks.

"Out with it," I prompted.

"The admissions office drapes haven't been washed . . ." he said, "ever," he added, throwing in a wince for good measure.

Washing drapes didn't fit on anyone else's job description, so the chore came home with the guy who wanted it done. Although Rip is blessedly tolerant of a lived-in home, he puts on the white gloves when prospective students are expected to visit his school.

I smiled my answer and tried not to think of how much

dust eight-foot-high draw drapes would have collected over several years.

"Thanks, honey, they're in the laundry room."

He wasn't taking my answer for granted, I knew. Had I for some perverse reason replied in the negative, Rip would have traded directions with me and washed them himself while I attended to the sofa bed. Equal partners. Division of labor and all that. Normally we stick to our areas of expertise or at least experience.

"You better hope they don't disintegrate," I shouted after him. Or get streaked by the rust in our dryer. Better to wash them tonight and dry them outdoors all day Saturday. It would mean rehanging them Saturday night or Sunday morning, but odd hours doing odd jobs came with the territory.

With Mother settled down in a borrowed nightgown, dozing even as the credits rolled on Garry's gangster movie, I finally made it into Chelsea's room for our talk.

She was in white flannel topped with a # 82 football jersey of yellow material pierced like swiss cheese. Her slippers were sad-eyed sheep with pink noses and brown ears. She was lying on the bright blue, red, yellow, and green quilt that covered a brass bed I found at a garage sale. Her hair, a more golden version of my own, was presently styled in a curly puff that looked a little like dandelion down and emphasized her dark brown, heavily lashed eyes. When she finally finished with her colt stage and filled out a bit more, she was going to be sensational. *Those* related problems I swore I would turn over to Rip.

I sat on the bed and fingered dandelion fluff off her forehead. Fact is I can never resist. As usual, my daughter squirmed.

"I understand your science experiment didn't go very well."

"Damn right it didn't. The—"

"Hold on there," I said. "What's with this 'damn' business all of a sudden. Dad told me you said even worse in front of your teacher today. What happened to my ladylike daughter? The one who lived here yesterday?''

Chelsea's lips compressed into a sneer. ''I'm just growing up, that's all. Everybody swears. Even you, Mom.'' A pair of stylized silver swans dangled from her dainty round earlobes, which happened to be cookie-cutter replicas of my own. The earrings jiggled and bobbed as if the swans were straining to take off.

I clasped my hands together and considered how to proceed. It was true I occasionally swore, and occasionally I allowed my children to hear me do so—a calculated lesson from my personal Parents Are People curriculum.

''Okay. Suppose I dropped a flowerpot on my foot. What do you think I might say?''

My daughter squinted at me and held her silence.

''No tricks. Pick a nice appropriate curse.''

''Goddamn it to hell.''

''Excellent choice. Now am I really, sincerely expecting the flowerpot to be damned to hell?''

''I don't know.''

''Think about this, Chelsea. Do I really want to send the flowerpot to hell?''

''No.''

''So why did I say 'Goddamn it to hell?' ''

''Because you dropped a flowerpot on your foot!''

I gave her a quiz-show buzz. ''No, honey. You're not thinking. I could have just said 'ouch.' I'll give you a clue. Dad was listening when I said it.''

A shrug.

''I said it for effect. I picked a nice colorful; phrase to make Dad feel sorry that I dropped a flowerpot on my foot— to get his attention.''

''I've heard you swear when you thought nobody would hear.''

''Letting off steam. I was angry at the situation.''

Chelsea frowned her impatience. "What's the point, Mom?"

"I'm trying to teach you about cursing. My personal opinion is that the sin is in the intention. Have I ever sworn at you?"

"No."

"That's right. And I never will."

"So what was so wrong about what I did?"

"Swearing at your science experiment? An interesting question. Why were you angry?"

"The thing wasn't working. It was so frustrating. Honestly, Mom . . ."

"Got it. You were playing to your audience."

"What?"

"You wanted your friends to know how frustrated you were."

"Yeah, I guess . . ."

"But what went wrong?"

"Mrs. Filmeyer was right behind me."

"You offended her?"

"I guess."

"So what does that tell you?"

"Don't swear when Mrs. Filmeyer is right behind me."

"Exactly. Pick your audience carefully. Very carefully. Also, if you're going to be risqué, I insist that you know the meaning of every phrase *before* you use it. No repeating what friends said until you know—literally—what you're saying. If you don't want to ask your friends, ask me."

Chelsea gulped.

"And one more thing. Words that spicy are more effective if they're not overdone. Save something for when you drop a flowerpot on your foot." I patted her knee. "Think about it."

She gave me a doubtful smile. "Do I have to think about it in my bedroom?"

"For a while. Can you look suitably contrite by break-fast?"

The next smile looked genuine, and my precious, coltish daughter even hugged my neck. It's tough when everything a kid does reflects on his, or her, father's career. Sort of like having a minister for a parent—rebellion is almost essential if the child wants an identity of his own.

All things considered, I felt lucky as hell.

Actually, a whole lot luckier than that.

When I walked into our second-floor bedroom, Rip was sitting on the edge of our bed wearing pajama bottoms and aftershave. He aimed the remote control and killed the eleven o'clock news. The phrase "inexplicable crime" spoken by an earnest female died along with the picture. It occurred to me that she could have been talking about almost anything.

"They cover the murder?" I asked.

Rip nodded and watched me undress. It was not an erotic experience for either of us. Married, yes. Erotic, no. As I slipped into something flannel, I skirted the horror of Iffy's death with peripheral details the news would not have cov-ered—George Mills, Julia, the muffler mess.

"You don't think you need a new car, do you?"

It is a truly perceptive husband who goes where you lead him. Gratefully, I crawled across the bed to where he had settled back with his hands under his head. "Nah," I assured him, and two or three wrinkles let go of their grip.

"Your turn," I prompted. "What happened today?"

He took a deep breath and released it. "More vandalism."

I sat up on an elbow. "What did they do this time?" Last week it had been paper towels in the girls' room toilets.

"Bashed the overhead lights in the locker-room hall. About four of them." The school halls were lighted by rectangular fixtures suspended on thick cords, each con-taining four long, expensive, fluorescent tubes. At the end of the locker-room hall an exit led out to the playing fields and the world.

Rip took another deep, reflective breath. "Probably one kid with a big stick, running like mad to stay ahead of the glass."

I grimaced. "Catch the creep?"

My husband said something that would have earned detention from Mrs. Filmeyer.

"After school?" I guessed.

"During practices. Everybody who was still around was outdoors."

I lay back and looked at the ceiling. "So who's angry at the school now?"

Rip rolled toward me. "We thought maybe the kid I tossed last week for cheating, or I should say cheating, stealing, general obnoxiousness, and suspicion of drug possession. But at the time it happened he was receiving mandatory extra help at his new public school. His principal and I exchanged sympathies."

"Anybody else?"

"Nobody obvious. There was the girl the other kid cheated from, but she seemed delighted to get off as easily as she did. The lacrosse coach threw Miles Pendergrass off the team for mouthing off and shoving him, but that's not necessarily enough." Rip thought for a moment but didn't come up with any more suspects.

"Friday afternoon?" he reflected. "It could be a former student with a grievance—real or imagined—a current student with a grievance we don't know about yet or one of those poor troubled souls who's just plain screaming for help."

"Any chance of an informant?"

"Maybe. If the kid confides in anybody—or brags about it." Rip exhaled heavily. "We may never know who did it."

His depression was troubling. Schooling kids is like putting messages into hundreds of bottles and throwing them out to sea. Why should one—relatively minor—unsolved incident bother him so much?

"Bryn Derwyn's too young to weather much of this," he explained. "It needs a flawless image, especially now."

"The fund raising?"

"Mm-hmm," Rip concurred.

"But that's so unfair," I said. "Every high school has its share of troubled kids. It comes with the age group."

"You know that, and I know that. And if Bryn Derwyn were even half as old as some of the other private schools around here, people would keep an incident like this in perspective . . ." He shook his head. "We just can't afford any negative publicity."

The world securely balanced on a fairy's wing, as F. Scott Fitzgerald put it. That little matter of a new gymnasium begun, then stymied by financial bad luck. If a private school isn't moving forward, it's dead in the water. Soon it starts to sink. Next Friday night Rip and I were hosting a party to recruit volunteers for the Capital Campaign team, parents with clout who were at the moment, so far as we knew, enthusiastic ambassadors for Bryn Derwyn Academy.

There was nothing to say to Rip that wouldn't sound Pollyanna, so I changed the subject. I tasted some of his aftershave with my tongue; our dog couldn't resist licking it off Rip's face every chance he got.

"Phooo," I said. "Barney must hate the smell."

Which proved to be the lesson of the day: sometimes perspective is everything.

❈ *Chapter 10* ❈

Rip dropped the front section of the Saturday morning newspaper face-down, shrouding the lurid headline about Iffy Bigelow's death under the back-page car ads. Gradually, my stomach-churning vision of yesterday morning faded as I watched my husband fiddle with his microwave pancakes and bacon.

"You want Patrice to help clean next Friday?" he asked before taking a bite. In a plaid flannel shirt and jeans he looked more like my own personal Robert Ripley Barnes than the buttoned-down necktie version the school got Monday through Friday. Which is not to say that he doesn't work weekends.

"You bet," I answered to his offer. A caterer would be fixing hors d'oeuvres for the upcoming fund-raiser kickoff, so even if the young woman who cleaned the school called in sick at the last minute, I could physically manage to be ready.

Neither Rip nor I kidded ourselves that the evening would be fun. He would be working hard to recruit his critical money-raising committee while I would be working hard to make a suspicious, disparate group of strangers feel comfortable enough to make friends with each other. At least the odds favored some stimulating conversation; couch potatoes don't volunteer to help out their kid's school.

In theory, my responsibilities were supposed to be a centerpiece for the serving table and a tasteful dress, but my personal list was a bit more inclusive—blitz the paper plague (those ubiquitous piles of newspapers and mail), wash selected windows, caulk a pretty far gone bathtub, and bathe the dog.

"What's for breakfast?" shouted our son. Since Garry had asked that question every day since he learned to talk, I considered it a form of "Good morning." Beneath his blue striped pajama bottoms were untied black high-top sneakers. Last year's maroon baseball shirt strained across his chest and pinched his armpits. His straight, medium brown hair was . . . unstyled.

"Go to sleep with your head wet again?" I asked.

He dismissed me with an expression of disgust. "When can we go, Dad?"

"Where?" I asked, placing a plate of pancakes within Garry's reach. They disappeared more or less like Dorothy and Toto.

"Sign up for baseball," Rip mumbled between gulps of coffee. "After that I'll drop Chelsea at Chrissie's and take your Mom home on my way to pick up the lawn mower. Any idea where Garry's birth certificate might be?" To certify that he's old enough for the team, something that does not prove itself to the naked eye.

"Baby books are in the cardboard box on the shelf in your office."

Rip propelled Garry toward his room with a swat to the rear. "Put on some pants and a shirt that fits." He winked at me. Down the hall I heard Chelsea in the shower, the beginning of an hour-long routine which results in that casually tossed together perfection teenagers manage so well. Me, I'm working on the reverse, looking well-groomed in five minutes.

Mom shuffled in, rubbing her eyes by poking two fingers under her glasses. I poured us some coffee and rounded the corner at the end of the narrow kitchen to join her at the pine plank table we use for all occasions. Behind us milky sunlight seeped through my dirty windows and illuminated the rest of the sprawling early American living room, Mom's gray hair and the pale blue terry cloth robe she had borrowed. She looked like a forlorn kitten wrapped in a towel.

"Breakfast?" I offered.

Mother sipped coffee without looking up. Then in the stillness she realized she must have missed something. "What, dear?"

"I asked if you wanted any breakfast."

"No thank you, dear." Her head tilted a couple degrees as if trying to regain some inner focus.

"Mom," I said, gently resting my hand on her arm. "Mom, I'm trying to understand about you and Iffy, but I guess I just don't. So I need to ask. Why do you care so much?"

Tears slipped down her cheeks. She lowered her head to fumble a tissue out of the bathrobe pocket. Then she sniffled and wiped and glanced at me with embarrassment. "I guess you wouldn't know. I guess I didn't know until this morning. I just woke up and felt . . . older." She rested her elbows on the table and straightened her back. "Iffy was part of . . . of my past, and I was part of hers. And now she's gone." She looked away, hid her trembling lips behind her hand.

"You were very close in high school." Mother had never described her teenage years in much detail, and I was eager to learn more.

She shook her head. "Not in the usual way. Not in the way you'd think. Winifred was two years older, a senior, president of the pep club I had just joined. She was beautiful, sophisticated. And she had these deep mysterious eyes that were absolutely fascinating. You could say we liked each other, but we had little in common."

Mother took a sip of coffee before she continued. "I guess it was around December Iffy took me under her wing," she said. "Some of the boys had tumbled to me and this amused her. She began giving me advice—what to wear, what to say. I suppose I became her pet project. I was enormously pleased, a popular senior taking an interest in me. Nobody could say a word against my idol.

"Then in March the word got out that Iffy was in trouble and the boy refused to—well, it was an awful scandal. You can imagine how I reacted. I made quite a fool of myself defending her until Iffy herself told me the rumors were true."

"She was pregnant?" The story was so engrossing that I actually felt some of my mother's disappointment and shock.

"Oh yes, dear. I believe the day Iffy admitted it was the day I grew up."

"What did you do?" My coffee was cold, so I set it aside. Mother followed my example.

"She needed a girlfriend, so I became that friend."

Naturally. Mother never adhered to conventions, instead simply did what she thought was right. I could picture her cutting school to support Iffy through an abortion. Right or wrong, to Mother it would have seemed the only thing to do. I wondered if something like that really happened, but felt I could only ask, "How about afterward?"

Mother shrugged philosophically. "You know how people are, dear. When they pass beyond a difficult time, they like to leave behind everything that reminds them of that time. I knew Iffy's worst secret, and that embarrassed her for quite a while."

"Did you ever see her?"

"Oh, we met accidentally now and then. I wrote Christmas cards; and of course she came to your father's funeral. I always felt it was her choice whether to see me or not, and she did call once in a while." When she needed someone she could use, was my guess. Mother might have grown up, but she never gave up—on anyone.

"Then when we talked last month, Iffy sounded different. Better. A little distracted as if something was on her mind. But she was sincerely friendly toward me, and I remember feeling that she'd finally forgiven me for . . . knowing. She invited me to Toland's for lunch and told me how grateful she was that I'd kept in touch. Honestly, Gin, she almost sounded as if I was her one and only friend."

Mother had been struggling to express herself, and when she finished and heard her own final words, she grimaced. "Sounds pretty egotistical, doesn't it?"

"Nope," I said, standing up because I was suddenly too annoyed to sit still. "Sounds entirely possible. I'll bet Iffy snubbed so many people getting where she was going that when she got there she was mighty lonely." I started to clear dishes with unnecessary vigor.

"Ginger Struve Barnes!" Mother glared at me openmouthed.

I leaned down to look her in the eye. "You *were* her friend, Mom. You're not being egotistical—you're just telling the truth. How many other people were as sensitive to Iffy's feelings as you? How many other people were there when she needed them?"

Mother's back straightened and her eyes gleamed. It was good to see some rosiness on her cheeks instead of in her glasses. My mother, who never coddled me that I can remember, who was in fact quite a trooper herself, had been sounding as old as she said she felt. I couldn't accept that. Not yet. While I could keep my feisty, offbeat mother behaving like herself, I planned to do it. For both our sakes.

I sat down and leaned on the table. "Think about it, Mom. Something was going on in Iffy's life. Something that made her want a friend she could trust. You, Mom. I'm sure she was working up the nerve to confide in you, but the murderer got to her first."

Mother shut her mouth and blinked. She was getting angry in a different way now, a healthy sign.

"I believe you're right," she said, slapping a palm on my pine plank table. An orange juice glass fell over and spread a puddle. "After Rip takes me home, I'm going to write down everything Iffy said at that lunch we had; but right now I'm going to get out of your way." Mother patted my hand into the orange juice. "I'll do whatever I can to help."

George Masterson Mills forgive me; I've been coerced by an expert.

Twenty minutes later Garry burst in the front door replete with a large-toothed grin and a neon-orange baseball cap. On the front of the cap was the black letter T.

"We're a Tiger this year, I'll just bet," I called after him. Always wild animals, never anything as daunting as gym socks or as tough as, say, grease stains.

"The girls ready?" Rip asked as he pulled the door shut behind him.

I reported that Chelsea was messing with Mother's hair-style, "but I'm sure they're ready to go." The previous night's teenage moodiness had washed down the drain with Chelsea's shower.

"What are you going to do today?" Rip asked.

I kicked the dishwasher closed and wiped my hands on a towel. "Gosh," I said. "Paint the inside of the dryer with Rustoleum?" For now the admissions office drapes hung safely on the clothesline behind the garage, begging the cool March sunlight to dry them before nightfall. At that rate the several loads of laundry bursting out of the hampers would take ten days to dry.

Rip treated me to a crooked grin. "I'm not out of socks yet."

I glanced out the front window—sharp blue sky, light breeze in the empty trees. Crocuses thinking about making a move down there under the dry grass. Plus it was Saturday, and my family members were all busy.

I folded my arms to wrap up my decision. "Actually," I said, "I wouldn't mind seeing more of the flower show."

❈ *Chapter 11* ❈

*A*s usual, prior to the flower show the *Philadelphia Inquirer* emphatically advised that public transportation was the way to go. Rainy days and certain off afternoons were also recommended. Faced with a sunny Saturday morning, I opted for the train into Thirtieth Street Station.

Once, waiting there for a train, a shabbily dressed young woman snipped a thin silver bangle off my wrist while hitting me up for cash. To get me to lean close enough, she had spoken just above a whisper. The station always reminds me that I can usually afford to be trusting, a bigger surprise than the theft and a lesson much more valuable than the five dollars I had paid for the bracelet.

So here I was again, older, better fed, buoyed by visions of spring, insulated from the cold and damp by suitable matching clothing, only one of a horde of similar women moving through the high-ceilinged marble railway station as carefree as if we represented all the material comforts of the world, which among us we probably did.

I couldn't help seeing Iffy and my mother over and over in the crowd—sweet, dutiful women on a frivolous excursion, harmless ladies. Nothing about them appeared to threaten anyone, let alone to inspire murderous fury. Of course, that impression was as misleading as the pickpocket asking for cash. Bespectacled, blue-haired ladies prove themselves tougher than tigers or grease stains every day. Sooner or later one of them will get sued for false advertising.

The *Inquirer* said special buses would be waiting along a certain curb to take us to and from the Civic Center. True to the printed word, two such vehicles squatted at the ready, one a Southeastern Pennsylvania Transportation Authority (SEPTA) type, the other a yellow school bus. Each sported flower show signs with a logo under it, except the school bus sign was done with magic markers.

The latest batch of train station ladies headed for the silver SEPTA bus and quickly clogged the corner with a slow, fat line. A young, round-faced black man eyed me from the driver's seat of the second bus and delivered his spiel: "Flower show bus, one dollar." He smiled. I smiled. I gave him a dollar and took a window seat in the middle. Slowly, the clump of women spun off a few individualists who joined me.

When our bus was two-thirds full, an elderly woman entered as far as the first step, glanced around and asked the driver in all seriousness. "Do you take men?"

"No, ma'am," dead-panned the driver.

"Oh, sorry," she said, then backed out and took her husband's arm to lead him toward the other bus. Our driver bounded after them and soon all three returned, the couple smiling dubiously, our driver wearing an all-out grin.

As the several blocks between the station and the Civic Center passed before my eyes, I tried to picture Iffy Bigelow even once being as gullible as that poor silly woman. The picture simply wouldn't work. Iffy grew up in Ludwig, as down to earth an upbringing as you can get. She must have trusted the young man who got her pregnant, but that experience surely exhausted her lifetime supply.

So yesterday morning it must have been someone she knew and felt safe with who drew her aside for a private conversation. No weapon could have been involved. The murderer needed both hands to choke Iffy with her own scarf. So trust, not force, propelled Iffy into that storage room; there was simply no other explanation.

When the bus stopped, I waited for most of the other women (and one gentleman) to disembark before me. Arm over the back of his leather seat, the driver beamed at his exiting passengers. When his eyes rested on me, they seemed to radiate even more warmth, as if by being his first passenger we shared some inside joke.

"Where'd you get the bus?" I asked, for his smugness gave him away even if the handmade sign and distinctly non-SEPTA vehicle didn't.

His eyes scrambled and widened with alarm. "You won't report me will you?"

I shouldered my handbag and sidled down the aisle. "Hey," I said. "Free enterprise—the American way. So where'd you get the bus?"

His head swayed on a limp neck. "My uncle Sid."

"I'll look for you later," I said and smiled. I had to, the guy looked so relieved.

Hanging back had been a mistake, even if it had satisfied my curiosity. All those chirpy, wide-eyed women and hundreds more, actually thousands, were now squeezing through the far left doors of the Civic Center, converging on the cattle chute into the upper level, standing in line for tickets, for programs, for the escalator, to check their coats. So far the only flower in sight in the broad upper hall was the stylized one on the omnipresent logo.

I made it into the ticketing area and paused, bracing myself to be trapped for hours inside the stifling crowd. Coping with a quantity of people that enormous demands a patience I don't usually possess. Down on the main floor I wouldn't be able to take more than a few normal strides in a row unless it was toward an exit. I reminded myself, firmly, of why I returned, and that gave me all the grit I needed.

While waiting to hand in my ticket, an opportunity for

information presented itself in the form of Scooter, the show official. I noticed her camel hair blazer cutting across the lobby through the crowd, apparently headed for a door on the inside wall.

Beyond the opening for the escalators, the Civic Center offices used to span the width of the building overlooking the lower level like a windowed cliff. Windows once faced the incoming upstairs crowd as well, but no longer. Now a wall of vertical wooden strips obscured the view, but it was fair to assume the offices were still there.

"Excuse me," I called, trotting to catch my quarry. Up close I could see that the blazer with its official ribbon was intended to make Scooter easy to spot, for underneath was a white, cowl-necked, knit dress that surely would have looked better on its own.

When the show official turned to face me, her medium brown hair swung forward, and she automatically tucked it behind her ears. Today instead of tugging an earlobe, she fingered the pearl earrings that complimented the dress. She was definitely dressed up for something. In her left hand she carried a wrinkled yellow bill of lading.

I extended my hand and reminded her, "Ginger Barnes from yesterday. I'm sorry, I don't know your name."

"Temple Bodell," she replied, returning my grip. The handshake was hearty, the accompanying smile a trifle eager. Murder seemed very much to be yesterday's problem. "You're Mrs. Bigelow's niece," she said, giving me the social eye-gaze.

"No, that was Julia," I said. "My mother and Mrs. Bigelow were friends."

Temple Bodell didn't seem to much care who I was as long as I was in a position to help her, which from her stance and expression I seemed to be.

"I've got to take this to somebody," she said, waving the yellow paper, "but do you have a minute?" she asked. "Maybe you can do me a big favor."

"I'll try."

I followed her through the side door, past a volunteer sentry, and down a narrow hall to the open expanse of desks I expected. Temple stopped at a near one and called across the room. "Donny, take a look at this."

Donny, a handsome young man in a white shirt and red braces wound among the relatively empty desks to relieve her of the paper.

After he returned to his desk, I asked, "What can I do for you?" My questions could certainly wait until I answered hers.

The chin-length hair swung its arc onto the woman's pale cheeks. "It's Mrs. Bigelow's entries. There are several of them, as you can imagine. Here, I've got a list. The rules clearly state . . . somebody has to remove them today." She shuffled papers and extracted the list. I took it because she pushed it into my hand.

"I'm sorry, but I came in by train."

"But you'll make arrangements, won't you? I've got the banquet in an hour and a half and, really, this shouldn't be my problem. The rules clearly state . . ."

"I can call Mr. Bigelow . . ."

"Wonderful. Great. Thanks a lot." She turned to shout across the room. "Donny, where did you—"

I touched the sleeve of her blazer. "Excuse me. I was wondering if you could tell me the status of the Grand Sweepstakes on Thursday afternoon."

"The what?"

"Thursday afternoon—the status of the sweeps?"

Her mind was across the room with Donny; I was lucky she even faced my direction.

"The awards will be made at the banquet at noon. I can't give you any information now."

"But I don't need to know who won, just the status . . ."

She was turning again, opening her mouth to shout. I

interrupted rather loudly. "How can I reach you after the show?"

"What?"

"In case I have a problem about Iffy's plants?"

Blank eyes. Mind elsewhere. One more try.

"Your home phone number, Mrs. Bodell?"

She scribbled on a slip of paper and handed it to me as she turned away, our whole exchange probably forgotten. At least with her phone number I could ask a few questions later, when she might have the leisure to answer them.

"Thank you," I murmured, but I was talking to myself.

There were a couple pay phones along the inner wall, and I used one to call Arthur Bigelow.

"Who is it?" he answered groggily. I felt awful about waking him up, but how was I to know? Best to get to the point and let him try to go back to sleep.

"Iffy's plants?" I could hear the change in his voice as he sat upright.

"Yes. I'm really sorry to bother you, but I was told they have to be removed today."

After a heavy pause, he said, "Give them away."

That wasn't the answer I expected. "Are you sure? They must be fairly valuable."

"What am I going to do with them now?" My heart ached for all the sad changes in his life. Why had I volunteered for this phone call? Had I volunteered for this phone call?

"Do you have anyone in mind?"

"No, Mrs. Barnes. Whoever you choose will be fine. Keep them yourself if you like."

Something more had to be said, but what? "Thanks, but I think I should find someone . . ." I was dealing with a lump in my throat. "I'll find them . . ." I almost said, "a good home," but that made them sound like puppies. "I'll find someone with a greenhouse."

I carried my new responsibility to the escalator line with my ticket. Give them to Temple Bodell? No, she couldn't wait to unload the problem of their removal; she surely wouldn't want it back.

They were prize-winning specimens—maybe I should keep them, i.e. go home, get my car, come back and carry them one at a time to the car, to my house, place them in the perfect light, water them, feed them, turn them, re-pot them, de-bug them, et cetera ad infinitum. Out of the question. I didn't want the plants either. Like many other luxuries I admired, I could enjoy them without owning them.

Yet the Civic Center was filled with people who probably would treasure Iffy's plants. As I worked my way through my agenda, perhaps a deserving recipient would emerge.

For now I turned in my ticket to the uniformed agent at the top of the second escalator and concentrated on the sensual pleasure awaiting me. My pulse picked up. I could feel a goofy grin spread across my face. Only the possibility of someone hearing me quashed an outright giggle. The fact that I'd been there yesterday didn't matter; yesterday I hadn't used the escalator.

Once I was twenty minutes early for a 5:12 p.m. train out of the old Reading Terminal. The only thing I had in common with the inhabitants of the seating area were a couple of loaded shopping bags, so I opted to wait just inside the double sliding doors posted with my departure time. Rocking from one sore foot to the other, I absorbed more and more of the elderly train station's dreary, decades-old grime and depressing disrepair. At first I was one of only a few politely spaced commuters, but as time crept along I became tightly enclosed by a crowd. Pregnant, exhausted, claustrophobic, I began to think my wait would never end.

Riding the escalator down to the flower show was like the doors opening for the train out of winter.

As fellow Pennsylvanians, Temple Bodell and her crew were not unaware of this effect. Every year they placed a splashy theme display at the bottom of the entrance, always a grand flight of imagination comparable to the quality of the competitive classes. This year's theme was "A Celebration of Spring," and the display no disappointment. Although I had seen it at ground level, it was much more impressive from above. It consisted of five angled wedges in a broken semi-circle with flowers planted in matching rainbow stripes. The wedges were probably ten feet tall and the planted areas about that wide. Remembering the lawsuit brought on by an overhead banner, I glanced up to find ordinary acoustical ceiling. Only the broken rainbow below drew you into the show by way of your own feet.

When I hit ground level, I stepped to the right out of the flow of the crowd to consider where to begin. An oval "Information" booth staffed by Pennsylvania Horticulture Society members stood directly in front of me. Since I needed information, I decided to begin there.

The booth was staffed by three people, two women and a man. Considering what I planned to ask, I calculated that a woman might be more accommodating.

Occupied with a visitor, the nearest female helper pointed her pen at the color coded maps inside the show program. The listener, a short brunette with slanted eyebrows, looked as if English were her second language. I moved around to catch the attention of the second woman staffer as she squeezed between her co-worker and some storage cabinets.

"Excuse me," I said, "I'm writing an obituary for the newspaper, and I wonder if you could give me some information about Winifred Bigelow?"

The woman pointed her nose at me and gawked. "No," she said. "No, I can't." So much for instinct.

Okay. "Sir. Excuse me." I walked around the booth into the view of the remaining purveyor of information. Displayed behind him on the inside wall were PHS T-shirts and aprons in bright solid colors. "Could you possibly give me some information about Winifred Bigelow?"

"What did you say it was for?" He was an aging man held erect by will power and a plaid shirt so crisp it could have been made of cardboard. The seriousness of his face suggested that any information he chose to impart would hold up in court.

"For an obituary for the paper."

"What paper?"

"*Main Line Courier.*" A fictitious name, or so I hoped. You never knew. "Can you tell me anything about Mrs. Bigelow? Preferably something my readers wouldn't have read elsewhere?"

The man's thin-skinned cheeks colored. "Sorry. I didn't know her that well."

Another man leaning against the counter had been watching me hustle around on my supposed errand. When the cardboard shirt dusted me off, he laughed. I turned toward a laconic grin hung in a wreath of inflated wrinkles, a sort of fleshy inner tube not fully blown up. He had some gray-black hair, some loose clothes, and the air of an idler on a pension. I might have liked him if he hadn't been laughing at me.

"Whyn't you try Howie Hancock. He'd prob'ly have lots to say. Or if ya can't find him, Beatrice Crumb." There was a joke on me in there somewhere, but I was too excited about the leads to worry about it.

Since Howie Hancock was the name of the man in the niche competition with Iffy, I asked, "Who's Beatrice Crumb?"

"Owns the Tuckahoe Nursery. Tall gal. White bun right atop her head."

"Thanks. I think I know what Howie looks like. Have you seen him today?"

"Yup."

I satisfied this obvious goad with a sarcastic scowl. "You want to tell me where?"

"Sure. I don't mind. Saw old Howie darlin' sipping his café au lait over the concession area about ten minutes ago."

"You want to tell me which concession area?"

A flick of a bony index finger indicated the middle of the long right hand wall, referring to one of the small refreshment areas around the perimeter of the show. I thanked him and started to leave, but the bony finger hooked my arm and reeled me in for a whisper. "Don't get too close, mind you."

Since I was nearly close enough to bite his nose, I had to ask what he meant.

"AIDS," he said, with a smirk.

I glanced toward the cardboard shirt, whose sleeves were folded crisply enough for a package. The information man was alive in there, though, because I saw him breathe.

"Least that's the word according to Iffy Bigelow." The bony hand swatted my shoulder, and the inner tube puffed up for a wonderful laugh. "Course you have to wonder how she knew."

Plaid Shirt huffed. "That's enough, Abe. You had your fun. Now move along."

Abe moved along, pausing only to slap his thighs and finish his laugh.

"Is it true?" I asked the shirt.

"I have no idea. But I'd be very careful about printing anything I didn't verify."

I gave him an "umm" to indicate I was too professional to respond to such a comment. "Can you at least tell me whether the Tuckahoe Nursery is here?"

"Yes, ma'am. Bea has a booth in the trade section. Second row from the left, third booth in. But don't be surprised if she's too busy to talk."

I nodded and thanked him. He obviously knew Beatrice Crumb well enough to use her first name. I was tempted to ask about her relationship with Iffy Bigelow, but my information man was already defensive and suspicious enough to turn hostile.

Instead I aimed for the concession area "Abe" had indicated. It doesn't take long to drink a cup of coffee; and if Howie had already rejoined the Saturday crowd, finding him would be impossible.

❈ *Chapter 12* ❈

Getting to the concession area Abe the Comedian had indicated meant passing between and around at least five major displays. Since the visitors ringed each commercial exhibit two or three deep, in a few narrow spots squeezing past meant waiting for a line to move enough to make an opening.

Flowers? I saw part of a dogwood tree over a couple of shorter heads and an azalea briefly through a gap, but viewing an exhibit all at once from twenty feet away was a pleasant memory, one nobody else would be taking home today.

The map in the middle of my program, which I opened during a particularly slow spot, showed me there were five snack bars on the side Abe indicated, not just one in the middle. Since his directions had been a trifle vague, I thought I'd better sneak through the first available opening and check all along that outer wall.

Opposite a pair of rest rooms, the first snack bar shunted its customers between a chrome railing and a rope suspended on posts. No seating. Strictly fend-for-yourself food. I shouldered my way past the rest room line, scooted past the rope and continued my search.

Their space unimpeded by lavatories, the middle two snack bars afforded some of the plastic Siamese seating

Mother and I had endured for hours yesterday morning. Odd pairings of apparent strangers shared a few round tables.

I recognized Howie nursing a paper cup at the centermost table. To his right a portly mother in a black-and-white printed dress spooned ice cream into the mouth of a toddler in an umbrella stroller. On his left—an empty seat just for me!

I started to rush for it but hesitated two yards away.

What would I say?

Studying my quarry for a clue to the proper approach didn't help. Howie just sat there mothering his coffee, a weary cherub, as much an ice-cream candidate as the tear-stained toddler strapped to the stroller. The air of nervous fatigue I remembered from the niche competition had rendered his face as pale as his thin curly hair and limp as his shoulders. Nothing came to mind but sympathy, and whoever pried open a murder suspect with sympathy?

One of those helpful cliches came to mind, the one about the devil hating a coward. I don't know why, but I always think of that when I'm planning to lie.

"Howie Hancock, isn't it?" I said extending my hand.

He blinked. He rubbed his coffee container on the table and blinked again. "Yes?" he said, as if it had been a trick question.

Unfortunately, the chair to his left possessed a drying ketchup/relish blob front and center. I did some hasty housekeeping with a napkin and carefully sat down.

With an air intended to be respectfully glum I remarked, "Iffy Bigelow spoke to me about you."

The young man's sensitive eyes were an interesting greenish-blue with brown flecks. They were also large and damp as if he were perpetually on the verge of tears. He looked away. "Please," he said. "No more."

I wagged my head. "She said she might have been wrong."

Suddenly those damp eyes poised over me like a tack

hammer. "Who are you?" His pursed lips remained as soft as the baby's in a current toilet paper commercial.

"My mother and Iffy were friends. I drove her here yes-. terday."

"And what do you want with me?"

"To ask if there's anything I can do. Mother was fond of Iffy, but she knew her . . . faults. She wanted to sort of . . . apologize." From what Abe at the information booth said, I had pieced together that Iffy started a damaging rumor, most likely that Howie Hancock had AIDS. At least I supposed it was a rumor. He looked healthy enough to me.

The young man sighed and a shoulder twitched. Then once again he regarded me with weariness.

"Do you have any idea what you're talking about?"

"Maybe not."

"Then why . . .? Of course. By now everyone knows what Iffy said at the preview Saturday night. But now you're trying to tell me she thought she might have been wrong?"

I shrugged, tilted my head, smiled.

Howie stared at me until I flinched. "She never intended to apologize, did she?" he pressed. "Iffy Bigelow believed every awful word she said. That's what made her so convincing."

He examined the far wall, maybe checking for cracks. "Stupid, irresponsible bitch. This has been the most hellacious week of my life."

"I'm sorry. Iffy was inclined to be . . ."

"Yes . . .?" Howie's soft round face had reddened in ominous blotches.

I shrugged. ". . . But she had a good heart."

The lips clamped into a rigid line. "Does she have any idea? Oh, of course not, she's . . ." A trembling hand flew to his forehead. "Please excuse me. I've scarcely slept. I probably need a good run—Tom and I used to run together every morning; you know, to sweat out the impurities. But after he left, I just couldn't, and with all this to worry about . . ." His hand waved in a tiny circle that encompassed the Civic Center. I took him to mean his entries in the flower show.

"Flowers are your livelihood?"

He glanced at me sharply.

Oops. "I didn't mean to offend you, but I'm strictly a spectator here."

"You're not a garden club lady? No quaint little shop in Glenside?"

I shook my head, and he reinflated himself with a breath. "Well, that's something anyhow."

"Mr. Hancock, what do you do?"

"You really are an outsider?"

"One hundred percent."

"I'm going to arrange flowers, professionally," he said. It seemed a rather small admission to follow such an inquisition, but he relaxed around his coffee cup in a promising way. A passerby bumped my chair leg just then, so I hunkered in. No distractions, please. Howie was about to confess.

"I've been developing a small following, so to speak, and Tom"—a small gulp—"Tom encouraged me to make use of it. The commercial art business isn't really satisfactory anymore, logos with bulldozers on them, pie charts on the computer. So Tom suggested I go into the flower business. Some corporations agreed to use me for their interior landscaping, seasonal displays, that sort of thing. But of course I hope to do weddings, private parties, and so on. Whatever it takes to survive, you know."

"Excuse my ignorance," I said, "but with all that going for you, why bother with the flower show?"

A small blush. "Oh, darling," he teased, playing the femme for me. "It's a wonderful vehicle. Of course it's risky as hell to stick out one's neck, but it's also quite a thrill. If you were writing this up, I'd probably tell you I love the competition. But you're not." The playfulness abruptly stopped. "You're not, are you?",

"No."

"Well, then I guess it doesn't hurt to admit I need all the exposure I can get. Word of mouth is essential in this business—paid advertising makes you sound like such a beggar."

"Reputation is money in the bank," I remarked, thinking mainly of Rip's PR problems, past and present.

"Exactly," Howie agreed. And then I remembered Iffy's irresponsible remark and what it had done to his personal reputation. He seemed to be thinking the same thing.

"Exactly who are you again?"

"My mother was a friend of Iffy's."

"And what was that bunk about an apology? To my knowledge Iffy Bigelow never apologized to anybody."

"Actually, I'm not entirely sure what she should have apologized for."

A sigh and distant gaze. "She got spiffed at the preview dinner and told some people . . . she said I was HIV-positive, that I was one of those Typhoid Marys who looked perfectly healthy but was the kiss of death."

I was genuinely shocked. "She actually said all that?"

Howie nodded with surprising composure, possibly because I was reacting for us both. "She was very spiffed and it attracted an audience. I guess she just . . . needed something sensational to say. She was very spiffed."

"But surely it isn't true." I had been growing fond of Howie Hancock; he had a sweet face and an appealing personality. And anyway I always warm to people who can laugh at themselves.

"No. It's an absolute lie. I've been tested. Last year, but then there was only Tom soon after, and he . . . but you don't need to hear all that."

"Could you have sued?"

"I doubt it. I quizzed an eyewitness, a waiter who was standing right behind her with a tray. He said she used 'probably' and 'looks like' and all those safe little phrases that indicate she's giving an opinion but unfortunately nobody hears. He thought she could say it was all a poorly worded joke. Anyhow, I haven't got money for a lawsuit, especially against the talent she could have hired."

"You said you had a hellacious week. Were people unkind? Did they avoid you?"

"Dear girl, you should never hope to have a week like mine." He rolled his eyes and tried a smile, but it didn't hold.

"What happened?"

"The freeze was in, naturally, but I've been through that. And I knew eventually the truth would emerge. Anyway, what did I care about strangers? It was Tom who mattered." Howie covered his mouth with his knuckles and blinked. The plump woman beside him chose that moment to jostle past us with her loaded umbrella stroller. I thought she bumped Howie's shoulder unnecessarily, perhaps even leaned that way on purpose to give him a good shot, but Howie paid no attention. I inched my chair closer to avoid further eavesdropping.

"Tom believed the rumor?" I asked.

"Oh no. Of course not. But he works for an ignorant bunch of stiffs, his words, not mine. Anyhow, he said one of them was at the dinner, unfortunately the partner who has it in for Tom, and if he ever found out we lived together . . . It was just an excuse. He's been wanting to leave for a long time. Still, I wish . . .." He wished the delusion had lasted much longer.

He washed me with those damp eyes. "Maybe I should have killed the bitch," he said. "It just didn't occur to me. Imagine that."

Sympathy. Oh yes. Sam Spade should have given it a chance.

❈ *Chapter 13* ❈

I told Howie I was very happy to hear he hadn't killed Mrs. Bigelow. He snorted. I asked him who did it. "In your opinion, of course."

"Spread gossip?" He snorted again. "Far too much of that going around already."

"Oh come on, Howie," I said. "You have a rather sizeable interest in somebody else taking the blame. Have the police spoken to you yet?"

This time a huff of disgust.

"They on to both your motives?"

Two raised eyebrows. "What do you mean?"

"I mean Iffy's rumor, which happened to ruin your relationship with Tom, and then the professional one."

"What do you mean?"

"I mean that you needed to win the niche category to launch your new business. Nobody remembers a runner-up."

"That's nonsense. I already have clients. Tom's a terrific salesperson. He has plenty of work lined up for me."

"But Tom is gone, and correct me if I'm wrong, but aren't flower jobs more or less one shot deals? A wedding here, a banquet there?"

"He got me those corporate jobs."

I raised my palms. "Enough?"

He sighed. Mentioning that Tom was no longer on the job had been superfluous. The fact hung around Howie's neck like a noose.

"You're right, of course. A blue ribbon, or better, would have been terrific publicity. But you don't fix a horse race by strangling one horse."

The reference made me wince, and I wasn't even sure I knew what he meant.

"Winifred Bigelow's death didn't help," he clarified for me. "I still came in second."

The comparison finally came into focus. "Gamblers prefer to bet on a sure thing."

"Of course. I'd have had to eliminate everybody who stood a chance of beating me." He blinked those limpid eyes and smiled slightly. "Not literally, of course."

He was saying that he didn't murder Iffy, or more accurately: killing her for that reason was ineffective and, therefore, illogical.

Howie and I sat there a moment reading each other. The tolerant amusement in his eyes made me wonder if he saw past the pressure from my mother all the way to my private reason for questioning him, my anachronistic opinion that a person should try to leave the world with a little more than her recipe for salsa pie. If he saw that, he also forgave me and in a way endorsed my sentiment. Nice guy, Howie Hancock.

"Who won?" I finally asked.

The pretty lips spread into a grin. He puffed his chest, spread his elbows, and cupped his hands as if hefting enormous boobs. "Helen Luedeke, dahling. Who else?" I laughed. Lord help me, I liked Howie Hancock. I sure hoped he wasn't a murderer.

I turned away for a moment and watched a vendor pluck a hot dog off a hot rack and drop it into a roll.

Who else, dahling?

I said, "Helen Luedeke, alias the Grande Dame of Niches, never left the area during the competition."

Howie wagged his head no.

"Did you?"

A glare.

"Okay. So who else had a motive?"

He sighed with resignation. "Walk me over to the trade section. I'm filling in for a friend, and I'm already late."

I scraped back my chair. "What about Beatrice Crumb?"

"Tuckahoe Nurseries?" He considered while he guided me through the maze of legs, animate and inanimate.

"I don't know any reason why Beatrice should hate Iffy. I guess you'd have to ask around. Joe Pescatore maybe."

Rather than fighting past the exhibits, he routed us along the outer wall. When he pushed through into an open expanse, keeping up earned me a nasty look from a man carrying a loaded tray.

"On second thought, Joe can't even swat a fly. Forget it," he shouted over his shoulder.

Where the lines of people waiting were contained by another rope, Howie bolted several steps ahead. I wanted to ask him more about this Pescatore person, but he abruptly wheeled to face me, raising a finger and both eyebrows. I kept my mouth shut.

"Alice Gifford," he said.

"Who's that?"

"The no-show." The person Scooter's niche arrangement replaced, the display that didn't count.

"Howie!" I complained. "Don't just tell me a name. Tell me why."

He glanced around us. Although people stood in line only five or six feet away, we were in a pocket of relative privacy.

Howie answered so cautiously I could scarcely hear him. "The accident in the parking garage."

"What accident?"

The young man's shoulders lifted individually, little impatient jabs in the air. "Thursday morning. I'll bet the police are questioning her already." The prospect brightened his face.

"Please, Howie. Start at the beginning."

"You'll remind them, won't you, if they forgot or something. Coming from me it would sound too . . . self-serving." A finger rested on his cheek. "Oh surely they've checked her out. Even Philadelphia cops are that smart."

I placed my fists on my hips and took a deep noisy breath.

"What? You really don't know?"

"Nobody knows everything." A twitty remark, but I was losing it.

Howie shifted his feet and held his elbow and told the story alternately to my nose and my collarbone.

It emerged that Iffy Bigelow's car was in the shop because she hit a passing car that swerved into Alice Gifford, who happened to be on foot. Alice was treated at the hospital for a broken leg and released. The accident occurred about six-thirty in the morning, about the same time I arrived with my party the next day.

No wonder Iffy had been a nervous wreck riding with me. The day after causing an accident, to her, anybody's normal speed probably felt like the pace at Indianapolis. Last accident I had, it took me two weeks to settle down, and all I'd done was hit a neighbor's mailbox. Throw in the guilt of injuring someone, the normal misgivings older people have about driving (my mother and I both knew her license was in her dresser drawer), compound those worries with anxiety over the sweeps, and anybody might become a bit testy. Especially an Iffy Bigelow.

"Okay, assuming an opportunity presents itself for me to mention this to the police. Who should they talk to for the unabridged version?"

Howie smirked. "Helen Luedeke."

"Helen? Why?"

Once again the self-amused flirt, he said, "Because, my dear, she was driving the other car. With those breasts, her driver's air bag didn't even bother to open."

Chapter 14

*H*owie led me across the corner of the commercial displays toward a trade section entrance. When he had room to get going, he had a springy, boyish stride, almost as if he were wearing basketball high tops instead of canvas slip-ons. But then I remembered he and Tom used to run together "to sweat out the impurities."

We jostled over to the third aisle from the left, skirting around the second shop in the row, a flat-topped hut, or more accurately the frame of a hut finished only to the waist. There the rectangular structure supported plywood tabletops. Small plastic pots of robust little plants were grouped by kind: miniature African violets in bloom, primroses of amazing color, variegated ivies, and a dozen interesting specimens I could not name. Abruptly, Howie halted behind a woman exchanging dollar bills for a closed paper bag. Other customers, mostly women, contemplated everything from the hanging plants that filled the ceiling frame to larger specimens crowding the aisle on the floor.

For a second I thought Howie was admiring a plant that looked like strung peas spilling from a pot, but he had indicated a rough wooden Tuckahoe Nursery sign dangling from a wrought-iron arm. My destination.

He turned to go.

"Wait!" I shouted above the crowd noise.

He paused, his body eager to hurry away.

"Maybe I can deliver an apology from Iffy after all," I said. Curiosity held Howie long enough for me to explain that I had been commissioned to dispose of Iffy's prize winning plants.

"You seem be the most appropriate recipient."

First he gaped at me with his soft mouth forming a pear of disbelief. And then he threw back his head and laughed.

I handed him the list.

"You mean it, don't you?" He laughed some more. And then he said, "You've got a deal. Thank you, Ginger Barnes. Where do you live? I'll send a bouquet for your birthday. Then he handed me his business card, a creamy white creation with an embossed rose underscoring his name in mauve, no doubt another Howie Hancock joke, which also happened to be a pretty good gimmick.

"Any idea where Alice Gifford lives? So I can direct the police, if they haven't talked to her already."

"Rosemont, I think. Not far from the college. Her husband's a professor or something. But it's probably useless. If somebody with a broken leg came here to kill Iffy Bigelow, we'd have heard about it by now."

"Still, I'll pass it along."

"Would you? That'd be wonderful." He seemed excessively grateful. It really must have been a tough week.

I thanked him for his help, and we shook hands. "Now don't forget to pick up *all* of Iffy's plants or Temple Bodell will chase you down on her scooter."

"Yes, Mother," he said with a wink. Then he bounded off through the crowd, every bit the dear he pretended to be.

Beatrice Crumb wore a denim skirt with deep pockets, a leather belt and boots, a white shirt with a mud smear on the sleeve, a tooled silver necklace trimmed with turquoise, and large lumpy earrings to match. Her silver-white hair was twisted unceremoniously into a knot on top of her head. She might have been thirty or fifty, but her face was just beginning to lose to gravity, and her eyes had squinted at more than thirty years of sunshine.

I arbitrarily put her at forty-two, partly because of the jaded way she detached herself from her customers. Or maybe I didn't like the squint of her eyes.

I circled the booth admiring the plants, including shamrocks in tiny square pots. An array of cut flowers wound into cones of green tissue were stuck into a plywood display board. I chose a bunch with rust-and-white mums, blue statice, and white baby's-breath to match our living room.

"May I help you?"

The voice belonged to one of Beatrice Crumb's assistants, a tall, robust woman who looked as stern as her boss.

"Not finished looking," I mumbled, sidling around to a position in front of the owner.

"Help you?" Beatrice asked.

I handed her my bunch of flowers and reached for my wallet. "Sorry about Iffy Bigelow," I said as I counted out money. "You were friends, weren't you?"

"Where'd you get that idea?" the woman asked. Grim black eyebrows crowded her eyes as she tucked her chin.

"From Iffy. I thought she said . . ."

"You're mistaken, and I'm too busy for this." She strode around a co-worker to the cash register. The co-worker passed me my change.

"Thanks," I shouted, but Beatrice Crumb was already across the booth waiting on someone else.

I told the helper that I wanted two big hanging plants but didn't want to carry them home today. "Where's your nursery? Maybe I can stop by next week."

She grabbed a folder from a stack at the end of the counter and shoved it into my hand.

"Did I say something wrong?" I pressed.

She looked at me scathingly.

I'm an adult; I knew I was blushing, but I also knew how to pretend I wasn't stung. With a certain graceful flair I stowed the folder in my shoulder bag and nestled the bouquet in my elbow like an award.

Twirling to take my place in the throng, I noticed the well-dressed, handsome figure of a man leaning on a post. He crooked his finger and I let him reel me in.

General Motors Mills said, "What the hell you doin,' girl?"

"Didn't you used to beat up people who called you 'boy?'" I asked. He grinned. "Then how about saying hello like everybody else."

He crossed his arms and centered his head against the pole. "Hello, Mrs. Barnes. What the hell you doin' here, Mrs. Barnes?"

"Buying flowers, George. What the hell does it look like?"

"Looks like you're pokin' your little white nose in a beehive, and I think you're gonna get stung."

I mimed a "moi?"

He surrounded my shoulders with a long arm and started me in motion beside him. It was probably my imagination, but people seemed to fall to the wayside to let us through. I hummed a little of the Miss America theme, "There she is . . ." George snorted into his mustache.

The last booth on the left sold Pennsylvania Dutch items—corn relish, shoo-fly pie, homemade noodles, also trivets and hex signs in two sizes painted on pressed board. Howie was accepting payment for a set of tacky salt and pepper shakers shaped like an Amish boy and girl. He stopped long enough to show me the thumbs-up sign, no doubt pleased that I would be diverting suspicion to the disabled Alice Gifford so soon—something I was not at all eager to do.

I fell a step behind and shrugged. Howie smiled and

nodded his encouragement. I wasn't going to get released from my "assignment" so easily. Considering his recent emotional battering, maybe giving Howie the plants had been a tactical error, a bit more bonding than I had intended. I sighed loud enough for George to ask, "What?"

"Nothing," I mumbled.

In front of us spread the Garden Cafe, yet another refreshment area for the suddenly hungry. This one was quite spacious, a large selection of food stalls surrounding a wide expanse of tables and chairs. The nearest seats were fairly empty, probably because they were farthest from the food. George held my chair. I dumped my flowers and purse on another chair and waited.

"You want any coffee?"

"No, and why don't you quit stalling."

George shot his shirt cuffs and rolled his shoulders. People with muscles always seem to be doing that, as if their clothes never fit right or they're inviting you to imagine them naked. When he pulled out a chair in preparation for sitting down, I noticed that the center seam of George's corduroy sport coat was indeed engaged in a struggle.

When he was settled, he said, "You're cleared," then he wiggled the knot of his kelly-green tie.

My eyes popped. "I was a suspect?" Now there was a frightening thought.

"Yeah, but the coffee cart lady remembered your red hair. We're still askin' around, but you can probably relax."

Light auburn. My hair is light auburn. "Did you take into consideration that yesterday morning was the first time I ever spoke to Iffy Bigelow?"

"Feisty redhead like you? An old bat like that? Hell, I figure you offed her just for makin' some crack about your driving."

"You . . . you're kidding, right?"

"Right."

I resumed breathing. He had guessed about the driving. My only connection with Iffy was that I drove her there.

The Pennsylvania Dutch booth lay in my line of vision. A glimpse of Howie gave me the guilts, so I made use of the opening. "Speaking of driving, did you know Iffy caused an accident two mornings ago?"

George offered no comment one way or the other.

"A woman who was supposed to compete in the same niche category was injured. Alice Gifford? The winner, Helen Luedeke, was involved, too, but she wasn't hurt."

"You didn't mention that yesterday," George remarked.

"I just heard about it."

"Oh?"

Watch your step, Gin.

George gave me the look that said, "Go on . . ."

"Yes, I was just talking to somebody about Iffy's plants— Temple Bodell asked me to find someone to remove them today—and the man who's doing it and I got talking. He was in the niche competition, too, and happened to mention that Alice couldn't compete because she had a broken leg . . ." Enough, blabbermouth.

"Mm-hmm," George said, not a bit fooled. "You seem to have a lot of acquaintances around here. Anything else you'd like to bring to the attention of the Philadelphia police?"

I caught myself hiding behind my fists, which were propped up by my elbows. Just snap on the handcuffs and take me away.

I dropped my hands to my lap.

"Not at this time," I said.

George let a little smile play on his lips. His eyes were also amused.

Meanwhile, his question set off a review of what I actually knew, most of which fell into the rumor category rather than fact. Except for the rumor Iffy started, which many witnesses would no doubt substantiate.

I glanced toward the Pennsylvania Dutch booth where Howie was occupied wrapping jars of apple butter and honey in tissue.

"There is one thing I'm sure you already know."

"Umm?"

I fiddled with an unused straw somebody left on the table, lifted it, dropped it. "The man I was talking to, Howie Hancock, was quite upset by something Mrs. Bigelow said at the preview last Saturday night." George sat back and folded his arms, the better to grill me in silence. "Do you know about the AIDS rumor?"

Silence. I lifted the straw, dropped it, pushed it around. George just watched.

"Do you know that Howie's lover left him because of the rumor?" I was feeling horribly disloyal to a trusting, gentle soul. But he *was* a very hurt human being who I just met. It wasn't for me to decide whether he was capable of murder or not. Despite feeling rotten, I also felt relieved.

George leaned on the table and let his hands fall on top of the straw. It bounced and rolled onto the floor.

George was thinking, no doubt about it. Although he couldn't or wouldn't admit whether any of my information was new to him, I'd have bet that some of it was. But just like last time, I probably only beat the police to it because of my proximity to the crime and the people involved. Eventually, one of the Main Liners would have squealed, even to a black city cop, if only to experience a moment of importance.

George scanned my face with a certain amount of warmth, this morning's first friendly overture. Until then he'd been one hundred percent cop.

"If you happen to *remember* anything else that you'd like to *remind* me about, you've got my number."

So that's how we were going to play it, I thought. That's how we were saving his face and my ass.

"If I *think* of anything else you should know, I'll call right away."

"Anytime," he said.

"Right," I said.

"See ya, Tink." He stuck out his hand, but first he rolled his shoulder.

"So long, George."

I collected my purse and flowers and headed home, so preoccupied deciding who to question next that I forgot my promise to the young man with the borrowed bus.

❈ *Chapter 15* ❈

When I got home from the show, there was just enough Saturday afternoon left to iron the Admissions office drapes and thaw a dinner of chili and onion rolls in the microwave.

Chelsea planned to stay overnight with Chrissie, and Garry had been joined by Dave (short and round) and Jordy (tall and thin) for an orgy of popcorn and action/adventure videos. Staying up and sleeping in was the name of the game, so the boys were kind enough to tolerate a leisurely dinner with the old folks.

The impromptu, down-home fun constituted a special treat for Rip, whose nurturing profession too rarely afforded him time to enjoy his own children. *Philadelphia Magazine* once quoted that a headmaster's job was like dancing with a bear: "You dance until the bear gets tired." Tonight the Bryn Derwyn bear napped while Rip teased three eleven-year-old boys and laughed at their mischievous jokes. Once I saw him glance at his watch; but when our eyes met, I realized it had been curiosity rather than impatience. The drapes could wait, till morning if necessary. So I scooped vanilla ice cream and heated hot fudge and poured my husband a second cup of coffee.

Around nine-thirty Rip and I finally tore ourselves away.

As I suspected, he had things other than drape-hanging planned for the morning—a little sleeping in of our own, then maybe some paperwork, a lazy start before the pressure of the Open House.

It isn't every combination of young boys I would leave unsupervised for even an hour; but historically the Garry, Dave, and Jordy trio were not big risk-takers. Given a Rambo scenario, I expected them to phone for help then alert the network news.

Yet at the door Rip reflected my mild anxiety over leaving the boys. "Keep an eye on things, sport," he told Barney as he fondled the dog's whitening muzzle.

On the short drive to the school Rip and I were content with a mellow silence. Yet pulling into the school driveway gave me a chill—something like when, as a girl, the light went off and my familiar bedroom suddenly became a closet of dark jutting corners and booby traps. I saw how someone might believe the school was haunted at night.

Sitting square at the top of a long drive, the main building was a large brick block with appendages extending up and out in many directions. Third graders still got lost in the Upper School wing trying to find music class. Not that it was so large—just a house with additions to accommodate three hundred forty-eight people in clumps of fifteen—sort of a brick castle built by a kindergarten class.

Rip parked in the front circle and began handing me broadly folded drapes from the back seat of his car.

"Feels like a refrigerator out here," I said, shivering as I accepted the awkward bundle.

While he fiddled with the lock on the wide front door, my eye strayed to the right end of the building. Just around the corner crouched the foundation of the future gymnasium, begun on the site of our former home. An extra chill seemed to waft across the shadowy mounds of mud and naked rows of cement block.

Although no traces of the demolished headmaster's house

remained, its ghost haunted my heart. I had decorated and cared for every inch of it long enough for it to become mine. Maybe when the capital campaign was successful and the gym covered the site, my mind's eye would no longer conjure up off-white siding and dark-green trim, a eucalyptus wreath or sheer white drapes or the smell of lilac in the spring.

Although a heavy dew had muffled the outdoor sounds, inside the school lobby echoed like a church. To the left behind a window and a door lay the reception area and administrative offices, the mail room and a copier—lots of desks and telephones and file cabinets.

A safety light glowed warmly, offering enough visibility to render the blue-and-gray lobby relatively inviting. Centered in the expanse was a hefty mahogany table with neatly arranged brochures, name tags and pens, plus a large fresh flower arrangement—all in honor of the Open House. The upholstered lobby chairs were temporarily absent, making space for the standing crowd everyone hoped would fill the room.

Rip unlocked the Admissions Office directly to the right of the front doors.

"No ladder," he observed. "Be right back." Around a corner toward the left he unlocked a fire door into the long, dark halls of the Upper School and eventually the maintenance area. Rather than flip the master switch and illuminate the building like a Christmas tree, Rip chose to find his way with the safety lights, something he could probably do with his eyes closed anyhow.

I turned on a floor lamp and spread the tweedy blue drapes across a leather sofa. Decorated along the order of an upscale living room, the Admissions Office balanced the formal with the informal—leather seating and a pecan coffee table, some Colonial prints and a few brass lamps.

I found the pin hooks for the drapes in an ashtray and managed to slip them all in place before Rip returned. For a while I stood staring out into the night, letting my imagination play, watching a car or two pass the end of the school driveway about a hundred yards away. It was Saturday night, and I supposed the travelers were heading to or from some pleasant social engagement.

Finally I heard Rip's footsteps and the clunks and rattles of one of the school's twelve-foot aluminum step ladders.

"Gin?" he called. "Can you get this door?"

Outside on the road a dark car slowed to a creep at the end of the driveway.

"Just a minute," I called to my husband.

No stop sign or traffic light would account for the car's slowing. Someone must be looking closely at the front of the school.

Casing the place? I was glad our car was parked prominently out front.

The police?

No. Township vehicles were two-toned; and as this long, sleek boat passed under the light of the school's sign, I could see it was dark, probably black. Also, I noticed the right rear was dented, since the strip of reflected light along the length of the car had a dip in it roughly where many gas tank covers were. But that was all I could see, no license plate, not even the make of the car.

A vandal? Putting a name to my suspicions made the idea seem preposterous. Only teenagers had warped, teenage reasons for damaging a school; and teenagers rarely drove long, black luxury cars, not even if their parents owned them.

Then I connected the car to the Open House and immediately felt better. Someone planning to attend tomorrow must be checking the school's location on the way to somewhere else, or perhaps timing the drive from home to see if sending their child to Bryn Derwyn would constitute an unreasonable inconvenience.

"Gin?"

"Right there."

I propped the fire door open with a wooden wedge and grabbed an end of the ladder. The office door we held open with a chair. We managed to chip the doorjamb paint anyhow, but after a few curses and a minute or two the ladder was finally in place.

Reaching the plastic tabs that ran the drape back and forth required Rip's longer arms. After he broke one or two of the brittle little devils, I climbed onto the window sill to support the heavy fabric and minimize the strain. The job wasn't really difficult or even time consuming, and there certainly wasn't any need for conversation.

If we had been talking, we wouldn't have heard the crash.

Some distance away, it wasn't especially loud or dramatic; but the way my heart took off you'd have thought somebody clanged cymbals right behind my head. Rip hit the floor first and stopped to give me a hand.

"A window?" I asked.

"Down the phys-ed hall I think. Stay here." He took out his keys and hurried out of the room.

He could have phoned the police from the Admissions office, so I knew he had something else in mind. I watched him cross the lobby and let himself into the main office, relieved that he hadn't turned toward the other way. The intruder didn't have to be a troubled student, not at all—it could be a nice full-grown thief or two after computers or camera equipment.

I kept quiet, listening for whatever I could hear. If the vandal didn't know we were there, maybe we could safely see who it was.

Time crept by as slowly as the black sedan. I felt exposed in the bright light of the small office, the only well-lighted room in the building, so I switched off the lamp and stood there hugging myself and biting my lip.

I could hear nothing. Behind Rip the main office door had clicked quietly closed on its compressor. If he were speaking on the phone, talking to the police, I could not tell.

If he had taken another route toward the sound of breaking glass, I could not see.

Then suddenly the building was bright as a circus. Hall lights were all Rip could control with a single switch, but it seemed that the place would stand up and sing. A distant door slammed, some furniture crashed, a masculine voice cursed once viciously, and then there was silence once more.

Rip walked toward me in the brilliantly lighted lobby, surrounded me with his arms, and breathed into my hair.

"Bastards," I said into his shirt.

"We'll see," he said, stroking my hair.

The police took only five minutes to respond, but five minutes is a lot of heartbeats, a lot of distance if you're running.

Although patrol cars circled the area and men searched on foot, nothing was found but some man-sized footsteps in the dew of the grass leading to and from the residential section at the back of the property. Nothing distinct, nothing of use. And nothing seemed to be missing.

In the end a patrolman took a statement from Rip, shook his hand, and the incident was over.

While Rip stacked half the classroom furniture inside the broken window (the frame was metal and wouldn't take nails), I called Garry to tell him why we were late, then finished hanging the drapes by myself.

Before we closed up to go home, Rip phoned Jacob, the man in charge of maintaining the property, to alert him to the problem. Jacob was scheduled to clean up and replace furniture after the Open House anyway. Now he would have to arrive early as well to repair the window mess. Although Rip took pains to downplay the seriousness of the problem, I could hear Jacob's outrage all the way across the office. Rip was forced to hold the receiver away from his ear. He turned toward me, shook his head, and smiled.

I smiled, too, as ironically as Rip. Good maintenance people always became very proprietary about their buildings, and Jacob was good. He sometimes drove Rip crazy fussing over little details, but that was far better than the alternative.

When our headlights finally swept past the shadows that shrouded our former house, I reflected that Jacob's feelings bore a surprising resemblance to some of my own.

Rip was exhausted. He drove the mile home with his shoulders slumped and his head scarcely above the wheel. I stroked his shoulders and caressed his neck with my fingers, as much to keep him awake as to express my sympathy. He needed a long, uninterrupted sleep to cope with tonight, to prepare for tomorrow.

He wasn't about to get it.

When we pulled into our driveway, the headlights washed over my modest little Nissan wagon. The maroon was streaked with red, the windows opaque with the lurid color.

Someone had thrown a gallon of paint on it.

✖ *Chapter 16* ✖

Rip and I leaped from the car and rushed toward the joke our serviceable little car had become. I wanted to stomp and scream and shriek.

But as always Rip's response was more rational. He gave the Nissan a scornful passing glance and continued toward the front of the house shouting, "Garry! Where are you?"

In ten seconds he was back. "Nobody's in there. Not even the dog."

Every limb went brittle on me and my brain became marshmallow Fluff. What did that mean exactly: nobody's in there?

Rip clutched my shoulders the better to hold me eye to eye. "The boys probably tried to chase the vandal. I'm going after them. You go in the house and call the police. Then *stay there*."

I nodded. I could tell I nodded because the movement made my head spin.

The dispatcher was polite. He took our address and said he'd send someone right away. "That's twice in one night," I pointed out.

"Yes, ma'am. We're on our way."

On autopilot I brought Rip's heavy camel hair coat out of the hall closet and put it on over the jacket I was already wearing. It covered my hands and my legs down to my shoes and weighed as much as armor. When I went out to stand in the driveway, the warmth of the hall came with me, except around my head. The refrigerator air did wonders for my head.

I had scarcely circled the car examining the Rorschach test patterns for psychological meaning, when Barney emerged from the shadows of the trees tugging Rip behind him on the leash. Then the three boys stepped into the driveway spotlight with eyes shining big and black. Their shoulders were squared and raised, their arms loose and ready. Even chubby Dave looked smug and manly.

"I see that Rambo won after all." But Garry misunderstood.

"No. We lost him." He was still breathless, but tall and proud.

I shot my hands to the ends of Rip's coat sleeves in order to grab my son's clothes. I felt like lifting him and shaking him, but I just grabbed tight.

"You get this straight, Rambo. What you did was irresponsible and dumb. We have police to chase crooks. They're trained for it. They're paid for it. Next time something happens, call a cop! Because if you don't, when I find out, you're going to mightily wish you did. You got that?"

Sometimes it takes a lot to get through to a Barnes. Garry's face was torn between disgust and disappointment.

"Could I just say something?" he asked.

I checked Rip's face. It was his kid, too.

"Yes, Garry. By all means tell us what's on your mind," I said.

"You've caught crooks. Nana says you're trying to catch one right now."

The brittleness in my bones was gone. I was unaware of possessing any bones at all.

I looked toward Rip for support. He crossed his arms and offered me a stern grin.

"Come on inside," I said. "We'll talk about this."

The three boys sat in a row on our long plaid sofa while Rip observed from the kitchen doorway. I had an idea that teachers confronted similar challenges several times a day, five days a week. My respect for them rose accordingly.

Pacing in front of the fireplace, hands in fists, I opened my explanation with the truth: "Sometimes private citizens help the police because they have, or can get, information that the police don't have, or can't get by themselves."

Three faces followed me as if I were reciting lines from a dull forties movie. If I didn't soon become more entertaining, they would switch the channel.

"That's all I did before. That's all I'm doing now."

"Gathering information," Garry summarized, nodding agreeably.

"Right. Whatever information I have I give straight to the police. Crook-chasing I leave strictly to them."

"Same as us," he said, confidence still intact. "We were getting information. We were finding out who threw the paint!"

"No, Garry. What you were doing was more in the line of crook-chasing."

We heard a knock at the door, and Rip slipped away to deal with the real cops—again.

I continued, "You guys did a very risky thing. What if the vandal was an extremely violent person and didn't want you kids to identify him—ever? What if it was more than one adult you were following? Nobody knew where you went, nobody was rushing to the rescue. You were on your own—you took a terrible chance."

"But Barney was along."

"That's the only thing you did right. Barney probably made so much noise, the vandal knew exactly where you were so he could go the other way."

Garry tilted his head and tightened his eyes. "I guess we weren't much help," he concluded.

"If we catch this vandal, it's going to be because we're smarter than he is," I said.

"I guess."

"You frightened us, guys."

"Sorry," they all spoke at once.

I embraced each boy in turn and gave Garry a motherly kiss. "Your hearts were in the right places, but your heads need a little time to catch up. Real bravery usually means using your brain instead of your fists."

Jordy was unconvinced. "How come they don't make movies about that?" he asked.

I tried to think whether anything by Rex Stout was available on film. The boys might get something out of a detective who solved murders by sitting in a chair pushing his lips in and out.

"Remind me to lend you a book," I said. Jordy groaned.

I wanted to join Rip in the driveway. "Get ready for bed, you guys," I told the boys.

"Can we watch the end of our movie?" Garry asked.

"What is it?"

"Dirty Harry."

"No!"

As they wandered away, my son consoled his friends. "It's okay. *Saturday Night Live* is almost on."

Perfect, I thought. Let them work up a mental sweat trying to catch double-entendres.

I shrugged back into Rip's camel hair armor and went back outside to speak with the police.

❋ *Chapter 17* ❋

*B*efore Rip turned off the light, before he kissed me good night, he turned his head on the pillow and narrowed his eyes. They were puffy and bloodshot and as formidable as I've ever seen them.

"You better have meant it," he said.

"What?"

"You know exactly what I'm talking about."

And so I did. "Leave the crook-chasing to the cops?"

He kissed me good night, turned out the light, and was snoring gently within the minute.

I, however, engaged in an unscheduled session of ceiling staring. "What if?" hissed the troll who lives to torment the sleepless. "What if it wasn't a student vandal either time?"

I discovered that at the ends of both rigid arms were fists full of blanket.

Worse, what if the paint on the Nissan was related to Iffy's murder? Why should anyone be that touchy about my inquiries? I thought back over my day. Answer: nobody should.

Most likely the person who broke the school window was frustrated because our presence interfered with his plan. So he drove straight to our house to vent his anger on Rip. Second best perhaps, but better than nothing.

Unless the emotional amateur who killed Iffy just happened to watch me with George Mills. I thought about that some more, about exactly what an observer of our conversation would have seen.

First the Miss America promenade, George's metaphorical hat in his hands rather than his mitt around my biceps. Different, surely. Confusing, perhaps.

Then at the table. He, or she, would have seen me conferring with a Philadelphia cop, chatting as casually as if we were friends, maybe even laughing a little, certainly lingering longer than a professional interview. On my part, no defensiveness to speak of; on his, an absence of the accusatory manner so common among cops. Take away any knowledge of our ancient friendship and the encounter still must have looked very much like what it was—me hypothesizing with the cop in charge of a murder case.

For another hour I tossed around how I felt about that, with Rip's feelings thrown in for good measure. The troll and I discussed how, much as everyone wants perfect lives for our children, warning them about every danger in the book never works. As parents, eventually we catch on that common sense is the lesson to stress. If you must, cross your fingers for your children when they cross the street, but first make sure to tell them about traffic lights.

With a husband or wife you just trust that they continue to remember the lesson.

I watched Rip sleep; and if there's anything to telepathy, we had a pretty good exchange. I told him I understood that he'd never let up working as hard as he did because doing less would mean caring less, and that was something neither of us wanted to change.

But I told him it was like that with me, too. Maybe I never outgrew asking why. Maybe I believed my mother's drill about us all being in this together.

"I'm me," I plainly admitted. "I may modify, but I probably won't change any more than you will."

I explained that at the moment I was incensed over Iffy's murder. "And now I'm worried about the possibility, however slim, that my peripheral involvement might endanger the ones I love."

I wound up by telling him I probably wouldn't sleep soundly until I got a few more answers.

As near as I could tell, Rip took it pretty well.

After breakfast, Rip started to help me razor-blade red paint from the Nissan's windows. The paint was oil-based, of course, or else a garden hose might have saved the car and the driveway, too. So, weather conditions permitting, it would be a fresh coat of driveway sealer and, insurance willing, a new paint job for the car.

But meanwhile the windows had to be scraped so I could drive.

We wore gloves. Rip's were too stubby to hold a little single-edged blade, so he took them off. Naturally, the blade immediately hit a bump, flipped over and bit into my husband's unprotected thumb.

"Don't you have an Open House speech to write?" I asked, interrupting his imprecations.

He blinked at me and shrugged. "Hello, glad you could make it—what the hell else do I say?"

"Too much if you don't have notes," I heartlessly pointed out.

"You sure?"

I playfully applied the toe of my sneaker to the rear of his jeans. "Go," I added, and he was out of sight in no time.

The morning temperature hovered somewhere between a jacket and a sweatshirt. I had begun with both, but shed the former within fifteen minutes because I got angry.

Working angry I also got focused, and the Nervous Murderer theory faded and pushed the Frustrated School Vandal theory to the fore. The troll wasn't totally wet, but in daylight his timing seemed premature.

On my Saturday trip to the flower show Howie Hancock was the only murder suspect from whom I'd learned anything. Since he had asked me as a favor to finger Alice Gifford, my apparent chumminess with the law had elicited an encouraging thumbs-up sign and a pleased smile.

Still, none of this theorizing meant beans without substantiating proof. Which made me put down my razor blade, flex my aching fingers, and head for my personal phone book.

Madge Neely lived adjacent to the rear of the school property in a tidy brick rancher of retirement proportions. She was a pest and a busybody, but she and her senile husband Newt had also been our closest neighbors when we lived on campus. Fortunately, a hundred yards of gently sloped grass lay between Madge's patio and our picnic table, mercifully making over-the-fence type conversation infrequent.

Now Madge's lay a hundred yards uphill from the foundations of the new gym, which may explain why I forgot about her until Sunday morning.

Madge answered in a brisk, birdie voice that had been awake since the crack of dawn.

"Good morning," I responded and proceeded to remind her who I was before I began to explain my call.

"Did you happen to notice any strange cars parked on your street between nine and ten last night?"

"There are always strange cars on this street. You remember. People get company—where else would they park?"

"In the driveways, probably, if they knew somebody. But the reason I'm asking is a window was broken down at the school, and it's possible the person responsible parked up on your street."

"Oh dear. That's a shame. But don't children usually do that sort of thing?"

"We're thinking older children this time, Madge. Old enough to drive a car. And if we knew what the car looked like we might be able to collect damages." Madge and Newt were never blessed with children of any age at any time. Consequently, the only thought they gave to schools was resentment at tax time. Bryn Derwyn, since it operated outside the tax structure, represented nothing to the Neelys but a source of noise and debris. In honor of the gym Madge had personally planted a row of pine seedlings that would probably form an effective barrier by the year 2020.

Her voice became grave. "I did notice Billy Cox's red Jeep outside the Margolises' at dinner, but then Jennifer and Billy left together about quarter to eight. At the time I just thought they were going to a movie at the mall. But they didn't have to go to the movies. . ."

Betty Margolis had been my neighborhood friend of convenience while we lived over there. The main things we had in common were children and a dislike of Madge's spying. I made a mental note to stop by Betty's someday soon with doughnuts and sympathy.

"Thank you, Madge. This car would have been there between nine and ten." And then I thought of one more question.

"How about a long black car with a dent in the right rear fender?"

"No. No, I'm sure I would have noticed that."

I was sure she would have, too.

The Open House was scheduled from two and four. Rip went early to check on Jacob's window repair, walk through the place, and do whatever else he does to get ready. After Dave and Jordy departed, I picked up Chelsea in my splotch-mobile, gave her spaghetti sauce instructions for later, and dressed in something suitably hostess—low heels for standing and a soft knit dress (kelly green in honor of St. Patrick's Day), which I formalized with some tasteful shell earrings and a matching pin.

Although my attendance at open houses is optional, today I had my own reason to volunteer: watching for that dented black car.

Luckily, Rip insists that I serve a valuable function when I'm there. Very few teachers are the thrust-your-hand-out, "Hi, I'm so-and-so" type. The parents of current students seldom understand why they're on hand, and the school heads (Upper, Middle, Lower) and Admissions Director all get tied up answering questions. Somebody has to ease the panic of that first awful moment inside the door. Somebody has to say, "Could we please get a little information from you before we send you off on a tour?" and somebody has to collar a student guide and put them together with the guests. "The faculty will answer questions in the assembly room," I add, winking to the visiting kid that the refreshments are in there, too.

Today there was an unusual crush right at two. The weather was ordinary for March, not warm enough to garden, not cold enough to hole up at home. No major sports event dominated the afternoon's television schedule. No holiday weekend to send people off on trips. Still, I've yet to determine a rhyme or reason why some open houses are packed and others are pitifully poor.

"Do you serve whole wheat bread in the cafeteria?" the tallest man I ever saw outside the NBA asked in complete seriousness. "Probably," I hedged. "One of the teachers could answer that better. But if you want a special diet for your child, some of the students bring lunches." Jack and his young bean sprout wriggled through the crowd toward a dazed-looking teacher.

"I just heard of your school. Is it new?"

"Twenty-three years." New compared to one that was chartered by William Penn.

"And how long has your husband been head?"

"Six years." Six long, hard years. You'll never know.

"Hello, I'm Ginger Barnes. . ."

"How does the state busing work?"

"In Pennsylvania if your township is within ten miles of our township, you are entitled to free busing. Twelve different townships bus to Bryn Derwyn at the moment." It's a relatively cheap way for the state to support private schooling, cheaper than educating all those kids publicly; but don't expect the bus schedule to be convenient.

"Hello, I'm Ginger Barnes. Could we please get a little information. . ."

I stole a glance out the front door. So far I hadn't been free enough to catch so much as the color of anyone's car, let alone check it for dents. I would have to escape during Rip's question-and-answer session.

"Could we please have a tour?" asked a generously patient woman with a frail-looking daughter.

Oh, lord, where were all the guides who were here a minute ago? "Be right back," I assured them. As soon as I tear your guide away from the cookies.

"I live in the neighborhood. Could I just look around?"

"Sure. Help yourself." One more guide available for our potential customers.

"Darcy Mayer's psychologist recommended Bryn Derwyn for my daughter. Is Darcy here?"

"Try the cookie table. But first could we get a little information. . . ?"

"Who's in charge of your computer program?" Through the door in the corner of my vision, a black car pulled into a parking space.

"Computers? The fellow over there with the purple plaid tie. Have you had a tour yet?"

A black couple and their son stood just inside the door. The boy wore a navy blue suit, white shirt, and red bow tie. While his parents shrugged out of their coats and glanced around critically, he blinked with bewilderment. I knew he could become comfortable, possibly even happy at Bryn Derwyn, but not if his parents were scared away in the first two minutes. Checking that car would have to wait.

Jack and the bean sprout were collecting their jackets from the clothes rack. "Get all your questions answered? Good. Thanks for coming. . ." I strained to see what they drove away. Something tan and square with a ski rack.

I looked at my watch. Three o'clock. Behind me an intense woman in a pinstriped suit questioned Rip about where Bryn Derwyn graduates went to college.

"We have a recent list in the literature you picked up," he replied. "I think you'll find they're mostly in the competitive range. It depends on the student, of course."

I touched his arm, showed him my watch. He nodded. "I'm going to answer questions in the assembly room in a couple minutes, if you'd like to join us there."

The lobby had thinned out. Inside the assembly area the short, shy, sweet lower-schoolers nibbled cookies and hung onto their parents' clothing. The ingenuously open-eyed or prematurely cynical middle-schoolers wandered in front of the bulletin boards or trophy cases as far from their parents as possible without actually hiding. Scattered elsewhere, the handful of older teenagers looking to transfer into a fresh start stood cowed or bored or belligerent beside their earnest, hopeful parents, most of whom spoke about their children as if they were not there.

Tony, the veteran English teacher, sidled up to me with a questioning expression. He was suitably tweedy, mustachioed, and bespectacled. One hand held an elbow while the other touched his cheek. "He's not going to give the Volkswagen speech again, is he?"

The speech in which Rip compares Bryn Derwyn Academy to the now-extinct Beetle—different but surprisingly well-loved.

I held a wrist to my forehead and swooned. Tony snorted, and I seized my opportunity.

"Do me a favor," I said. "Stand in the back and make sure he smiles."

"Isn't that your job?"

"Not until we get home."

Tony stuffed his fists in his pockets the better to smirk.

"And keep an eye out for newcomers, will you?"

"I take it you've heard the new speech."

I rolled my eyes.

My coat was locked inside Rip's office, so I pretended I didn't need it and sauntered outside as if the chilly air were welcome. It was not. I hugged myself in my thin green sleeves and strolled and breathed and tried not to shiver.

In the parking lots on either side of the main driveway about thirty-five vehicles huddled close to the building. Only three were black or even dark in color, one of those a station wagon and another a small and sporty Jaguar. The most promising one that I had seen from the lobby turned out to be an Oldsmobile in impeccable condition. Shivering mightily, I trotted back indoors to be met by the first wave of exiting guests.

"Good-bye. Thanks for coming. . . Good-bye, thanks for coming," I began to chant. Sorry none of your cars has a dent in its rear. "Good-bye. Thanks for coming. . ."

I eased deep into the warmth of the room, but my shivering wouldn't stop.

❋ *Chapter 18* ❋

I love Mondays. On Monday everybody in my house goes back to school except me and the dog. Theoretically, I'm in control of my own time.

"Barney," I'll say, "let's do laundry." Barney's brown eyes devour me lovingly as he wags his plumy red tail. "You bet," he agrees. "Let's do it." If I said, "Barney, let's go stick up a convenience store," he'd wag his tail and say, "You bet—let's do it."

After the Open House, I had finally rust-proofed the dryer drum. So today I looked forward to an afternoon of folding and ironing in front of an old movie I taped for the purpose— something starring Bing Crosby as a priest. St. Patrick's Day didn't inspire too many hit movies.

When the phone rang about ten-thirty, I was standing in a rhododendron bush under gray skies wondering why so much housework involves rubbing something. I dropped my sponge into the bucket and splashed my foot, fought my way out of the bush into the yard, rounded the corner, crossed the patio, yanked open the back door, and grabbed the receiver just as the answering machine kicked in.

"Just a minute," I said while Rip's voice instructed us to wait for the beep.

"Call me, darling. I'm at home," my mother said.

"Mom, I'm here. What is it?"

"You're there. . . ?"

"Yes. In the flesh. What can I do for you?"

"Well, since you asked, can you go over to Iffy's and pick out something for the funeral? It has to be done today, and I said yes before I remembered I promised to go with Mrs. Savitch to the ophthalmologist."

"You've been talking to Arthur Bigelow again."

"Just to offer my sympathy and see if he needed anything done."

The offer would have begun with, "Why don't you let me. . ." and finished with ". . . solve every problem in your life."

"It really doesn't matter much what you choose, although she looked lovely in pink. Maybe a suit with a nice lacy blouse. I think I noticed a white one with ribbons."

"How am I supposed to get into the house, Mom?"

"A key?"

I would call the office on that one.

"And then, of course, you know where the funeral home is."

"Certainly." The office would be able to tell me that, too.

"All right, then. Good-bye, dear."

My wet foot was cold and it had begun to drizzle outside, but I finished washing the last window just for the satisfaction, the home caretaker's paycheck.

Speculations about Iffy's murder stimulated by Mother's call kept me company while I worked. I decided I was curious about Joe Pescatore, despite Howie's hastily canceled thought. Perhaps he had some reason to be prejudiced. That sweeps information wouldn't hurt either.

Once again sitting on the plaid living room sofa, I removed my wet sneaker and sock and dug Temple Bodell's phone number out of my purse. A woman answered the phone with a very Spanish, "Yez?" pausing to indicate that it was my turn to talk. She probably wouldn't understand me, but I was free to try.

"Is Mrs. Bodell there?"

"Yez?"

"Can she come to the phone?"

"No phone. Headache."

"Will you please tell Mrs. Bodell that Ginger Barnes called, and I'll call back?"

"Yez?"

To warm my foot I folded it Indian-style under me then opened the Eastern Main Line phone book on my lap to check Arthur Bigelow's office number.

Cloris, the chunky secretary with the chopped hair, said she had errands to run during lunch but would leave me Arthur's extra key in an envelope on her desk. "You needn't return it. Just leave it inside the house where Mr. Bigelow can find it again." The kitchen counter sounded just fine to her.

As Cloris recited the address of the funeral home, in the background I could hear her boss ask, "That Cynthia Struve you're talking to?" and then come on the phone without waiting for an answer.

"Cynthia?"

"No, this is Ginger, her daughter. I'll be delivering the clothes to the funeral home, and I needed . . ."

"Thanks. Thanks very much. I can't . . . I really can't . . ."

"No problem at all."

"Your mother also offered, and I decided to take her up on it. . ."

"What's that, Mr. Bigelow?"

"The rest. Iffy's things. Your mother offered to . . . to do something with the rest of her things."

"Donate them, or consign them?"

"Yes. But first I want her to check with my daughter-in-law and Iffy's aunt. See if they want anything."

"And Julia?" I asked. She was taller than her aunt had been, but some things might fit.

"Yes, I suppose so. Please tell Cynthia she's right—I'd appreciate it very much. Ordinarily, my secretary could have done it, but she's busy with her own packing right now."

"That's right, she's leaving." His easy dismissal of Julia had wearied me of his conversation.

"Yes, moving back home the end of the week. Carol and Iffy's aunt will be here Wednesday for the funeral. Perhaps your mother can check with them then. After that, she's free to take everything away."

"Fine."

I guess it's healthy to be realistic, but Arthur Bigelow's clean sweep made me feel a little hurt for Iffy. Sure, it was my mother's suggestion he was responding to, and she could have made it at a later, more tasteful time. But Arthur Bigelow could have waited, too.

Under my leg and the Main Line phone book, my bare foot was marvelously warm. I prolonged the pleasure by looking up one more number and writing myself a note.

After lunch, I showered and changed into "errand clothes" that would blend into the Main Line ambience: dry socks and green duck boots, tan corduroy jeans, and a turtleneck from L. L. Bean, plus a green slicker in honor of the drizzle.

Straining to look irresistible, Barney positioned himself between me and the front door, smiling and sweeping the oval braided rug with his tail. Neither of the kids would arrive home until dinner; Garry had an after-school baseball meeting, and Chelsea was scheduled to re-do her science experiment. I may have been thinking that spoiled older dogs deserve extra consideration, or maybe it was the pathetic way he said "please." But I stroked Barney's whitening chin, gazed back at those dark brown eyes and told him, "Let's go stick up a convenience store."

"Wow, you mean it?" he danced, almost peeing on the floor with excitement.

✳ *Chapter 19* ✳

Already the inside of Iffy Bigelow's closet smelled stale. The clothes seemed dusty and tired. Even the sable coat looked limp.

I found a soft crepe suit in a pastel rose still in the cleaner's plastic bag, and I easily located the lace and ribbon blouse Mother remembered.

In the wire racks along the floor I discovered a pair of low-heeled shoes to match the suit, but they weren't orthopedic. I didn't want to think what the undertaker would do if the shoes didn't fit, but it was like telling me not to think of pink elephants. For good measure, so to speak, I threw a pair of cumbersome white orthopedics in a grocery bag along with the matching shoes.

Then came the undergarment and accessory dilemma. My stomach was turning by the time I collected panties and stockings and a pair of pearl earrings I hoped were fake. "Mother, you owe me," I muttered as the grocery bag filled with intimate items.

On a mirror tray edged in silver filigree were Iffy's cosmetics—foundation, powder, eye shadow, pencil, mascara, perfume. I collected them all in another grocery bag, ran down a mental checklist, and got the hell out of there. Arthur Bigelow's clean-sweep decision still struck me as cowardly, but now I realized it wasn't anything I wouldn't have done myself.

From the car Barney woofed hello as if he hadn't been dozing, and I pretended I hadn't caught him at it. I turned off the radio and took the entire five-mile ride to the funeral home to shake off the feeling of invading Iffy's privacy.

An earnest middle-aged woman whose eyebrows might have been pinched together by a clothespin relieved me of Iffy's belongings just inside the funeral home door.

"See you Wednesday," I remarked in passing. Who knows what to say in those situations?

The woman blinked as if I were bright daylight, offered a dubious "Yes," then silently toddled away. It was a relief to return to my car.

Heading home though the busy traffic along Montgomery Avenue, my subconscious started clamoring for attention, blanking out blocks at a time. To safely sort out my thoughts I pulled into one of the many front-yard office parking lots interspersed with private homes and apartment buildings.

The address I had doodled while warming my foot was somewhere nearby. It belonged to the Rosemont professor whose wife Helen Luedeke accidently injured in the Civic Center parking garage. There had been only one Gifford family with an address in the vicinity of the college.

I took out the well-worn map booklet kept under my seat, the one I bought when we first moved across the river. Since the Main Line was rife with streets that changed names or suddenly veered off at unexpected angles, for the first few weeks I used it just to get home from the grocery store.

A quick check confirmed that Tangier Avenue was only three zigzags from a nearby traffic light.

"What the heck," I told Barney. "Let's take a look."

The Gifford's neighborhood was older with broad, flat yards, no sidewalks, and private driveways about six car-lengths long. Formidable houses, mostly Colonial in style, looked in perfect proportion to the tall, thick-trunked oaks that sheltered them like annuity funds set up before the invention of income tax.

"If there are trash cans, it must be Monday," I thought, noticing that the whole road was temporarily disgraced by an assortment of cans with the occasional cardboard carton thrown in for variety.

Twelve-seventeen Tangier was brick in the Federal style, with pairs of black-shuttered windows on each side of the front door and duplicate windows directly above. Softening the severe symmetry, a sun porch or solarium with its own slate roof and white-edged windows huddled to the right. Overgrown boxwood and a few tall, delicate hemlocks grew up close to the house, their obvious age confirming that the place had not been built yesterday. Under five or six huge shade trees the front yard consisted of exposed roots and packed clay. If Alice were a gardener, she spent her energy elsewhere.

In order to think, I stopped my car off the road just short of a black plastic trash can (Sears, guaranteed to hold its shape for five years against any manner of abuse). Now that I was here, how was I going to inveigle a conversation with Alice Gifford, preferably inside her house where I might learn more about her?

I had the Nissan in reverse before I acknowledged what I was doing, then in first before I could change my mind.

The collision occurred at about five miles an hour, the trash can lid ricochetting off a tree trunk and landing in front of my right wheel. The can bounced ahead to the left, spewed stuff into the Gifford driveway, rolled evasively once to the right, then lay like a stunned boxer propped on plastic elbows.

Unfortunately, the impact also slammed Barney's chest into the back of my seat and his chin into the back of my head.

"Sorry," I apologized, rubbing both his head and mine.

I got out, found an empty bread bag to protect my hands

from goo, then proceeded to clean up coffee grounds, wilted lettuce, a red-and-white millk carton, and some sticky junk mail as best I could.

Which, fortunately, wasn't all that well. Even from the Gifford's front doorway, a couple piles of gunk remained visible, and of course my car was parked where the trash can once sat. Satisfied with my ploy, I contemplated what to say while I waited for Howie's favorite murder suspect to answer my knock.

The moment dragged while I weighed my lecture to Garry, Jordy, and Dave against the promises to my mother and myself. Then I realized the cause for the delay and felt infinitely better. Alice Gifford would be on crutches.

As it turned out, I could have outrun Alice Gifford if she'd been in decathlon condition for her age, which was over seventy. She opened the door with fiercely alert eyes peeking out from the baseball mitt that was her face. She was four-foot-eleven and shrinking. The white cardigan trimmed with embroidered flowers swallowed her arms down to her knuckles. All her youthfulness had been sucked into hair thick with luxurious white and gray waves.

"Hello, Mrs. Gifford, I'm Ginger Barnes. I just wanted to ask you a quick question, but my foot slipped and I bumped your trash can. Would you mind if I came in for a second to wash my hands?"

"You know me?" she asked. In Pennsylvania skin as thick and leathered as hers could only be acquired by relentless exposure to Florida winters.

"Well, yes. I know *of* you. Someone pointed you out. Your talent is quite respected, or should I say *feared*, among the flower show people. My mother's friend, Iffy Bigelow, especially worried when you were competing against her. And Helen Luedeke!"

"You a reporter?"

"No."

"Too bad."

I closed my mouth, then opened it again. "May I come in? I was hoping to speak with you for just a minute."

"I don't know what . . ."

"I won't be a minute."

"Oh, why not? I'm not going anywhere." She lifted an aluminum crutch and closed the door behind me. "Come this way. You want a cup of tea?"

"That'd be great."

"Grab a mug from the kitchen, will you?" Alice stabbed an elbow toward the back of the house, then swung herself off toward the right.

Soon I was standing in the middle of the dustiest, mustiest, messiest accumulation of possessions I ever saw outside of my children's bedrooms. Actually, the Giffords' neglect outdistanced the Barnes offspring by miles when it came to dirt, since I saw to it that beneath the teen and pre-teen paraphernalia a certain level of sanitation was maintained.

In the Gifford's entrance hall, for example, were a towering wardrobe, a cottage bureau with a white marble top, three wooden chairs, a wrought-iron floor lamp, and a threadbare rag rug of indeterminate color. All available table surfaces were in use, the bureau alone displaying a chipped brown bowl, three ears of Indian corn, a bunch of keys, an embalmed pheasant, black mittens with holes in the tips, and a white marble elephant.

In the kitchen, which I found by squeezing between the wardrobe and the bureau, cans and dishes cluttered the wooden-edged linoleum countertops. Several brown bags and a few pots had found their way to the floor. Two filthy dish towels and an apron hung high on a clothes tree that Alice probably could not reach. And on the floor near the back door cat food ossified in a frying pan beside a yellow plastic water dish.

I washed my hands with the gray bar of Ivory on the drain board and dried them on my corduroy pants. Then I found a mug inside a white wooden cabinet with glass doors. I washed it with hot water but didn't dare dry it on anything.

Since there was no kettle on the gas stove, I followed instructions only as far as they went and carried the mug with me in search of my hostess.

Until now, all the flower show people I'd met had exhibited an extraordinary affection for style, for appearances. As artists working in conjunction with nature, attractive surroundings seemed to be a high priority, perhaps even the major thrust of their lives.

Already, comparing the fussy perfectionism of those floral designers with the Gifford's disastrous household asked too much of my imagination. Either the Gifford's had suffered a blow of life-altering proportions, or I had the wrong house.

Passing through a book-gorged, vaguely green and burgundy living room, I looked for hints that it had once been different. Here and there an item confirmed my suspicion. A graceful lamp, a crystal ashtray, a tooled leather bookmark—the debris of a lifestyle that had died. My heart ached to think what had prompted the change; but whatever it was, tragedy or simple old age, I dared not ask. Whatever had ruined Alice Gifford's competitive zest, erased her pride, it was her private business and none of mine.

Entering the glass solarium filled with tropical plants, two sweet-smelling citrus trees clawed at my hair while a cat deposited black hair on my pantlegs. Perhaps the garbage smell offended him, because he tiptoed around my duck boots and went away sniffing.

Alice had ensconced herself in a white wicker armchair beside a round table and an electric kettle. Her well-plastered leg rested on an ottoman, her crutches beneath her on the floor. On the table Lipton tea bags mercifully encased in white paper were lined up inside a rectangular ceramic thing, and an open sugar bowl smudged with fingerprints contained a tarnished silver spoon.

I laid my green slicker on the floor and sat on a matching

love seat across from the odd little woman. Meanwhile, she poured and dunked my tea bag for me. "Sugar?" she asked politely. "I don't keep lemon."

"I take it plain, thanks," starting now.

"So you want to gossip about the flower show. Fire away."

Had I said that? "Well ..." I sipped my plain tea and thought quick. The tea wasn't so bad, no coffee aftertaste.

"Well," I tried again. "You know about Iffy Bigelow's ... unfortunate death."

"Yes I do. Only a matter of time, if you asked me. Always putting on airs. Who'd you say you were?"

"Ginger Barnes, Mrs. Gifford. My mother was an old friend of Iffy Bigelow—from high school."

"Humph. Didn't know Iffy had any friends."

"From high school. They didn't keep up too well, but they were friends. Iffy invited Mother and me to the flower show with her niece, Julia, on the day she was killed."

"Julia, you say? I don't know any Julia."

"Iffy's niece."

"Didn't know Iffy had a niece."

"Yes. Well, the murder has my mother all upset. She figures it had to be someone who saw us with Iffy at the show, maybe another one of their friends."

"I don't think Iffy had friends."

"Yes, well, Mother's worried that because we were with Iffy that day maybe the murderer might come after her ... or us."

"I don't know why."

I wasn't sure I knew either. "Maybe it was one of the other competitors."

"Another competitor? Whatever for? Spoil the fun, wouldn't you say?"

This conversation was not going the way I hoped. "Maybe Helen Luedeke?"

"Now you're getting to it. That windbag. More up front than up top, if you know what I mean."

"I understand that she won the niche competition."

"Yes she did, dammit. Do you know she put me in the hospital with her idiot driving? Just got home."

"So I heard. What happened exactly?"

"Sped up when she should have stopped."

"I'm sorry. I guess I don't understand."

"Who'd you say you were?"

"Ginger Barnes."

"Well, pay attention. I'm telling you what happened."

I clamped my lips tight.

"Your Bigelow woman was coming this way . . ." Alice waved her sweatered right hand in front of her right to left. ". . . and Helen's big heap was going along the building this way. . . " She swished her left hand from her chest outward. ". . . then bam." The hands intersected sending the left one off into the air.

"Where were you when all that happened?"

"Walking to the door with my best African violet, that's where."

"Let me see if I'm picturing this right. You're in the underground garage walking toward the door."

"Yup."

"Helen's driving along the length of the building toward you?" The building would have been on her left, just as it had been on mine when Iffy freaked out.

"Yup."

"Iffy's coming down a side aisle from the right."

"Yup."

"Helen sees Iffy headed for her and . . ." I paused, momentarily confused.

". . . and speeds up and hits me."

"What?"

"Your hearing bad? Who'd you say you were?"

"Didn't Helen's car hit Iffy's car?"

Alice shook her head sternly. "Nope. Other way around."

I pictured the scene again, and it came out Helen speeding

up instead of hitting the brakes, smacking into Iffy's car and Alice Gifford at the same time.

Alice gave me an exasperated glare. "I told you. Helen hit the gas. I don't know. Maybe she thought she could get past before your Bigelow woman came close, but probably she's just as idiot. She sped up and hit me, and Iffy hit her."

So she must have a dent in the right side of her car.

"Yup."

I hadn't realized I'd spoken aloud.

"What color is Helen Luedeke's car?" I knew I said that out loud, but I didn't get an answer. Alice was shifting her broken leg on the ottoman, grimacing with pain.

"I'm sorry. I should go. Thanks for the tea." I could make one more pertinent stop before I needed to be home.

"What'd you say your name was?"

"Ginger Barnes."

Her eyes narrowed shrewdly. "Well, Ginger Barnes. Your driving could use a little work, too, if you ask me."

That was when I realized Alice Gifford's wicker armchair offered a clear view of the curb.

❀ *Chapter 20* ❀

*B*arney expressed an interest in squirting one of Alice Gifford's trees, so I let him. I felt a little bad about her watching from the solarium, but what the hey? He certainly wasn't going to kill any grass, and I didn't know when I'd find another convenient rest stop.

It was after three-thirty, and I was divided about how to spend what was left of my cloudy afternoon. The information Alice had given me about the accident was indeed as provocative as Howie had expected, and I was eager to learn even more about Iffy's enemies. Yet I also needed to get ready for Friday night's party. Consequently, I thought of Beatrice Crumb.

According to the pamphlet still in my purse, Tuckahoe Nursery was located on Skippack Pike in Blue Bell. I tuned in some oldies and subjected Barney to my singing while I crossed over the Schuylkill on 476 and threaded my way halfway back to my hometown. Occasionally I needed the windshield wipers for road spray from an earlier sprinkle, but so far the rain held off.

Soon after turning onto Skippack I pulled into a semi-circle gravel parking area deeply rutted by runoff. Beatrice Crumb's office consisted of a small cedar-shingled shack darkened by dampness and trimmed with Williamsburg blue window boxes and shutters. Beyond this a row of three glass greenhouses pointed toward an outdoor spread of hardy trees and shrubs.

To the left just inside the door a broad plywood counter supported a cash register and a thick roll of white paper with Tuckahoe Nursery printed all over it in brown script. To the right were a limited selection of flower pots and fertilizers and a few lawn ornaments.

Apparently, the emphasis was on their greenery, unlike the places that try to be everything to every gardener. Nobody was minding the cash register, but through one of the three doors down to the greenhouses I could hear voices.

"You mess up again, Rodney, and you're out of here. I won't tolerate that sort of carelessness."

A male voice mumbled something I couldn't hear.

"Nonsense. Who else could it have been?"

Another mumble.

Then louder, "That's quite enough, Rodney. Get back to work."

Beatrice Crumb immediately appeared in the doorway. Beneath the white bun, her middle-aged face was flushed. Yet she did not seem embarrassed or even surprised that I was there. She merely asked, "May I help you?"

Over her shoulder I noticed a young man wearing a red bandanna pirate-style on his head shamble off through the brilliant tables of impatiens and geraniums.

"A couple of hanging plants, I think. I'll just look around." Now was no time to question the woman about her differences with Iffy Bigelow. Better to find something to decorate the party, then casually bring up the subject. Still, I could see this wasn't going to be easy.

My quarry grunted and turned her attention to the cash register. But then recognition clicked and she looked at me pointedly. "Have I seen you before?" she asked.

"The flower show?" I shrugged. "I took your brochure."

I extracted the crumpled item from my purse, smiled, and put it back.

Beatrice Crumb's pale eyes narrowed skeptically and returned to her register tape. For a business person her personality needed work.

I excused myself with another smile and stepped down into the left greenhouse she had just vacated. Rodney, the pirate, was gone. Partly looking for him and partly shopping, I strolled to the far end of the humidity-fogged glass building, enjoying the earthy smells and the brilliant reds, pinks, and white filling the three long rows of tables. Beneath my feet dribbles of water ran toward drains in the cement floor. My duck boots were right at home.

At the far end I wiped a peephole in the window of the padlocked door to the back lot. A long aluminum shed blocked much of my view of the outdoor expanse, so I made my way through the connecting enclosure to the middle greenhouse.

This room was even headier with the smell of loam and leaves, mostly of the houseplant variety. Overhead were lush hanging ivies and ferns and a few plants dripping with fancy purple and hot pink blooms delicately tipped in white.

No one in sight. Since access to the third greenhouse was blocked by a sawhorse, I strolled back to the center door to glance through its steamy window. Several yards down a path the young man with the bandanna worked bare-armed pushing a wheelbarrow of saplings. I could just hear the crunch of gravel and jingle of his unbuckled black rubber boots through the door.

"What do you really want?" a stern voice close behind me demanded.

I started and gasped and wheeled around with my hand protectively at my throat. "Do you treat all your customers like this, or am I just lucky?"

Beatrice Crumb stood like a post, her black eyebrows

locked in a scowl. "I don't forget people who ask me about Iffy Bigelow."

"I take it you weren't exactly friends."

"That is none of your business. Now if you want to buy a plant, I suggest you do so. If you're here about Iffy, I suggest you leave."

I yearned to say something clever and sharp, something that would pierce her in the wallet if not in her hide; but I never think of those comments until I'm halfway home. I settled for marching rather stiffly through the doors.

In the gloomy seclusion of my car, I scowled myself. Driving all the way over here had netted me nothing. I already knew that Beatrice Crumb's sore tooth was Iffy Bigelow. I still didn't know why.

Across from the nursery lay a quiet residential street. Just past the right hand house sat an Exxon gas station with a Mobil station diagonally across the traffic light from it. Houses occupied the other two corners. Clearly a neighborhood planned by a committee.

The office door sign had proclaimed that Beatrice closed down her business at five. Since there were no customers at this hour at this time of year, I understood. Furthermore, I approved. Only half an hour for me to kill.

I drove over to the Exxon station and used their phone booth to call home. Nobody was there, of course, but I instructed the answering machine to tell Chelsea not to let her brother eat any snacks until dinner was ready. I also told her how to start the chicken, and that I'd be a little late. It wasn't a lie, just an abridged version of the truth.

I then parked the Nissan on the residential side street pointing toward Skippack Pike and Tuckahoe Nursery, but sheltered by two huge clumps of sticks that in a few weeks would be bushes. I couldn't see every inch of the nursery's parking apron, but I would be able to catch when either of the three remaining vehicles moved.

"Barney, how about a little walk?" He leaped into the front seat and licked my ear.

During the twenty minutes that Barney and I loitered across from the parking lot, traffic on the pike picked up and became a moving distraction. Cars waiting for the light to change often blocked my view but also kept us from becoming too conspicuous.

If anyone were inside the two end houses, which I came to doubt, they probably thought I had the most finicky or constipated dog in captivity. Since he was walking on empty, so to speak, Barney engaged in lots of lackadaisical wanderings and prolonged sniffs, ideal for surveillance, although it made me appear a little dim—especially when it began to rain.

Finally, a young woman in jeans and a light jacket emerged from the front door of the nursery, trotted to her car through the downpour, and departed. I guessed her to be yet another employee who had been working out of sight. She was not the rude clerk who gave me the brochure at the show.

A minute later both Rodney and Beatrice Crumb stepped out, the latter pausing to lock the front door with a key.

"Let's go," I told the dog, but naturally—very naturally—he was making a substantial deposit on the nearest lawn. If it was five p.m., it was time for Barney to go. With an old dog, who needs a watch?

The nursery owner climbed into a white Chevy while Rodney headed for an aged green thing with a blue left front fender.

"Come *on*," I urged.

Barney eyed me with scorn.

The white Chevy backed around to face Skippack Pike for a left turn. If Beatrice saw anything but traffic, she saw my paint-splotched station wagon, probably also me and the dog.

An opening presented itself, and she joined the homeward bound.

I tugged Barney's leash, and he finally obliged by galloping around to the driver's side.

Open the door, wait for Barney to jump in, climb in myself, turn the key, push back my hood, wipe rain off my face . . .

Rodney's car must have needed a tune-up because he sat gunning the irregular engine long enough for me to take a position at the end of the little side street. Right? Left? I couldn't signal because I didn't know which way he'd turn.

The latest red-light traffic was nearly cleared before he eased into the eastbound lane, a left turn for me. By the time two cars crossed my path and I could follow, my heart and head were pounding. After the corner, only one car separated me from Beatrice Crumb's employee, but in the poor visibility from the early twilight and the gloomy rain one was enough to make me worry.

When his old gas-guzzler got going, it could sprint like a colt, an ability Rodney demonstrated at every opening. I was grateful for the numerous commuters in front keeping a safe pace on the slick road.

Windshield wipers thumping along with my head, we traveled three miles or so along Skippack until it merged with Bethlehem Pike at the edge of Flourtown. Now nobody was between us, the one car having turned off onto Joshua Road.

Maybe the young man had recently been stopped for speeding or maybe he had spotted me, but for some reason, he crawled through the entire business section of Flourtown, only speeding uphill as he approached the conglomerate corner with Papermill Road and Stenton Avenue. There he eased into the left lane as if he were aiming for Stenton rather than the continuation of Bethlehem or the other right turn; but with four choices of direction at that light, I was just plain lucky he decided to stop instead of gunning through on yellow.

Waiting for the light, I fretted whether he was watching

me in his mirror, then I realized he probably hadn't done anything to make him expect a tail. After that, I simply concentrated on not losing him anywhere along Stenton or through the several turns he made into what I supposed was now Erdenheim.

At the northwestern edge of Philadelphia Erdenheim represents a tightly populated assortment of housing somewhat more affordable than its neighboring Chestnut Hill. Parts of the area were also slightly less desirable. The young man I was perhaps foolishly following led me to a neighborhood I'd never seen before, but busy and clean. Not wealthy, but not slovenly either. He pulled into a small parking lot beside a bar. To go in there alone would be more than daring, it would be crazy. I decided to accost Rodney outside instead, holding Barney on his leash.

I shouted his name through the rain as he shambled toward the door of the bar. He had removed the red bandanna; and if I hadn't seen him get out of the blue-fendered car, I'd never have recognized him.

He turned toward me like something out of a movie, blowing smoke from a cigarette into the rain. The red from the neon sign that labeled the place turned the smoke pink before it dissipated in the heavy air. Rodney's hair was long and honey-blond, quickly going dark as it got wet. His face was too angular and thin to be beautiful, but he was masculine and attractive anyway. The muddy cut-off sweatshirt he worked in had been replaced by a blue nylon jacket with knit cuffs, the kind that usually had the name of a sports team lettered across the back.

He tossed the cigarette butt into a puddle then stood there with his thumbs in his pockets waiting for me to approach.

"I don't do trios," he said.

"Excuse me?" I said.

He waved an elbow at Barney. "I don't do trios."

"Oh. This isn't . . ." He was kidding. I quickly put Barney back in the car.

I thought he was kidding. "This isn't . . . I just want to ask you about Beatrice Crumb."

"You a clown or something?"

"What?"

"A clown." The elbow gestured in the direction of my car. Really with the gray sky and the rain and all it didn't look too bad, but I could see his point. It did look as if I should have had flipper shoes and a rubber nose in the back seat.

"Is it all right inside? I mean could we talk inside?" The rain was steady and chillingly cold. Rodney was too macho to shiver or even blink at the raindrops, but my teeth were chattering.

He turned on his boot heel and strolled toward the door. I trotted along behind. It was a public place, and Rodney seemed to be a regular enough guy. I already knew he didn't do trios.

Then he passed the neon light, and I could read the back of his jacket. HOT ROD, it said in flaming red.

Oh please.

He held the door for me then led me toward a booth along the far right wall. In between were drab wooden tables with men in work clothes wearing drab wooden expressions. A television blabbed the network news down at them from a corner of the oval bar, which dominated the left half of the room. Somebody shouted, "Hey, Hot Rod," then shut up quickly. Nobody was eating. I noticed a lot of beer bottles, but primarily I was busy trying to shrink.

Rodney gestured me into the booth then signaled the bartender with two fingers. "You buyin'?" he asked. I was the one who wanted something after all.

"Do they serve food here?" I asked.

"Sure. You want something?" He was very proud of his belonging here, very intent on me knowing it. Also, something about the pure exaggeration of his movements suggested that my presence elevated him a notch in the barroom social order. He was too young for it to be otherwise.

"No, but you go ahead. I can't stay long."

When the bartender delivered the beers, the bottles wore glasses in my honor. Rodney said, "Did you want something else?"

"No, beer's fine." I tried red wine in a local bar once before. The bartender took five minutes to find it and then it was warm and sweet.

Rodney ordered a cheese steak with onions and fries, then blinked at me with a pair of exceptional blue eyes. The nose was a hatchet with fringe, but below the mustache his lips were nice and his hair was clean—probably the purpose of the bandanna. But the eyes set him apart. They were warm and humorous. Looking at those eyes, I felt very conscious of my femininity.

"Why do you want to know about Bea?" he asked. "She owe you money?"

I tilted my glass and poured, took a sip and relaxed against the booth. "No. It's much more complicated than that."

Briefly, I explained about the murder and what happened to my car. "That's why I'm checking out a few suspects on my own." It was a shortcut, but it got there.

He was interested, I could tell, although he tried not to show it. "So what does that have to do with Bea?" he asked.

"Something happened a while ago between her and Mrs. Bigelow. I'm trying to find out what it was, and I thought you might know."

His eyebrows flicked up then down. "Why should I tell you? I work for the woman. I don't need trouble."

"Come on, Rodney. I heard her chew you out."

He shrugged and leaned on his elbows, the beer bottle resting between long-fingered hands.

After a minute, he fixed me with those eyes. "I only been there three months. But I know Amy, and Amy'd know."

"Is Amy the young woman you work with?"

"Yeah. She's Bea's niece, but we have sort of a thing . . ."

"A duo?" I teased.

He laughed a little uncomfortably. "Yeah. But Bea don't know."

"Can you find out for me?"

"Depends. You really springing for the beer?" His eyes were teasing now, friendly. He was going to enjoy getting my information for me, even if he wasn't sure why I needed it.

"And the cheese steak, too," I told him.

"Wow. Big spender."

I wrote my name and phone number on the Tuckahoe brochure and pushed it across the table.

"If a man answers . . .?" he asked.

"Just ask for me," I finished.

"Must be nice."

I smiled back at him.

The cheese steak and fries arrived just then, and the smell made my mouth water. I put a twenty on the table, and shook hands with "Hot Rod." He gave me a cigarette squint, a wink, and said, "Later." Just like in the movies.

Feeling proud of my ingenuity, I stepped into the rain and pulled my hood over my head. Today's accomplishments far surpassed the satisfaction of ironing in front of Bing Crosby. Perhaps even George Mills would be impressed.

A brief glimpse of the red paint on my car instantly set my thinking straight. Someone had been furious enough to kill.

Possibly someone I had spoken to today.

I would do well to remember that.

❋ *Chapter 21* ❋

For a change Rip's car was in the driveway when Barney and I got home. In the kitchen the man himself stood with a fistful of silverware. Behind him Chelsea poked at her roast chicken with a knife.

"Garry! Come feed the dog. Dinner's almost ready," Rip shouted.

"Barney run away?" he asked. An Irish setter trait—they like to break loose and keep going. Barney's a bit elderly for much distance, but established procedure is to grab a leash and drive after him. Barney running away would have explained my being out with the Nissan at dinnertime.

"Nope. I was with another man."

Rip gave me a quick kiss as I went by on my way to check the table. It appeared that we were having chicken, canned corn, and potato chips.

"You taste like beer," my husband remarked.

"I told you . . ."

"Didi Martin's been corrupting you again." He clucked and shook his head. "Honestly, that woman . . ." He gazed at a spot on the wall. ". . . reminds me of my college roommates."

I opened a jar of applesauce and stuck in a spoon.

"How is she?" Rip asked.

"Fine, I guess." I'd ask her tomorrow at lunch. We'd been friends since the playpen and knew each other better than sisters. We also liked each other better than sisters usually do, which is not to say we were not vastly different. Didi owned a beer distributorship, was usually single, and maintained a romantic fondness for men despite all experience to the contrary. With Didi for a best friend, I led a varied and surprising vicarious life. I believe she would have said the same about me.

I hugged Chelsea and thanked her for making dinner. "Next week maybe we'll move up to baked potatoes in the microwave."

She wrinkled her nose. "They all had antennae, Mom."

"Oh." Time for the grocery store.

On the car radio I heard that Tuesday's weather was expected to be dry and mild. Since both kids were between after-school activities, I spent dinnertime negotiating their help raking leaves Tuesday afternoon. Nothing motivates you to finish tiresome chores quite like entertaining strangers.

The kids dropped their dishes off in the kitchen and departed for desks and homework. On school nights television is *verboten*. Rip scraped and I loaded the dishwasher.

"I want to go away on vacation," he said solemnly. The two weeks of spring break began Saturday.

"We've had this discussion before."

"I know."

"We agreed we can't afford to go away."

"I know."

I put in the last dish and began to knead Rip's shoulders. "I'll add it up again," I promised. Tuitions, mortgage, new clothes dryer, et cetera, et cetera. Private school personnel always seemed to have their noses pressed to the candy store window. Still, we'd never trade the lifestyle for any other, and in today's economy most teachers tended to agree. They were grabbing the jobs and hanging onto them for dear life.

"Any more information about the vandal?" I asked. We were into the wiping up stage, Rip around the corner doing the table.

"Nothing new. Nobody bragging, no informants. We've still just got Miles Pendergrass, whose grandmother happens to have one of the foundations we've approached."

"Why Miles again?"

Rip stopped wiping to shake his head. "He mouthed off at Charlie, the lacrosse coach, for something or other and got benched. Then he sort of attacked Charlie and they got into a little shoving tussle. Charlie had to throw him off the team."

"Will he be missed?"

"Some. He's a big sturdy senior, but no college sports prospect. With his attitude he might have been more of a liability than an asset."

"But you don't like him as the vandal."

"It would make him too much of a brat. He's spoiled, but not usually out of control. His parents are away, though. I don't know . . ."

"Anyone else?"

"You mean beside assorted malcontents we weeded out over the years?" He thought again. "Not really. A couple to watch, but nobody specific."

I debated with myself again about whether to mention the murderer idea and answered myself with a resounding no. Hearing more about Miles, I bought the vengeful spoiled brat possibility wholesale. If the grandson messed up the school's chances with the family foundation, too bad. Those things happen.

Later I was looking through the Barnes family finances as promised, paying a couple of bills while I was at it, when the phone rang.

"Mrs. Barnes?" a tentative, but decidedly masculine, voice asked.

"Rodney, I thought you'd never call."

"Listen, we gotta cut the crap. Amy's here."

"Seriously, I thought you'd never call."

"I told you I would."

"And so you did. What did you find out?"

"Lemme put Amy on." I could hear him drag on his cigarette before he changed hands to give the phone to his girlfriend.

"This will have to be quick," a tense female voice told me. "My mother is upstairs, and if she comes down . . . it's bad enough that Rodney's here."

"Okay. Why does your aunt hate Iffy Bigelow?"

"You won't tell her I said this?"

"Absolutely not."

"It sounds really stupid."

"Yes . . .?"

"Well, okay. It's just that when my aunt started up her first nursery business, that Bigelow woman said something that made the business go under."

"What did she say?"

"That's what sounds so silly. She just told some people that the plants Aunt Bea sent Mrs. Bigelow's garden club for the flower show were worse than the ones she sent some other garden club."

"I see what you mean. That doesn't sound like much of a reason to hate somebody."

"But it could be," Amy corrected me, "if you knew Aunt Bea and you knew what happened afterwards. Hold on a minute." She mumbled something to Rodney that sounded like "Don't go," and "Okay, see you tomorrow."

"What happened afterward?" I prompted.

"Aunt Bea lost some really big order. She always thought it was connected to what Mrs. Bigelow said. Then she couldn't pay her bills, and pretty soon she lost her business."

"When was this?"

"About four or five years ago."

"But now she's doing fine."

"Yeah. Seems to be.

"Hey," she asked, "was Mrs. Bigelow really murdered?" She sounded hopeful, a bit titillated by the thought of her aunt as a suspect. But then, she was scarcely twenty. Before experience taught me otherwise, hurricanes and fire and death were just the special effects put on by life.

"I'm afraid so," I answered Amy.

"Wow."

"Listen, if I came back to talk to your Aunt Bea again, would she know who told me about this?"

"No way. I just heard her and Mom talking once. Aunt Bea still thinks I'm a kid."

"You're sure."

"Positive." She huffed scornfully.

"Thanks, Amy. I appreciate your talking to me." Now I knew what I would be doing tomorrow. "Thank Rodney for me, too, will you? He's an okay guy."

"God. Tell that to my mother."

❈ *Chapter 22* ❈

"We'll take day trips," I consoled my husband from my pillow in the dark. "Lancaster, the zoo, maybe Baltimore's inner harbor."

Rip grunted.

"And Franklin Court. Garry loves Franklin Court." There was a special bank of telephones for dialing lots of famous people. A recorded message tells you what they might have said about Benjamin Franklin. "*You* love Franklin Court."

"They don't have a beach on South Street." The educator's annual winter blahs, a direct result of being trapped in a building with children affected with cabin fever.

Rip kissed me good night, and before I fell asleep I resolved to help the man escape his pressures somehow, even if all we could afford was a sunlamp.

Morning breezes dried what the rain had washed the day before. All the colors seemed more distinct—the red-tipped branches whipping the cold blue sky, the deep brown of the soil, the red paint slopped all over my car. Pretty soon I was going to have to take time for estimates, but not this week. Iffy's funeral was tomorrow, our party Friday. Plus I never had patience for fixing minor things when I was preoccupied with something major.

After my family departed for the day, I made a half-hearted effort to restore household order until an hour when Tuckahoe Nursery would be open. Then I left Barney home with a rawhide bone and made the twenty minute drive back to Beatrice Crumb's business. As damning as Amy's "inferior plant" story seemed, going to the police with unsubstantiated gossip would be irresponsible, if not libelous. Yet as much as I looked forward to confronting Beatrice Crumb with what could well be a murder motive, my sweating palms and racing heart seemed acutely aware that this suspect was not on crutches.

Amy was sweeping the office when I stepped in. I had seen her leave the night before; but although she knew I might come, she had no way to recognize me.

While her aunt remained behind the counter immersed in a thick catalog I shielded myself with the door and jerked my head toward one of the greenhouses hoping Amy would get the message and leave. Her blue eyes squinted at me, then widened. I nodded. She was an attractive brunette, slender and young with a graceful dignity about her. Rodney showed good taste.

"Aunt Bea, I'm going to start watering now," she said.

From behind the counter the nursery owner glanced over the half-glasses she'd been using to read the catalog's fine print. She wore an embroidered yellow sweater and a denim skirt similar to the one I'd seen on Saturday. For some reason I expected to see knitting needles poked through her prematurely white bun. She said, "Help you?" to me. Then she actually saw me and said, "Get out."

I strolled around to face her.

"I'll leave in a minute. I just thought I'd better talk to you before I talk to the police."

"The police! What the hell—?"

"I've heard that you had a reasonably good motive for killing Winifred Bigelow. But before I tell the police I'd like to hear your version. Maybe it won't sound so incriminating."

Jeez, Ginger, why don't you hand the woman a gun and make it easy for her. I squeezed my hands together tight and tried not to sweat.

"Who are you?"

"Let's just say I have a personal interest in who killed Mrs. Bigelow." At least Amy knew I was there, and Rodney's heap was parked out front.

"Well, it wasn't me, and you can tell that to the police when you see them."

"I'd be glad to, but why should they believe me?"

Beatrice Crumb watched me, and I watched her while a great deal of thinking went on behind her impenetrable countenance. "You'll keep asking, won't you?"

"Anyone, anywhere."

"Then pay attention, because I'm only saying this once." Some trembling went on around her eyes, but then the stiff expression returned for good. Settling herself against the tall stool behind her, she removed her glasses and glared through the window off to my right. Thinly suppressed hostility enlivened the hazel eyes she turned toward me.

"I suppose it's true that 'Iffy Bigelow,' as you call her, cost me two years and all my savings." She paused to press her lips together hard. "She told people I delivered inferior plants to her garden club for their flower show exhibit."

"Did you?"

The eyes slashed at me. "What do you know about forcing plants?"

I gave her a "nothing" head shake.

"Well, it happens to be highly scientific, very painstaking, and quite chancy. It takes months and many, many more plants than you need to fill an order." She put her palms on the counter. "My business was just beginning to catch on; I had to deliver my best. And that's what I did."

Quite possibly her best wasn't good enough, but now was not the time to point that out.

"You grow everything here?" I asked.

Her pause and facial expression told me it was a dumb question, that the place wasn't big enough for anything but retail trade.

"No," she answered. "I've always had a property in Montgomeryville—a farm, greenhouses."

"So Iffy was dissatisfied and made a point of telling others . . ."

"She said I showed favoritism toward another club. It was a vicious lie; but the wrong people believed it, and some very crucial orders were canceled. Three months later I was out of business."

"And you blamed it all on Iffy Bigelow."

Beatrice Crumb stared hard at me. "You're damn right I did. You would have, too."

"But you're okay now. How come?"

Her eyes narrowed. "Because this time I made certain I had deeper pockets, secure sources, more advance orders . . ."

She regarded the way I was waiting. "I suppose you'd like me to be grateful to the bitch for hurrying things along, so I could finally do it right. Don't be naive."

"Okay, I won't. Where were you Friday morning?"

"During the murder? Setting up my booth at the show, going back and forth between my van and the booth." In other words, no one place with witnesses.

"Too bad," I said.

"Isn't it just?" She was squinting at me again, studying me like a dart board. She pushed a telephone across the counter.

"Go ahead," she said. "Call the cops. Don't waste another minute."

I waved her away. "No rush," I said. "Know anybody named Joe Pescatore?"

She folded her arms, straightened her back. I took that for a no.

And a good-bye.

* * *

Didi and I had arranged to meet at the Pizza Hut in Bryn Mawr at noon. It's the one where the two stalls in the ladies' room are set sideways. To get to the second you have to go through the first. To leave, you might have to wait for someone else to finish and let you out. Unique. I always went in to see if they had fixed it yet.

Didi wasn't there when I arrived, so I took a booth next to a sunny window and wondered who my best friend would be today. In our high school's production of "Oklahoma" she played the part of Ado Annie ("I'm just a girl who cain't say no") and, in more ways than one, she never got over the experience. You might say that Dolores "Didi" Martin is an actress without any professional or amateur stage ambitions. She's too busy playing her own schizophrenic self.

Her energy and unpredictability so exhausted her first husband, Harvey, that he eagerly exchanged his beer distributorship for the freedom to marry an older woman with two shy little girls. They moved to Arizona, where I understand Harvey doesn't even need to mow grass. Didi says she preferred beer to Harvey anyway.

I was reading the menu for something to do when an unmistakable voice asked the entire Pizza Hut, "What the hell did you do to your car?"

I glanced around at several curious faces.

"Didi, for goodness sake sit down and I'll tell you."

She sat, and the lunch crowd politely averted their stares.

Today Didi's fine, blond hair was in a French twist, and the sickeningly fit figure it topped was sheathed in black wool jersey. She might have been a ballet instructor or a model. Or she might have sold cosmetics at Bloomingdale's. Actually, one time or another she'd done all three.

"A little vandalism trouble at school," I answered.

"On *your* car? Bet it has something to do with that murder you saw."

"I didn't see it, Didi. I was just there."

She shrugged off the difference.

"Anyhow my car had nothing to do with it." I didn't want to talk about my car.

Didi practiced a skeptical expression while the waitress took our orders. To prevent people listening in on a conversation about murder, while we circled the salad bar I asked about Didi's latest news.

"I've given up on George," she announced.

"Oh?" Last month George topped her list, something to do with a strip tease on Valentine's Day.

"He brought his son over Sunday and actually expected meat and potatoes for dinner. The whole domestic bit! Then while I barked my hands on the icicles in my freezer, he and Danny—who is nine, by the way—sat on my sofa and put their feet up in exactly the same way and watched a demolition derby on cable. I mean really! With ninety-two channels on the satellite dish, they couldn't find anything more entertaining than a bunch of idiots deliberately smashing cars?"

"You didn't feel like cooking dinner."

"No." She held an anemic cherry tomato between steel tongs for a moment before tossing it onto her plate.

"Maybe next time maybe we should try their pizza," she said.

I grunted agreement.

"What else is new?" I asked.

We strolled back through the red-and-green paisley decor to our table. "The Beverage Barn needs a roof. Like tomorrow," Didi lamented. "I may have to take another job."

All of Didi's part-time jobs were amusing diversions of limited duration, not unlike an assortment of doomed sitcom pilots.

"I thought you made a killing on some stock."

"I want a new car."

"Feast or famine—the story of your life. Did you ever stop to think you arrange it that way?"

Didi wrinkled her upturned nose and sneered. On her it was a very cute expression, conveying both her distaste for my honesty and the fact that she had no intention of altering the pattern of her life. To her, security was boring. Didi spent a great deal of energy avoiding boredom.

"So tell me," she said, hunkering down over her salad. "What did the body look like?"

"Please—I'm eating."

"Okay, then just tell me who did it." Despite the desperation that drove me, Didi had been quite proud of my previous deductive success. Now she seemed to expect a repeat.

"I don't know. There are lots of possibilities." I explained about Julia, who Didi dismissed with a sniff and a wave of her fork; Howie, a thoughtful "hummm" and Helen Luedeke.

"However, she was making a scene with my mother at the time of the murder . . ."

"Cynthia? How is the old dear?"

"The same. So the only way this Luedeke woman could have done it was to hire a killer—"

"—who choked the old lady with her own scarf. I don't like it." Didi kicked the anemic tomato off her fork with a pink fingernail.

"The tomato? Or Helen Luedeke as the murderer?"

"The Helen idea. Too complicated. What about the husband? Usually it's the husband."

"He was flying to California. He got there late, but that's beside the point. He was in the air at the time his wife was killed."

"You sure?"

"Far as I know."

Didi frowned. "Who else?" she asked.

The waitress dropped off our check, but Didi held her arm. "Two personal pan pizzas," she said. "Pepperoni?" she addressed me.

"Sure," I agreed. "And more iced tea." The waitress blinked and removed the check.

"So who else?" Didi persisted.

I told her about Beatrice Crumb.

"She reluctantly admitted Iffy probably did her a favor, but the operative word is reluctant. She really hated the woman."

"So why wait? Why didn't she choke Iffy four or five years ago?"

I sucked the last of my old iced tea through the straw. "I don't know. Opportunity? Less chance of getting caught?"

"I like the husband for it," Didi insisted.

Our pizzas came. Before I dug in I loosened my size nine jeans to accommodate the size eleven I'd be if I ate as much as Didi. What-ifs about Arthur Bigelow buzzed inside my head.

"So what have you been doing?" my slender friend asked, breaking a string of cheese with her finger.

I knew what sort of answer she wanted, and it wasn't details about my party preparations.

"This morning I had the pleasure of choosing Iffy's burial clothes."

"Oooh. What'd you pick?"

I told her. "So why didn't this Arthur-husband choose something, or just ask his secretary to do it?"

"Arthur couldn't face it, and his secretary's busy. She's moving back to wherever she's from at the end of the week. Anyhow, Mother offered."

"And then remembered a previous commitment." Didi knew my mother as well as I did.

While we finished most of our pizza, I talked about Garry's athletic aspirations—"Bully for him," she said and gave a good laugh over Chelsea's science experiment fiasco.

She then departed to meet with a roofer, a real hunk, she claimed, "with hairy arms and a big black moustache." Next week she would learn about the pregnant wife at home with the four other kids. But in the meantime he would quote a fair price for the Beverage Barn's roof, flirt with Didi until he got the job, and give us something to joke about at our next lunch. Already I looked forward to that lunch.

I checked my watch. Our discussion had reminded me about the information I wanted from Temple Bodell—the status of the sweeps prior to the murder. One-thirty. Plenty of time to visit her before going home to rake leaves.

But first, that women's room. After two iced teas, the architecture was no longer my prime concern.

⌘ *Chapter* 23 ⌘

The phone book/area map trick got me to the right East Falls neighborhood but the wrong house. In answer to my ring a gentle older man brought his walker with him to the door and told me the curved driveway to my left belonged to Bodells. I apologized for bothering him. "No bother," he assured me, revealing the loneliness he carried along on each difficult step.

It occurred to me that Arthur Bigelow could be headed for a similar old age; that is, unless he had already arranged for something better. Younger companionship, perhaps, and so often the convenient secretary. Cloris Huber?

Absolute nonsense. Something Didi would think, but not me. Cloris's appearance did not suggest a man in her life, either now or in recent years. Also, the idea was somehow repulsive—Arthur Bigelow was bereaved, an indirect victim of Iffy's murderer, not the man behind the crime. *Didi*! I mentally scolded. *Stop playing with my mind*!

The short bumpy drive that hooked uphill to the right placed Bodell's square graystone above and behind the old gentleman's house. I left my car at the curb and walked. Breezes came in short gusts that mussed my hair and chilled me through both the light jacket and sweater I was wearing.

A cream-colored Volvo wagon sat in a corner of the narrow

drive, suggesting that someone was home. Beside it a tall wooden gate painted brown blocked entrance to the back yard. Since the rest of the barrier consisted of almost leafless boxwood hedge, I could easily see a greenhouse nestled against the house and about an acre of terraced yard.

I hurried toward the front door between fat oaks and thin hemlocks on the downslope and fragrant trimmed bushes that hugged the house. The arched door was tucked into a stone alcove flanked by two ornate wrought-iron lamps. I couldn't find a bell, so used the iron knocker, which surprised me by chiming deep within the house.

After three long minutes, Temple Bodell finally responded. She wore an aqua velour sweat suit and held a wet towel to her forehead. The swishy brown hair that always swung into her face needed a good brushing. She gaped at me blankly through the opening.

"Ginger Barnes, Mrs. Bodell. I couldn't reach you by phone, so I decided to stop by. I hope you don't mind."

The sockets around her eyes appeared bruised and puffy, not as if she'd been hit, but as if she'd been ill. I promised to make my intrusion brief.

"You have something to do with Mrs. Bigelow, don't you? I remember now. You took care of her plants for me. Come in."

She led me across an expanse of dark hardwood floor into the sitting area of a dimly lighted living room. The furniture gave a sparse, open appearance—wrought-iron with a lamp shade, wrought-iron with two cushions, wrought-iron with magazines—or amazingly solid lumps in rust and white—toasted marshmallows big enough to sit upon. A sculpted area rug still striped by a recent vacuuming complmented the deep peach of the three painted walls.

Yet it was the rear wall that dominated the room. Comprised entirely of glass, it offered a mural-like view of the tiered back yard, beginning with a patio that had been carved out of rock. In summer it would be especially picturesque and cool.

"The woman who answered your phone yesterday kept saying yes, but I don't think she understood a word I said."

"Placida," she concurred. "Cleans for us once a week. Usually she doesn't answer the phone, but since I couldn't lift my head . . ." She waved a hand to finish the sentence. "Please have a seat," she directed me. "My migraine isn't quite gone." She eased herself onto a white sofa and gently lay her head against the cushioned armrest. Then she carefully draped the wet towel across her forehead.

I thought of how frazzled she appeared assembling her niche and how much worse after the murder. I expressed my sympathy and again promised not to stay long.

"Have the police given you a hard time?" I asked.

"Friday, and again Sunday . . ." Her voice came slowly; I could almost hear the throbs of her headache.

"Then they are interested in Iffy's competitors." I remarked almost to myself.

"Her competitors? What do you mean?"

"Weren't the police asking you about the people involved with the show?"

"Some," she admitted. "But mainly things about layout, what I saw, who I saw."

"By any chance did they question you about the Grand Sweepstakes standings on Tuesday and Thursday afternoons?"

Temple lifted her head. "No. Why should they want to know that?" Alarm brightened her puffy eyes before pain squeezed them shut.

"You probably know that Iffy Bigelow was involved in the car accident that broke Alice Gifford's leg Wednesday morning; and, of course, Iffy was killed early Friday."

The show official sat up and dropped the wet cloth onto her sculpted carpet. The hasty motion seemed to make her head swim, so she clasped it between her hands. "You think the two are connected?"

"Let's just say the coincidence has been on my mind, and before I say anything to the police I'd like to see whether the idea is absurd or not."

"It was a car *accident*. It happened by *accident*."

"Probably," I agreed. "But Helen Luedeke sped up instead of applying her brakes. That might have been panic, but it also could have been deliberate."

"Deliberate!" She winced with alarm then picked up her towel. "What exactly do you mean?"

"I don't mean it was planned exactly. That would have been impossible. But either Iffy or Helen Luedeke could have taken a lucky opportunity to cause the accident. If, say, Alice Gifford was winning the sweeps, Helen Luedeke might have wanted to . . . to disable her. Or maybe Iffy was aiming for Helen. Or none of the above. As you say, it may have been an accident pure and simple. But if the sweeps standings suggest a motive for malicious endangerment, or whatever the legal term would be, I think the police should know."

"You really want to tell the police about this?"

I nodded. "But only if the standings suggest a connection. If they don't, I won't say anything."

Temple wagged her head and covered her eyes with the wet towel. "I hope there's no connection," she said. "Lord, do I hope there's no connection."

"We are dealing with murder," I reminded her.

"Yes," she said. She removed the towel and stared at me. Her eyes were red. "I'll find out. I'll look it up."

"Is the information handy?"

"No. Penny has it. I think I can get it, but . . . but not today. I'll borrow everything from her and read it myself, but not right now. I really shouldn't drive. I can scarcely see, and I'm feeling a little sick."

I'd known others who suffered migraine headaches; so it was no surprise she felt nauseous, especially after what I'd been suggesting. ''Really, it can wait until you feel better. But if you can manage to do it soon, I'd be most grateful. It could be nothing, but it might be quite important.''

''Yes,'' she said. ''I'll try.''

''I'll show myself out.''

''Thank you,'' she said. I had the impression she needed to cry.

Personally, I felt relieved; and after a few miles in the car, I figured out why. Nothing I had learned so far necessitated a telephone call to George, an act that—despite his offer— would have neared the limits of our understanding.

No, another offhand conversation would suffice, possibly at tomorrow's funeral.

❈ *Chapter 24* ❈

*R*aking leaves with the kids was a lot of laughs. Little wind swirls kept undermining our efforts to the point where Chelsea and Garry got the giggles and began throwing armfuls of leaves at each other. Consequently, what should have taken an hour took two. But by dinnertime the corners of our front yard held three heaps of leaves about eight feet in diameter and three feet deep.

By then we all were too hungry and chilled to stuff them into the township-required brown paper bags, so we threw plastic paint tarps over two piles and an old sheet over the third. A few rocks from the garden border held them down so the rest of the job could wait a day or two. The tarps were the first thing I thought of when the wind woke me early Wednesday morning.

Iffy Bigelow's funeral was the second.

Replete with natural contrast, the day was suited for a burial. March earnestly pursued its blowhard reputation. Snug under the covers I listened to the house produce squeaks and pings and thumps as if a platoon of poltergeists were rehearsing for Halloween.

Scraping breakfast plates into the sink, I glanced up through the window to see high treetops drunkenly circle and sway. Overhead the neighbor's pines hissed like surf while I kissed my family good-bye at the door. Down the street a trash can threw its lid and rolled helter-skelter. All while the rising sun spread a tolerant smile, and daffodil spikes timidly inched upward.

I dressed in a navy wool suit, found a hooded tweed coat in the back of a closet and chose comfortable shoes for standing and walking on grass.

When I picked Mother up about mid-morning, she had on a black dress and that horrid black pillbox with dangling cherries. Since she originally brought it out of the attic to keep Iffy company in her outdated "lucky" outfit, wearing the hat today struck me as touching, even appropriate. I hooked Mother's arm over mine, and we walked toward my ugly Nissan in silence.

The Kraftner Funeral Home and its parking lot covered half of an Ardmore block. Between the brick and macadam it appeared ready to outlast most anything or anybody. I parked in the back pointing toward a neighboring tree and guided my mother around to the front door. Normally she survives funerals like a cork on a high sea, but today suggested both a very bad night's sleep and a case of identifying far too closely with the departure of a long-standing friend.

The tight-lipped woman who had taken Iffy's clothes from me guided us across the carpet-muffled lobby to the largest of three chapels. The room was off-white and gold, giving a candlelight impression without the actual presence of candles. At the end of the center aisle Iffy's open casket glowed with polish. The familiar pale rose suit and lace-and-ribbon blouse exuded a feminine dignity. Without them, I'd never have known who was in the casket.

Not that the undertaker had done a poor job, for he must have worked miracles to overcome the ravages of so violent a death; it was simply the absence of life. Without that spark, to me anyone would look as if they belonged in Madame Tussaud's wax museum. For some, including me, that makes enduring a funeral easier. To others the pure reality of death is on view, daring them to look it in the face.

It was clearly such a struggle for mother as she approached her old friend. The wrinkled lace handkerchief in her hand trembled in anticipation of a prolonged torture. When at last Mother reached her destination, she slowly lifted her chin to center Iffy squarely in her line of vision, but it didn't last. The chin took a sharp turn to the left, and the handkerchief rushed to rescue Mother's eyes from a sudden spillover. Patting the edge of the casket twice, she turned to take a seat.

I remained a moment longer, hoping for some profound revelation; but as usual, my head was too abuzz with selfish life to fully absorb what was going on around me. Or maybe I was simply too frightened of death to confront it. I regarded Iffy's remains with my useless hands uselessly holding each other, admired the profuse display of flowers left and right, then turned to join my mother far in the back.

From my seat I scanned the room trying to catch sight of Julia Stone. There was a bowed brown head in the second row I was pretty sure was her, but it was difficult to be certain until she finally turned to watch someone approaching the casket. I couldn't tell how she was holding up.

"Doesn't she look natural?" a newcomer near me remarked aloud to her companion.

"Aren't the flowers lovely?" her friend observed.

For ten more minutes people filtered in, paid their respects and quietly took their seats. Among them were Alice Gifford, aided by a large man in unpressed tweed whose intelligence identified him as her professor husband. She spared herself the trip to the casket, simply shrugging her coat onto the end seat of the row neighboring me. When her husband squatted in the aisle to slip her crutches under the chair legs, I could see a shiny outline on his pants pocket where he kept his wallet.

After the padded chairs were nearly filled with what

looked like eighty or ninety people, Arthur Bigelow was ushered in followed by a young couple with two small, frail children. Before taking his seat, the widower bent to touch the arm of the older woman beside Julia. As soon as the family settled down, the minister took his place behind a podium.

"Dear friends," he began, "we are gathered here to celebrate the life of Mrs. Winifred Bigelow . . ." Mother perked up, and I stopped listening.

Judging by the clusters of different-aged women, I determined that the garden club/flower show contingent was well represented. None of the backs of female heads looked like Temple Bodell's swishy hair, but Helen Luedeke was present, as was Howie Hancock. They had positioned themselves on opposite sides of the room.

George Mills sat alone in the rear row, his elbows resting on his knees, his head sweeping the scene like the video camera in the ceiling of a bank. A tan trench coat that resembled a dozen others in the room helped, but he still remained painfully obvious.

The rest of the gathering was predominantly business acquaintance types—polite, suited men who had greeted each other with "How fortunate to see you—we'll talk later" expressions. Although they appeared to be listening to the eulogy, the slightest distraction—a cough or a sneeze, the drop of a glove—set their faces aglow with that time-is-money religion.

Evidently, Arthur had a lot of clients. I was surprised to notice the Duvalls among them. Their daughter, Connie, was a student at Bryn Derwyn. In fact the Duvalls would probably be at Friday night's fund-raising kickoff.

" . . . talented . . . untimely death," the minister droned on. I practiced self-hypnosis staring at the back of a blue-tinted head.

Then finally the room stood. Everyone lowered his head to receive a benediction, and it was over.

"If you'll wait just a moment for the family to depart, there will be a receiving line in the lobby."

As he walked by, I noticed Arthur's square yellow face and hollow eyes, his stapled-on expression. He carried a black hat to go with his black cashmere coat over gray pinstripes, black-figured tie, white shirt. He looked worse than Iffy, less real. Behind him the young couple followed, leading their anxious children by the hands.

As soon as they passed through the doorway, murmurs of delayed greetings erupted, hands shook other hands, people put themselves together with their coats, and the room began to empty. Being toward the back, Mother and I were among the last to escape, but so was George Mills. He worked his way over to us, greeted Mother then asked me, "You going to the interment?"

"Yes, are you?"

"No," he said. "But I'd like to talk to you." Although I had hoped for just such an opportunity, his all-business tone of voice made me wonder if I was in trouble.

"I have to take Mother back to Bigelow's and then home. You want to meet somewhere around four?"

"That McDonald's near the Conshohocken entrance to the expressway?" Its location offered a quick return to the city for him and a brief trip home for me.

"Sure."

I had been watching for Julia while Mother and I eased toward the receiving line. Now, as I noticed her talking just a few paces off, I found myself confronted with the Bigelow family. The son extended his hand to me. "I'm Arthur Junior and this is my wife Carol," he said. Their boy tugged his coattail while their daughter twirled in bored circles behind the row.

"Ginger Barnes," I managed to say. "I'm so sorry about your loss."

"Yes, thank you."

Mother was already murmuring something to Arthur

Senior, leaving George stuck between us, apparently tongue-tied.

I gestured with my left hand. "I'd like you to meet Lt. George Mills. George is with the Philadelphia police."

Appraising glances were exchanged during a hearty hand-shake, but nothing verbal. "George, I think you said you had to go; and, Mother, we ought to put our car in line."

George nodded good-bye, glanced at me gratefully, and strode for the door.

Just as Mother and I stepped outdoors Howie Hancock swooped in to intercept me. "So have you told him?" he asked without preamble.

Throughout the parking lot cars were jammed at odd angles, drivers slowly extricating themselves with polite smiles and waves. With such an exhibition of Sunday manners it would be several minutes before I could jockey the Nissan into line.

"Tell who what?" I asked Howie.

"You know. Tell that cop about, you know . . .." He glanced around us before he whispered, "Alice Gifford."

Mother had focused her considerable curiosity on Howie. "I'll meet you in the car," I told her. Mercifully, she took the hint.

"Yes, I did. But honestly, it's hard to imagine a tiny old woman on crutches accomplishing something as physical as Iffy's murder." Across the driveway I noticed Julia being helped into a car by a tall, studious man.

"But it wasn't me!" Anguish moistened Howie's eyes and seemed to make his pale hair stand on end. "Oh tell me they don't think it was me."

"I really couldn't say what the police think." Inside the car Julia slid across the front seat to nestle up against her companion.

"What about you? What do you think?"

I tore my attention from Julia to give my answer the

proper emphasis. "Howie, I don't really know you, so how could I know whether you'd do something like that or not?"

"But you gave me those plants. Doesn't that mean you believed me?"

I thought back to Saturday and my earlier impressions of Howie Hancock. I had believed him, and the plants were a small gesture toward telling him so.

"Yes, Howie, I guess I believe you."

"Thanks," he said, and his hands danced to my coat sleeve and back to his side. "Don't forget now, flowers for your birthday."

We had reached a conversational lull, the perfect time to part company, but there he stood, hopeful and pathetic. I remembered again how emotional his week had been and how adrift he must have been feeling without his companion Tom.

"You going to the cemetery?" I asked.

"Oh no."

As I regarded him, I realized he might be able to fill in some background. I asked what he knew about Alice Gifford's past.

His eyes widened, but he answered eagerly. Around us cars were beginning to move. He tailored his reply accordingly.

"Used to be a big gun in arrangements about five years ago. Rather flamboyant, you know—took chances. Judges loved her. But then suddenly she dropped out."

"You think Iffy had anything to do with that?"

"It's possible, isn't it?"

I had to agree. If Iffy had originally caused Alice to disappear from the flower show scene, she might also have posed a serious threat to her return. Such a scenario might not contain a motive for murder, but that would depend on what happened.

I thought aloud. "Then why would she come to the funeral?"

Howie shrugged, unable or unwilling to say more.

I realized I had been writing off his desperate accusations as simply that—desperate. But if something actually happened between Alice Gifford and Winifred Bigelow and that something was serious enough, Alice's husband might have become involved—especially if he believed Iffy instigated the automobile accident that injured his wife. On crutches, she made an unlikely suspect, but Gordon Gifford had no such limitation. Also, professors don't exactly punch a time clock.

As Howie and I walked toward our respective cars, another idea of much lesser importance stopped me. "Howie," I called over to him. "What if I said my birthday is Friday?"

He beamed. "A bouquet on your doorstep by noon." He spread his hands and bowed.

"I'm really just giving a party, but I'll display your card."

"Say no more. Spring colors?"

"Royal blue dishes and off-white napkins."

"Done." Then his eye caught sight of my Nissan. "What *happened* to your *car*?" he asked with more of his old spirit.

I didn't like broadcasting that information across a parking lot, but I had to say something. "We had a little trouble with vandalism at my husband's school."

I opened my door and stuck one leg inside.

"Gin-ger," Howie sang. "You're forgetting something."

My manners? What?

"Your add-ress."

I told him and he wrote in a little notebook on the roof of his car. I waved good-bye and eased the Nissan into the caravan heading for the cemetery.

Julia and her companion were already out of sight.

❈ *Chapter 25* ❈

Winifred Bigelow's interment offered a wide selection of discomforts, physical as well as psychological.

Whenever your hand got too numb to hold your coat collar closed, a wind gust would break from behind the high-rises across the street and steal all the body heat you had managed to hoard.

While the minister rocked from foot to foot and read elevated prose to our small gathering, the diabolical wind also had its way with the strip of gray hair that, indoors, stretched across his empty pate. The flailing lock incited such an hysterical giggle from one of the female listeners that the spiritual leader temporarily lost his place in the Good Book.

During a silent moment the youngest Bigelow grandchild whispered loudly that she wanted her lunch. Her brother sneezed into his sleeve.

Julia laid her white carnation upon the casket while her gentleman clung to her other arm. I couldn't see her expression, but just the symbolic act summoned up that spooky business with the lily and gave me a shiver.

Then the wind got playful again, and most of the flowers

the rest of us put down rolled off into the cavity underneath. My experiment with folding the stem into a V caught on with a few fellow mourners, mostly corporate types I noticed.

Helen Luedeke probably didn't mean to smack hers down as if swatting a fly; she probably thought it would adhere better with a firm wrist, but the flower bounced off and landed at her feet. Since she could scarcely see past her mink to the ground, retrieving the carnation to try again involved an awkward stoop complete with splayed elbows and knees.

During the final benediction, I wondered why Helen was even there. Bidding farewell to an adversary? Gloating? Impossible to say.

Although the rest of the culled-down gathering was composed mostly of strangers, there was one face missing I had expected to see—Arthur Bigelow's secretary. In the car going back to Bigelow's I commented about her absence to my mother.

"Probably guarding the house, dear."

"You think so?"

"Thieves read obituaries, you know, for when the house will be empty."

"Some world we live in."

"Yes, dear, it is," she said. I had no idea which way she meant that, but it wasn't the day to ask.

For Mother, the morning's ritual apparently served its purpose. The facing of facts, the enforced good-bye—both seemed to provide her with that essential sense of closure. During our drive, I noticed her jaw had leveled with resolve. Cynthia Struve would carry on.

At Bigelow's she would ease into conversations with sincerity tangible enough to embrace in your arms. No one would be a stranger, even if they thought they should be. While condolences were meted out, Iffy's personal odds and ends would also be fairly and discreetly shared—today, before airplanes could whisk away opportunity. The Struve brand of compassion is extremely practical.

The driveway and street of Arthur Bigelow's brick Tudor were jammed with a variety of vehicles. Being a straggler proved an advantage, however; because the first slot at the end of the drive already had been vacated. By now I was accustomed to my lurid maroon-and-red paint job and not especially concerned about causing a stir. I pulled right in.

Cloris Huber (Mother must have been right about her housesitting) silently accepted our coats and headed for the stairs. Her hair was still fuzzy and chopped, her figure still round. Only her bearing was different. In the office she had been dutiful, not especially gung ho, but dutiful. Today the vacuous expression magnified by her glasses could only mean distaste for her chore or callous detachment. Thursday and Friday in the office would be a waste of time. Then again, Arthur Bigelow probably wouldn't accomplish much himself.

To the left, the living room was peopled with clusters of two and three. In the gaps the deep reds of the oriental rug and matching drapes were still visible. One of the flower women stood with her hand supporting the elbow of the arm that held a plastic wine glass. So intent was she on her conversation that she could only be thinking, "I'm stuck here, but I'll be damned if I'm going to look uncomfortable about it." Pretty soon, hungry or not, she would disengage and search for an hors d'oeuvre. Funerals and cocktail parties are often remarkably the same.

"You hungry?" I asked my mother.

Her ears were up and her nose alert. "No, dear. You go ahead." She had her eye on Arthur, who was drinkless and backed against the staircase by a woman in a bad dress. As Mother searched for the means for his rescue, the cherries on her hat bounced back and forth like little red tennis balls.

I leaned down to kiss her affectionately on the cheek. She sputtered, stuck out her tongue to remove a hair, and dismissed me with a curt, "Didn't you say you were hungry?"

I eased around a couple of men foolishly standing in the doorway to the dining room and contemplated my approach to the spread on the table. Clockwise? Counterclockwise?

"Good afternoon," a throaty man's voice addressed me. "I believe you had quite a time locating me last Friday. I'm Dr. Willoby McDonald." Julia must have pointed me out.

He was as tall as Rip, probably six feet one or two, but unusually thin; his brown herringbone jacket draped from shoulder to fingertips as if nothing were inside. His tie protruded over a gold bar, the pattern displaying irregular navy blue diamonds, yellow blobs, and red dots. His shirt was crisp blue; slacks, well-creased charcoal; shoes, buffed cordovan. His hair was taupe, and meticulously trimmed in a style that flattered his narrow face. There was a bit too much of it in the eyebrow department, but that small untidiness managed to point up every other impeccable detail of his dress, except hue, of course. Either he was color blind or possessed a unique sense of humor.

I stuck out my hand, promising myself a plate of chicken salad real soon. "Hello, Doctor. How is Julia doing?"

After our shake, he linked his hands behind his back and glanced across the table to where Julia spoke with an elderly woman, the one Arthur Bigelow had greeted just before the eulogy.

"She's well, thank you." His smug smile said, "thanks to me."

"Are the police giving her a hard time?"

McDonald eyed me abruptly. "What do you mean?"

"Last I heard they liked her pretty well as a suspect."

For some reason he blushed. "Impossible." His eyes strayed toward Julia again, and so did mine. What I saw was a demure, simple woman paying avid attention to everything her older relative said. It was easy to agree with her psychiatrist, so I did, adding, "Your interest seems to be pretty personal."

The chin jutted protectively forward. I waited for a denial, but she was still there in his line of sight, and he quickly crumbled under the weight of his affection.

"Julia's the kindest, sweetest woman I've ever met."

"That's . . ." A word, I needed a word. Not *risky*, not *unethical*. ". . . lovely," I said. Then for some reason I threw in, "Good luck to you both."

I was reaching for a piece of celery spread with speckled cream cheese when a question occurred to me. "Doctor," I said, turning back to him, "has Julia by any chance indicated whether she witnessed the murder?"

He had scooped up a tea sandwich and now paused to chew. Answering questions without the crutch of another question seemed foreign to him, like stepping on land after weeks at sea. He scowled and wiped his lip with a pinky finger. "I've tried to expose that moment to light, of course, to help her deal with it, but, um"—he tossed his hands—"nothing yet." Then he glanced at the floor as if playing back tapes of her therapy sessions in his head.

"Any guess?"

He looked at me. "I prefer not to guess."

"Not even a hint one way or the other?" I jiggled my shoulders the better to coax an answer out of him.

Willoby McDonald shook a skinny finger at me. "Perhaps the police should be giving you a hard time."

I smiled and picked up a plate. "Just look after her, Doc," I said. "Somewhere there's a guilty conscience running around untreated."

He peered at me with a certain amount of indignation.

"I'm here, aren't I?" his expression conveyed. His eye held mine significantly as he sauntered around the table and slipped an arm around Julia.

He meant to be reassuring, I know; but just to be safe, I memorized the rest of the faces in the room.

❈ *Chapter 26* ❈

Someone had fussed over the table display—polished silver and crystal on lace, a bouquet of blue iris and pink lilies in the center. I decided it must have been Cloris again, and I wondered how she felt about Arthur's old-fashioned chauvinism.

Twenty years ago fixing your boss's coffee and fetching his matches were unquestioned endeavors, as natural as waiting on your husband at home. Equally natural were the office romances such pampering engendered. Sometimes the heel returned to his wife, but with reasonable regularity the wife hired an expensive attorney instead—often enough to give simple creatures like Cloris a fatal case of hope.

Her leaving town bothered me. Originally I had dismissed the idea of a boss/secretary romance as ludicrous, but that was when I imagined Arthur returning the sentiment. I had forgotten about the category of sad souls who adore but are ignored. How many of them have bumped off the competition only to find their situation unimproved? Worsened, in fact. Closely observing Arthur and Cloris together might reveal something or nothing, but either way I would have my answer.

The buffet plates were a little small for lunch but better than plunking a couple of canapes on a napkin. I attempted to satisfy my nervous appetite (without appearing too indelicate) by eating an olive, putting a tea sandwich on my plate, eating a tea sandwich, putting a paté cracker on my plate, eating a pickle, palming a lump of cheese.

Then I threaded my way toward the living room. It was the hangers-on I wanted to infiltrate rather than the genuinely bereaved. So I skirted past Mother and the Bigelow daughter-in-law, the kiddies eating crackers on the stairs, Arthur and the whole hallway bunch.

From the direction of the front window seat in a small, offhand way a woman said, "Maybe they deliver pizza."

Helen Luedeke tilted sideways toward her and whispered loudly, "Arthur's yard man probably couldn't find anywhere to park."

I eased by and headed toward an emotionally detached garden club woman and her companion.

"Oh, thanks," she said, winching a lump of cheddar off my plate between two professionally manicured nails. While stowing the cheese into a mouth as perfect as an orthodontist's ad and as formidable as a trash compactor, she showed every intention of ignoring my actual person. Before she could swallow I said, "Aren't you surprised that Alice Gifford isn't here?"

"Why?" she questioned with green-lidded eyes. Slippery black hair, cheeks rouged with sable brushes, she was one of those women who look perfectly groomed when they drop their children at school, but have nowhere useful to go afterward.

Her companion's mouth was not engaged. "Alice Gifford? Not in our club. But didn't she lecture us once on medicinal herbs?"

Mrs. Perfect skewered a sandwich and completed the process of ignoring me. "You were saying . . .?" she prompted her friend.

I nodded to the second woman with a cocked eyebrow and left them to their gossip.

The instinctive need to be welcomed by someone pressed upon me; I offered my remaining food to four men stuck at the far edge of the room by the fireplace.

They all took something then stood there wondering why I didn't leave.

I put the last olive in my mouth. "Cloris did a nice job, didn't she. Good food." Obediently, they all put their selections in their mouths.

I addressed the tall one with the pocket watch. "I suppose Arthur will really miss her."

"Oh? She's leaving Bigelow and Associates?"

"Yes. Moving home."

"Oh." He eyed my empty plate.

"Surprised Joe Pescatore's not here," I ventured. Howie's quick accusation and even quicker retraction still piqued my curiosity.

"Don't know him," said the one on the left. Each eyed the other and mumbled and shrugged their ignorance.

"I'll just . . ." I circled a finger over my empty plate. The men grunted that they didn't mind.

As I went past, Mrs. Perfect was saying, "It must have been rusty, but they should have gone to one of those cheap places advertised on TV instead of trying to fix it themselves."

Mother and Carol Bigelow were gone from the hallway, and so were the two children. I imagined Carol beginning to lead her kids off to naps and Mother chiming in, "While you're up there . . ."

Cloris hesitated in front of me as I ambled toward her in the hall. "You finished with that?" she asked, looking pointedly at my plate.

I told her no. She continued into the living room, gathering empty cups and napkins as she went. Arthur was still four feet away, talking by the staircase, but he hadn't given her a glance. Nor had she looked at him.

I gave the table another go, picking up a second plate and

loading it with finger food. I wanted to learn something from these people, and bribery seemed to be the preferred approach.

Beyond the dining room and Arthur Bigelow's study was a small hallway accessing a powder room and the kitchen. Presently entering the dining room from that hall was the granny with the white hair whom Arthur had greeted and whom Julia had conversed with earlier.

Carrying her collected disposables, Cloris entered the dining room and gawked at the granny. The old lady was too intent on walking with a cane to pay much attention to anyone, but for some reason, Arthur's secretary hastily cut wide to the left of the table and disappeared into the second kitchen entrance at the opposite edge of the room.

I set my two plates on the buffet next to the wine and hurried over to the old woman. "We haven't met," I began. "I'm Ginger Barnes. My mother was very good friends with Mrs. Bigelow."

The woman stopped her forward progress and looked up at me. "Bring me a cup of coffee, will you? My legs haven't recovered from the airport. Cincinnati was all right, but Philadelphia . . ." She made a sour face.

"Black?" I asked.

"Cream and two sugars." She eased onto a lyre-backed dining chair against the wall. After I got her coffee from the buffet, I sat across the doorway from her. She accepted the cup as if it were her due.

"So sad about Mrs. Bigelow," I murmured. The old woman was primarily interested in the cup and saucer on her lap. "Are you related?" I asked. As yet, I had not determined who she was.

Her head lifted. Behind silver-rimmed lenses a spark had ignited in a pair of faded brown eyes. "Iffy was a beautiful girl," she said with surprising heat. "I told my sister to watch out—she'd be a handful when she started seeing boys.

She agreed with me, too. 'Lila,' she said, 'you were right.' And I was, too.''

''So you're Winifred Bigelow's Aunt Lila.''

''After my sister was gone, I tried to keep up with Iffy best I could. She didn't care. Didn't answer my letters. She was too young, too busy. But I was there for her when it counted.''

The woman cast her eyes around the room, dismissing it with disdain. ''She wouldn't have had all this but for me, mind you. She's lucky she had me to set her straight. Could have married one of the bums she started out with. But I set her straight.''

A wrist weakened by age lifted the dainty teacup toward her lips. I didn't speak for fear the vibrations would splash hot liquid on the woman's fingers. A young man used the lapse in conversation to dart between us.

Aunt Lila droned on. ''We knew what was what, the Macleish girls did. Didn't have a sou, but we knew what was what. We got by. I was awfully good to Iffy. She could have been better to me.'' She wagged her head, lamenting Iffy's lack of gratitude.

No wonder Cloris had avoided the woman. What a contrast she made to the man with the walker who directed me to Temple Bodell's driveway. ''No trouble,'' he had replied to my apology. To Aunt Lila everything and everyone seemed to be too much trouble.

When she paused to sip, I told her it was nice meeting her but I had to go. With bitterness as a steadfast companion, she didn't need me.

As I wandered past the stairs with two plates of food, Mother descended with Julia Stone and a bulky brown paper bag.

''Sweaters always come in handy,'' she said, and Julia didn't disagree. Rather she nodded a quick hello to me and excused herself, darting through the office toward the increasingly popular powder room.

Mother spied someone she wanted in the dining room, so I headed the other way. I didn't need her eavesdropping while I asked leading questions.

Just inside the living room Arthur Bigelow addressed Helen Luedeke and another woman. "Our gardener drives a truck," he said. "I don't know who it belongs to."

I stepped forward. "It's my car, and it got vandalized!"

Apparently I used more volume than I had intended. Cloris looked up from the dish she was removing from the coffee table. Mrs. Perfect and her companion stopped gossiping and inhaled simultaneously. The pocket-watch owner faltered in mid-sentence, and Helen Luedeke widened her eyes at me and said, "Oh dear!"

"Sandwich?" I offered.

Helen ignored me, but Arthur Bigelow accepted something pink spread between whole wheat then strolled toward the pocket-watch group. Cloris scuttled toward the kitchen.

I stepped more obviously into Helen's conversational range, "I talked to Alice Gifford the other day," I told her casually. "Haven't you been co-competitors for a long time?"

She blinked. "No, not in years." When she moved her head, diamond studs flashed beneath her fuzzy gray curls.

I handed her one of the plates so I could eat something myself, a bleached white tea sandwich spread with something green. It tasted like dough.

"Oh, that's right," I continued. "She said she had been away from the flower show for a while, but I forget why."

"I really couldn't say," Helen told me. She swerved her cowcatcher toward another track and offered my plate of food to Willoby McDonald, who sat alone on the window seat. The woman remaining from Helen's previous conversation stared at me.

"Do you know why Alice Gifford stopped competing?" I asked. "It wasn't Iffy was it?"

The woman took a paté cracker and sighed at it. Her

brown hair hadn't so much grayed as faded. She was my height, but softer by twenty-five years. Her blue eyes were clear and sorrowful. She put the cracker back on the plate.

"Oh no. Her son had leukemia. He was a bachelor, so Alice gave up everything to care for him. I think she still lectured a fair amount, but everything else went on hold."

"She lectures on medicinal herbs?"

"Oh yes. All over the world."

"But this year she came back to the flower show."

"Yes," the woman agreed. "Her son died last summer. She wanted to see her friends again, pick up her life."

"What a shame about her leg," I said. I was feeling truly sorry for her and her husband, also miserably guilty for believing either of them capable of murder.

"Yes."

"So I was mistaken about a rivalry with Helen and Iffy." I wanted to write off the car accident once and for all.

"Alice is a marvelous arranger. When she's entered, everyone is her rival."

It was true before; I supposed it might become true again.

"But there's never been anything especially personal about it?"

"No, of course not. It's all good clean fun." She took back the cracker and bit it decisively.

I handed her the plate.

The pocket-watch bunch had departed. Looking very perplexed, Arthur Bigelow stood by himself in the hall with a package in his hands. All over the white wrapping paper brown script said, "Tuckahoe Nursery." The delivery must have just arrived.

"Want me to take that?" I asked.

He handed it to me. I discarded the paper and set the pot of five fragrant purple hyacinths on a living room end table. The plastic holder displayed a card that read, "Condolences from B. Crumb."

I returned to Arthur. He seemed temporarily buoyed by having friends in his home, but his eyes betrayed a weariness waiting to overtake him. I thought his cheeks had decent color, but that could have been from wine.

"You have something around for dinner?" I asked. He smiled at my Mother-like remark, which I had uttered without thought.

"Art Junior, Carol, and I are taking Aunt Lila out," he said.

"Will your family be staying a while?"

He shook his head. "I wish they were. Unfortunately, Art's in sales, and a day off is a day without pay. With a young family, that makes quite a difference." I could well imagine.

"They live in Akron?"

"Yes. That's why we had the, uh, funeral today. To, uh, give them time to come in. And Aunt Lila from Cincinnati, of course."

"If there's anything Mother and I can do . . ."

"Thanks. You and Cynthia are doing quite enough. She said you'd both be back tomorrow to finish." Thursday before a Friday party? Sure, why not.

Again, I felt uncomfortable about the speed with which Iffy's presence was being erased. Some remark was needed. "I guess it's best to get it over with."

"I have a lot of adjusting to do," he agreed. "I might as well start."

"Will you be home?" I wondered—to let us in and help with decisions.

"No, at the airport then the office." He dug in his pocket and extracted his spare house key. "Let me give you this before I forget."

I looked at him. We both seemed to be contemplating life's greater blows. He squeezed my shoulder with his hand, firmly pressed his lips together, then wheeled to face a couple who were donning their coats. Others were headed upstairs to get theirs.

"Dorothy and Basil." He extended his hand. "Thank you for coming."

I looked at my watch. Better collect my mother and take her home, too—George would be waiting.

❊ *Chapter 27* ❊

I found Mother in line behind two other people waiting for the powder room. She agreed she would be ready to go after accomplishing her current mission.

The dining room was empty but for a few latecomers picking at a luncheon spread that was two-thirds gone. Tea sandwiches had been a hit, probably on the merit of sheer bulk; the celery and the paté only so-so. More lumps of Swiss cheese remained than cheddar, but both piles were in battle disarray. All but one of the decorative strawberries were gone. I snatched it up and ate it on the way to get our coats.

No one was in the upstairs bathroom, so I stepped in to wash the strawberry juice off my fingers. The spacious facility came complete with a deep claw-footed tub and lots of rectangular white tile. A tall window with a broad sill overlooked the roof of Iffy's greenhouse, the back yard, and a detached garage. As I peeked through the eyelet curtain, Cloris lugged a big green trash bag along the walk that led to the garage. If she ever had a crush on Arthur Bigelow, today would have cured it.

Searching for the coat repository, I discovered Aunt Lila snoring under a comforter. Lifting my coat from the same bed didn't faze her one iota.

Downstairs the powder room line was exactly as it had been five minutes before, except Mother and the two women ahead of her had begun to fidget and frown.

"Really, some people are so inconsiderate," the second in line said to the first, loudly enough to be heard in the middle of the dining room.

"I've been here at least ten minutes," she added with disgust.

I told them the upstairs bathroom was empty, and both hustled past me toward the stairs.

Mother shrugged. "I might as well wait," she said.

"I'll meet you in the hall."

Since I had a few moments to spare, I looked into the kitchen, hoping to compliment Cloris on her hostessing efforts. Nobody was there.

When I got to the hall, the front door was open, allowing rude little gusts of wind to blow under my skirt. Arthur had stepped outside to see off his son and his family. I guessed they were taking the kids for a change of clothes or just a change of scenery before dinner with Aunt Lila.

I threw our coats across the hall railing and wandered into the living room. Willoby McDonald remained alone on the window seat.

"Where's Julia?" I asked.

"I think she went to help in the kitchen."

"Nobody was in there a minute ago."

"Well, you know. She might have stopped to talk."

Scarcely anyone was left for her to speak with, and as shy as she was I couldn't imagine that happening anyway.

"Gin-ger!" Mother's voice carried clearly through Arthur's office to the living room.

I ran. As the closest thing to a medical doctor in the house, Willoby McDonald ran, too.

Mother stood rigidly by the powder room door. Her hands clutched each other in front of her skirt. Her face was wide with alarm.

"What is it? Mom, what's the matter?"

She blinked up at Willoby McDonald. "Do something," she said. "Julia's in there."

McDonald pounded the door with his fist. "Julia! Julia, are you all right?"

I concentrated on Mother. "Why? What's wrong. Did she ask for help?" I asked.

Mother bit her trembling lip. From the powder room came a sort of whimper and a scrambling noise.

Willoby shook the doorknob, which rattled but did not turn. The room was locked.

"Julia, it's Will. Talk to me, sweetheart. Open the door so we can talk."

Silence.

"Julia, honey. I'm here. I'll take care of it, just let me in."

More silence.

The psychiatrist glanced at Mother and me, sharing his fear and frustration.

"I'll get a screwdriver," I said. Mother sighed one of those "isn't she clever" smiles.

The kitchen drawers yielded nothing but kitchen junk. But the noise had drawn the remaining few people, three women, and Arthur Bigelow.

"Arthur," I called to him. "We need a skinny screwdriver. Where do you keep them?"

"I'll show you." He led the way through a door in the corner of the kitchen downstairs to a small disused workbench set on a cement floor. In a metal box were an assortment of dusty, rusty tools. Holding it away from my navy blue suit, I carried the whole thing upstairs.

Fortunately one of the screwdrivers was narrow enough to poke through the hole in the doorknob meant for such emergencies. The lock cooperated beautifully when I found the right slot and twisted the screwdriver. The knob turned and the latch moved freely in and out and everything. Except the door still wouldn't open. Julia had blocked it with something.

I looked inquiringly at Arthur.

"There's a tall bookshelf thing, for towels, and . . . and books. It's fairly heavy," he explained.

Willoby McDonald had given off crooning to Julia. Now he leaned against the wall distraught and useless.

"The hinges," somebody said, but the hinges were snug inside the doorjamb out of sight.

In a glance Arthur and I read each other's minds. Force was the only answer.

He held the doorknob unlatched and began to shove with his shoulder. The door shuddered and moved a half inch, just enough to remain unlatched. Repeated shoves yielded nothing and threatened to break Arthur's shoulder. He was, after all, in his seventies. The only person there strong enough to help was McDonald, and he flinched at each blow as if Julia herself were being bruised.

"Stop," I told Arthur. "There's a better way. Will," I leaned down to speak up at the psychiatrist's hanging head. "Can you kick the door open with your foot?"

Asking him something directly snapped him out of it. He whipped off that brown herringbone jacket and loosened that horrendous tie.

"Stay back, Julia," he shouted. Then he cocked a long leg, and gave the door a resounding flat-footed blow with his tasseled cordovan.

The bookcase inside broke and fell over. Something on it had been glass, or something it hit was glass, because we heard it shatter on the tile. A brief series of bangs and thumps also followed as books and other items bounced their way to the floor.

In the silence that followed I noticed the smell of a terrified human being beneath the flowery fragrance of the powder room. When the voice fails, the body uses other ways to say, "Get back. Don't touch me."

And so does the mind.

Julia Stone was far, far out of reach. Her arms and legs and body crouched, shivering with fear, between the toilet and wall. She had wrapped one arm across the back of her neck to fend off attack. Otherwise she held herself perfectly silent and still.

Will McDonald jumped over the mess on the floor and gently lifted her chin. "Julia," he said. "Oh, Julia." Her face was colorless. Her eyes, empty of all recognition.

McDonald hugged her head to his chest and took a deep ragged breath. Then he scooped Julia into his arms and carried her out of the small room. We all fell away like peons before royalty.

Julia's young doctor placed her carefully on the living room sofa, and Mother covered her with her coat.

"Stay with her while I make arrangements," Will requested. Mother kneeled on chubby knees beside Julia and soothingly petted the poor woman's hair with her hand.

Arthur dismissed the few remaining stragglers with hollow assurances that were nevertheless effective. "She's with her doctor," was the operative phrase. As they left, each woman grasped Arthur's hand and offered a mournful face. "What more must you endure?" they seemed to wonder. Also, "What if it had happened to me?"

I kept expecting to see Cloris, but she must have left before the problem had been discovered.

About fifteen minutes later, without sirens or fanfare, an ambulance arrived. Orderlies quickly took over, and with one eye on the gurney Dr. McDonald guided me out of Arthur's and Mother's hearing.

"She'll be guarded twenty-four hours a day," he said.

"Where?" I asked. I hadn't thought about where she was going at all, and now I panicked to think of her returning to somewhere as public and crowded as Norristown State Hospital.

"It's small and private. Out in the country. I don't think I'll tell you—or anyone—where."

"Do you think she saw something?"

"Or someone," he corrected me.

It made sense. I was no doctor, but something had touched off Julia's withdrawal. If she had indeed witnessed her aunt's death, then a reasonable explanation would be that she had come face-to-face with the murderer again—within the last hour.

One of the stragglers? No. A murderer who thought he was recognized would never stay around.

Of course, the recognition could have been one-way. Maybe Julia saw the killer across the room and hid before he or she saw her. It was possible, and I fervently hoped true.

Willoby told me, "If you call my office, they'll tell you Julia's catatonic. Call me at home if you want the truth." Whatever that may be.

"Do you think she'll ever be well enough to testify?"

McDonald buttoned his brown herringbone jacket and squared his shoulders. Then he tore his eyes off the back of the ambulance and fixed them on me.

"Let's just get her back and worry about that later."

❈ *Chapter 28* ❈

The parking lot in front of the McDonald's where I was to meet George lay in two sections to allow for the steep slope of the property. To avoid George's professional curiosity, I tucked the Nissan into one of the lower slots and walked uphill to the fast-food restaurant.

The day's wind had dampened, and serious gray clouds blanketed the hilly, recently rejuvenated community of Conshohocken on the opposite bank of the Schuylkill. I couldn't see the river, but I knew it was just downhill from the Mobil station and the Tower Bridge high-rise across the street. Past them to the right Route 23 zigzagged through gaps in the rock into the privileged territory of Gladwyne. To the left lay the small industrial town of Bridgeport.

Consequently, the intersection was well-used, especially by bridge traffic heading onto the facing expressway entrance. We don't have all that many bridges across the river, and this gathering point justified the existence of the McDonald's and the gas station as well. From here, there were no other direct roads into Philadelphia either, which explained why the Schuylkill Expressway became inadequate the day it opened.

For some odd reason a thick, dance-hall cylinder covered with rectangular mirrors hung just inside the door to the restaurant. George sat just behind it on a white, simulated bentwood chair feeding himself French fries the way Rip feeds Barney leftovers—without thinking. His moustache smiled and unsmiled as he chewed.

He had on a thick black-and-brown sweater over his white shirt and tie. It looked affected, like an executive pretending he behaved differently on a weekend. The trench coat he wore to the funeral was folded over the back of the booth.

When I sat down, the youth polishing the next table retreated behind a center divider bordered with three-toned brown tiles.

George pushed a wet cup of Coke toward me, a straw stuck through the lid. Since he had another one just like it, I accepted thankfully. I had to swirl the melted ice to fix the flavor, but just the idea of it helped me relax. Probably conditioning from all those commercials.

"Want some?" George asked, bouncing fried potatoes forward in their greasy container the way you might offer a cigarette.

I thought about it. "Yes and no," I said.

"Know what you mean," he agreed. Then he pinched a bunch between a thick finger and thumb, shrugged, and ate them.

"Exactly what've you been up to?" he asked not quite casually.

"Let's see," I began. "Monday I picked out something for Iffy to wear to her funeral and visited a woman with a broken leg. Then I got thrown out of the Tuckahoe Nursery."

He was alarmed. "Why? What'd you do?"

"Nothing. I was just trying to buy some flowers for a party. The owner remembered I thought she and Iffy Bigelow were friends, and she decided she didn't like my face."

George grunted. "And what was this person's name, may I ask?"

"Beatrice Crumb. Turns out Iffy caused her first business to go under."

"How the hell . . .?" Trying to control some anger, he rattled the ice in his Coke then decisively set it aside. "You have this information on good authority?"

"A relative who works there."

George sighed. "Whose relative? Yours?"

"No, hers."

He relaxed enough to retrieve his Coke.

I touched his arm with a knuckle. The sweater was cotton. "George," I said. "Is Julia Stone still a suspect?"

"Why?"

"Because something happened at the reception after the funeral."

"Oh?"

"She had a sort of spell. Well, she sort of went crazy. Not berserk crazy—scared crazy. She locked herself in the powder room and wouldn't let anyone in. We got her out, but she was totally gone, George. I'm worried that she'll never come back. Do you think she might have recognized the murderer?"

"Whoa, there. Back up a minute. According to your mother's account of last Friday morning, Julia never saw the murderer, just heard her aunt saying 'no' to someone."

"So you believe my mother?"

George evaded me. "Julia has a history of mental illness, right? And so far we don't know that she witnessed anything."

"Even without my mother's report, we know she either saw the murder or found the body right after it happened."

"Unless she did it herself."

I made an irritated noise. "She didn't, George. She—" I searched for an argument that didn't sound too sentimental"—doesn't have the guts."

George rolled his eyes, the professional dismissing all amateurs.

"Don't go snobby on me, George. Think about what

happened and give me an answer. Do you think Julia might have seen the murderer this afternoon?"

He considered the possibility for thirty seconds and then said no.

"No?"

"No."

"Why not?"

"You're just plain assuming too much. You're assuming she saw the killing, and then you're assuming the killer frightened her this afternoon. It doesn't make sense. Why react so late in the day? Why not at the funeral home or the cemetery?"

"Okay," I was becoming annoyed by his logic. "What do you think happened?"

"I've had some experience with loonies, excuse me— with the mentally ill. Their minds just don't work like everybody else's. They're not logical. They are unpredictable— that's the one thing you can count on. Things set them off that would never set off anybody else in a million years. A goddamned bunch of flowers could have done it."

He noticed my face and softened his voice. "Look," he said. "Julia Stone had an extremely stressful day, after a terrible shock last week. That alone could have caused a breakdown."

I shrugged. Maybe he was right. I didn't know.

"Or there's another way to look at it." George leaned toward me and took my hand in his. The youth around the corner pointedly resumed wiping mottled green Formica. "Maybe the guilt got to her."

I reclaimed my hand. "Her doctor thought she saw somebody, too."

George straightened, his hands retreating across the table with him. "Whose idea was it first?"

I couldn't remember, so I regrouped for a flank attack.

"Do all the family members have alibis? Except Julia, of course."

"The son and daughter-in-law you mean?"

"Yes," I agreed. "And Arthur." Aunt Lila was too old and lived in Cincinnati anyway.

He flexed some of the tension out of his shoulders. "Art Junior and his wife were in Akron last Friday morning. Confirmed. Arthur Senior—we don't know."

"Wasn't he on a plane?"

"The plane was delayed. He says he was at the airport waiting for it, but we haven't verified that yet."

Plane delays can be determined from anywhere with a phone call—lots of people verify their departure time before every flight.

"Do you think you could place him at the flower show?"

"We haven't yet."

"What about Helen Luedeke? I know she was arguing with my mother when Iffy was killed, but do you think she might have hired someone?"

George lifted his chin. "To imitate an impulsive murder? Unlikely."

I disagreed with that assessment, but George held firm. "It's unlikely, Gin. Unlikely enough that we're pursuing the more likely possibilities first."

"Like Beatrice Crumb?"

He scowled and grunted, unwilling to reveal whether anything I had told him was new information.

"But what if all the likely suspects get ruled out?" I asked.

"Then we look into the Helen Luedekes."

I had to be satisfied with that. Lightly, I said, "So how was your week, darling?" He laughed a little and smiled.

"I can tell you that one minute Mrs. Bigelow was bitching that a plant inspector was too slow, then suddenly she shut up. The inspector thought Mrs. Bigelow had recognized someone at a distance, but she didn't turn her head to see who it was."

Dutifully looking for bugs on the clivia, no doubt.

I asked George if he remembered Sally Metz, the aide with the hair like yellow fur. "I think she went to the hort section after she was through with the niches."

George shook his head no. "Sally was still at the niches when Mrs. Bigelow took her plant to be inspected. We're checking on who was in the hort section; but if the killer was someone Mrs. Bigelow trusted, it would have looked like two friends meeting. Who'd remember that?"

Mentally, I tallied it all up. The police were nowhere.

"What happened to your car?" George asked. So much for trying to park out of sight.

I described the break-in at the school, explaining how Rip threw on the hall lights and scared the person away, "but when we got home that's what my car looked like."

George considered my answer while he swept his hamburger refuse onto a tray and set it on the table behind him.

"School-related?" he asked.

"Probably."

"But maybe not."

"Maybe not," I agreed.

He wagged his head. "That first time? You fed me information like you were passin' out hors d'oeuvres. So I thought, okay, let her talk to her lady friends. Couldn't hurt . . ."

"And just might help," I interjected with a hint of sarcasm.

"And just might help," he agreed. "However, I did not expect you to go so far out of your way to stir up trouble. You've had your fun, Gin. Now I think you better back off."

I folded my arms and regarded him. He was paying more attention to his hands than to me, so I said, "You disappoint me, George. I thought you saw me the way I expect my friends to see me. Instead you sound like every other male chauvinist . . . pig."

"Now, Gin . . ."

"Don't patronize me, George. My information has been

damn helpful to you. Admit it: I learned as much as you did
this week, if not more.''

I stood, slung my bag over my shoulder, huffed. George
didn't move.

Then he rose slowly until he towered over me like a threat.
''Where the hell you think you're goin', *Mrs. Barnes*?''

I squared up to face him as effectively as possible. ''Home
to chat up my lady friends on the phone. Where else?''

''Well, sit down. We ain't through. Also, you owe me
eighty-nine cents for that Coke.''

❈ *Chapter 29* ❈

$\mathcal{A}$lthough George and I talked long enough to get past our little tiff, neither of us came up with one new thought about Iffy's murder. So when the McDonald's began to fill up with dinner customers, we ceremoniously shook hands and parted company.

I was happy to hear Temple Bodell's voice on our home answering machine listing the standings of the sweeps Tuesday and Thursday afternoons. Iffy was in the top five both days, but Helen Luedeke only on Thursday. In other words, both women could have won by Saturday, but Helen was on the rise while Iffy had dropped from second to third. The show official stated these facts with strain in her voice, as if she needed more aspirin. I took some for her.

Rain lashed the house all through dinner. Branches scraped the siding and splashes of water swung from window to window like a fire hose out of control. After a dessert of cookies and instant cocoa, Chelsea snuggled under her comforter with a reading assignment; and Garry, who swore he finished his work in study hall, holed up in the TV room in pajamas with the dog.

Rip donned a London Fog, kissed my nose, and pressed through the rain to the car and a fundraising call—more parents he needed to solicit as part of the capital campaign.

It always depressed me a bit to have him out evenings, even for a good cause, but I especially hated the thought of him out in the downpour. He wasn't any too pleased himself.

At least I could plan a cozy homecoming. With that in mind I lit a fire in the big walk-in in the family room, certainly the last of the year. Each log I used was one less to lug back to the woodpile.

I changed into a sweat suit and fluffy slippers and poured a glass of burgundy from the open bottle in the refrigerator, zapping it back to room temperature in the microwave.

Then with my legs under me on the sofa, watching the flames jump and waver, listening to the roof holding off the rain, I thought of Julia with her arm covering her head and I shivered. Willoby McDonald said I could call his home to ask after her. I had his number handy, too. He answered on the second ring.

"She's sedated, comfortable, safe," he told me. "It's going to take time."

"I wonder," I began tentatively, "could her condition have been brought on simply by the strain of the day?"

"Yes, certainly."

"I mean you thought, we both thought, she saw something that set it off. Have you given that idea any more consideration?"

"It's too soon to know anything definitely."

"You see, I was wondering if maybe it was more the power of suggestion that made you say that."

"What do you mean?"

"I wondered if maybe I put the idea in your head in the first place."

"By suggesting that Julia may have witnessed the murder rather than simply discovering the body?"

"Yes."

"You thought you might have psyched out the psychiatrist?"

When he put it that way, it sounded awfully presumptuous.

My cheeks began to burn. But they say no question is foolish if you want to know the answer. I was genuinely interested in his answer.

McDonald obliged. "It wouldn't be the first time that happened. We like to think we're only swayed by facts, but that doesn't really matter just now, does it? We have to protect Julia as if the worst were true: that she recognized a murderer and the murderer knows it. To behave any differently would be unconscionable, wouldn't you say?"

"Yes," I agreed. "And thank you."

If Julia recovered, or to put it more positively, *when* she recovered, it would be nice for her to be cleared of all suspicion. As usual, the urge to do something kicked in. But what?

The fire sizzled and spat. The rain splashed and spilled. Rip was elsewhere speaking to strangers, selling them on the idea that Bryn Derwyn Academy was a valuable entity worth supporting. My children were busy growing up in other rooms, and I was sipping wine in front of a fire wondering why I should be so warm and safe.

I got the Main Line phone book out of the end table and opened it on my lap.

Five Pescatores were listed. No Josephs. None of the people who answered even heard of a Joe Pescatore.

I went to Rip's office for two more phone books.

Finally, a Norristown Pescatore asked, "You mean Mary Jo?"

I almost said no, but since I was running out of phone books, I asked, "Is she the one who has something to do with flowers?"

The woman laughed. "She plants them, if that's what you mean."

Bingo. "By any chance was she acquainted with a woman named Winifred Bigelow?"

"Jo worked for her a while back."

"Are you sure?"

"I'm her mother. Of course, I'm sure."

"Mrs. Pescatore, I wonder if you'd mind giving me your daughter's phone number."

"It's unlisted. Why do you want to speak with her?"

I needed a persuasive reason, something vague. I crossed my fingers and said, "I'm considering a little landscaping job, nothing big, and I think it was Mrs. Bigelow who mentioned your daughter's name. She thought Jo wouldn't mind earning a little extra on the side."

"Jo Pescatore?" I soon asked the young voice on the other end of the line."

"Yes."

"My name is Ginger Barnes. Your mother gave me your number. I wonder if I could meet with you briefly to talk about Winifred Bigelow? I promise not to take much of your time."

"I, I don't know . . ."

"At your convenience. Anywhere you say."

"I don't think . . ."

"You used to work for Mrs. Bigelow, right?"

"Yes."

"This could really be important. I promise I won't keep you long."

"My mother gave you my number?"

"Yes."

A little sigh. "Then I guess it's all right. How about Saturday?"

"Could you possibly make it sooner? Please?"

"It's that important?"

"It might be."

A small moan. "Okay. If you can stop in around nine tomorrow morning I could give you a few minutes. But if it stops raining, I'll have to go to work."

She gave me directions to her apartment then held me on the line with a hesitant little noise. "Does this . . . does this have anything to do with Mrs. Bigelow's death?" she asked.

I thought it might, but I told her I honestly didn't know.

Chapter 30 ※

Rip came home about nine, drenched and exhausted. His smile was crooked, his shoulders limp.

"How'd it go?" I asked.

"We'll get something," he answered.

To me, soliciting donations would feel like begging. Fortunately, Rip reasoned that people with excess money needed something to do with it. I've also heard him say, "Educating young people offers a lot of value for the dollar." He just didn't realize how often he would have to say it.

"Cup of decaf in front of the fire?" I suggested.

He glanced at the warm hearth. "Sure."

We sat on the floor with the sofa for a backrest and our feet toward the coals. For a few minutes we held hands and caught up on the events of the day; but when we ran out of news, I tucked my head on Rip's shoulder and in thirty seconds he was snoring. I woke him and led him upstairs to make his day's end official. Then I battened down the rest of the Barnes' hatches, Chelsea and Garry and Barney, lights and locks, and so on. Thirty seconds was all the consciousness I had left when I hit my own pillow.

Sometime during the night the rain stopped, and enough moon lighted the woodsy yards behind us to allow Barney to see deer. Or maybe he smelled them first, but anyhow his throaty territorial bark woke me and possibly half the township. Irish setters are not renowned for their watchdog capabilities, but Barney and his neurotic predecessor each came through enough times to earn a lifetime supply of dog food. After your dog scares off a prowler even once, you learn to tolerate the false alarms.

"Thanks, Barn," I told him drowsily, "but just now we'd rather sleep than watch deer." I couldn't see them anyway, just smoky clouds blowing across a waning moon and deep black shadows in the woods. I got a hand on the dog's collar and led him from the patio window to Garry's room where I shut him in. When he couldn't see outside, he had no incentive to bark.

I returned upstairs to bed, shivered a minute and a half under the covers, then fell back to sleep.

When our alarm went off with soft rock music, it was like poking a pillow with a broom handle. Much as both Rip and I tried to sleep around it, eventually we got the point. Chelsea was already in the shower. Rip and I grunted good morning to each other across the pillows. Thursday had begun.

I kissed Chelsea good-bye in front of the stove where I was occupied frying Rip's eggs. The morning felt good, homey and normal. But then Chelsea came back.

"Forget something?" I asked before glancing at her face. It was white, her eyes wide.

"You better come see this," she said.

I turned off the stove and hurried to her side. Through the glass of the storm door I saw that two of the leaf piles had been combined under the old sheet we used as a spare tarp. Lying on top was a stuffed skeleton costume with its arms folded across its chest.

"Rip," I called up the stairs. "Look out front."

"Who do you think did it, Mom?" Chelsea asked. "School kids?" She was trying to be worldly and calm, as if pranksters put effigies in our front yard all the time and the only point of interest was who happened to put this one there.

Except she was still only thirteen and not quite that jaded. She bit her lip and hugged her aqua ski jacket closed and cast Rip a worried glance when he ran down the stairs.

My husband wore only corduroys and an unbuttoned blue shirt, so he didn't run into the yard. He just stood with his arms wide staring at the funeral pyre somebody had built on our lawn. Then he came over and wrapped his arms around Chelsea, who began to cry.

Over her head Rip jerked his chin toward the kitchen wall phone next to me. "Place the call, will you, honey?" he said. Reassuring Chelsea came first.

"What's she crying about?" Garry asked. He stood in the hallway in his Phillies pajamas and socks, rubbing his left eye with a fist. Rip released Chelsea and squatted in front of him.

"Somebody played another trick on us out front," he told our son. "Chelsea found it, and she's a little upset."

Garry rushed to the front storm door, which was frosted with condensation. Clearing a swath with his sleeve, he looked out and pronounced the spectacle, "Awesome—and it's not even Halloween!"

The police dispatcher said she'd send someone right over.

❈ *Chapter 31* ❈

The policeman who responded to our call yawned during Rip's rundown of our recent vandalism experiences. I assumed he was at the end, or maybe the very beginning, of his shift.

He closed his notebook, which contained our name and address.

"You run that school, right?" he remarked, squinting at Rip with his head tilted. "So wouldn't you say it's probably a student prank? I mean, unless you irritated some neighbor and they have a pretty childish sense of humor, this looks more like your department than mine."

"We haven't irritated any neighbors." Rip was clearly irritated by this policeman. "In fact we scarcely even see our neighbors unless we're walking our dog."

The cop tapped Rip on the chest with his notebook. "That could be it right there, Mr. Barnes. Some people really have it in for dogs."

"No," Rip said. "No. Almost everyone on the street owns a dog. Why aren't you taking this seriously?"

"I beg your pardon, Mr. Barnes," he glanced at the skeleton costume stuffed with leaves. "But I don't know exactly how to proceed here. You sure there isn't a kid you gave a tough time recently?"

Rip's cheeks looked pinched. "Last night was a school night," he said. "We've never had teenagers do anything on a school night before."

The officer's cynical smirk was not wasted on my husband. Rip knew quite well that students sometimes oversleep in the morning and occasionally doze off in class, indicating who-knew-what sort of late weeknight activity. Yet my husband was worried for the safety of his family, and he wanted to believe the police could make the vandalism stop.

If ever I were going to admit my connection to a murder investigation, that would have been the time. But what would I have said? "My mother's friend got killed, and I was there"? It was easy to imagine what the cynical cop's response would have been. Unless several others connected to the flower show had gotten effigies on their lawns, he would continue to insist that a student was responsible for our problem.

Circling around the leaf-mound funeral pyre a final time completed the officer's efforts on our behalf. Rip pivoted on his heel and muttered all the way into the house, leaving me to deal with the amenities.

"Lucky everything was wet." The officer punctuated this remark by shutting his car door.

"Why?" I asked.

"Don't they usually light these things on fire?" He glanced at the sky, smiled good-bye, and backed the car out of the driveway.

When my stomach lurched back to normal, I too noticed that the day was clearing nicely. Overhead, the earlier indefinite haze had become a promising pale blue. Under my feet the ground felt soft but not sodden from last night's drenching—a perfect day for planting things, if that happened to be your business.

So Jo Pescatore would be going to work after all. If I wanted to speak with her, I would have to hurry.

After seeing off my husband and son (Chelsea had taken

her bus), I hurried through the dog-feeding, dish-stacking, door-locking business I couldn't escape into the rush-hour traffic nobody could escape. Luckily the young woman's apartment was merely across town and around a corner into Berwyn.

The apartment building faced Lincoln Highway, as Route 30 was called in that section. It was just another inconspicuous brick structure three stories high, two apartments wide. The left-hand driveway led to rear parking. I used the back stairs as instructed and knocked on the plain birch door labeled 2B. Chain locks and dead bolts clattered and snicked, and suddenly I was facing the young woman with the plain glasses and long yarn-like braid whose graceful efficiency I had admired at the flower show. Today she wore a yellow oxford shirt over a white T-shirt printed with some slogan I couldn't read, well-washed jeans, and low leather work shoes.

I introduced myself and thanked her for seeing me.

She opened the door for me to enter. "Have we already met?" she asked.

"I was looking for someone at the flower show. I asked if you'd seen her."

"That's it," she concurred.

The lingering smell of coffee, toast, and eggs greeted me, probably because the aisle-shaped kitchen lay straight ahead. Off to the left a living room spanned the depth of the apartment.

Jo gestured for me to sit on a brown, fifties-modern, wood-and-foam sofa next to a sleeping gray cat. Behind my head in a wide, deep window extraordinarily healthy plants basked in the morning sun. Their shadows dappled the rest of the room, including the brown tweed carpet, the orange wood-and-foam chair where Jo sat, the dusty television screen, and the otherwise blank white walls. Behind Jo, a rectangular opening passed through to the kitchen.

"I'll have to leave for work soon," she prompted shyly.

"If it hadn't rained last night, I'd be there already." She said it because it was true, not because she didn't want to speak with me (which she clearly didn't), or because she was aggressive toward other women (which she clearly wasn't). She had waited for me because she said she would, probably fixed herself an unusually elaborate breakfast to kill time; and, now that I was later than planned, she was worried about her job.

"I appreciate your waiting for me, and I promise not to keep you long. You're obviously a very responsible employee—I saw you working at the flower show. So please tell me, whatever happened between you and Mrs. Bigelow?"

A wince passed across the young woman's pale countenance. She probably used gallons of sunscreen in her line of work, and certainly a wide-brimmed hat. The only hint of feminine pride was the long, fuzzy, medium-brown braid hanging well below her waist. I'd have dotted those exposed earlobes with the tiniest of turquoise beads.

But as I watched, Jo Pescatore's expression flickered like the shadows of her houseplants, showing me why adornment was intrinsically wrong for her. She was one hundred percent natural, the type who would be true to herself and truthful to others. And her face was even more fascinating to watch than her hands at work had been.

She was looking at the base of a floor lamp, or rather that's where her eyes were aimed. She appeared to be seeing a personal failure of some sort, judging by the sadness in her eyes.

"I don't see . . ."

"Please. What can it hurt? I just need to know what Winifred Bigelow was really like."

Jo Pescatore was polite; she didn't ask why I needed to know. Or maybe she didn't care to prolong our conversation by the length of an explanation. She just fixed me with big Bambi eyes and said, "She fired me."

With only half my attention I watched two enormous tears race down her cheeks and drip into her yellow shirt. My brain was attempting to process some current information, to connect it to something held in storage . . .

"I'm really sorry to make you uncomfortable, but have you any idea why?"

Small-boned shoulders shrugged under the two masculine shirts. "She just said she didn't need me anymore."

"I take it this wasn't at the end of the summer," when the old excuse might possibly have been true.

Jo wagged her head no.

"Were you getting along before that?"

Jo bit her lip.

I gave her a verbal nudge. "She was demanding and abusive, wasn't she?"

Behind the wire-rimmed glasses, the young woman's eyes grew huge. "How did you . . .?"

"She was that way with everybody. Did she lie about you, too?"

"Not that I . . ."

"So basically she bossed you all around until she finally let you go."

Jo's chin dipped slightly.

Just so. But what did it mean? As difficult as Iffy Bigelow had been, she could have had this girl in tears every time she came to work. It seemed unlikely that Iffy had verbalized her preferences to Jo or her husband or even herself, but she probably wanted an employee who didn't make her feel like such a bitch, somebody who could take her abuse a little more stoically. Perhaps a welfare case or a person with a limited understanding of English.

I expressed this thought to Jo Pescatore, and if possible the Bambi eyes grew even bigger. "She did hire . . . how did you . . .?"

"Lucky guess."

Meanwhile, my mind had completed its match-up, and it

was time for me to ask, "Why did you phone her the other day?"

"What do you mean?" Jo leaned forward, attempting to convey bafflement instead of shock, but she was far too ingenuous to be convincing.

I told her I heard her voice on the Bigelow's answering machine.

"I didn't . . ."

"Yes," I insisted gently, "you did. I listened to it several times." I leaned toward her. "There's nothing to be ashamed of. It sounded as if you were trying to do Mrs. Bigelow some sort of favor, but then you changed your mind. Considering what she did to you, I'm surprised you called at all."

Jo tucked her chin down tight. She wasn't sure what to do with the hands in her lap.

"She really wasn't that bad to me," she said. "Probably I just didn't understand what she wanted me to do."

I took a deep, calming breath and asked what it was Jo intended to tell her former boss.

A one-shoulder shrug.

"She was murdered, Jo. Maybe even while you were on the phone."

The eyes flashed their panic at me. "But that couldn't have had anything to do with . . ."

"What couldn't have, Jo? What did you want to tell her?"

Jo bit her knuckle, turned her head, dragged in a breath. Her hand dropped to her lap. Her eyes dared to meet mine.

"I was going to tell her something I overheard, something that seemed . . . odd. At first I couldn't figure out what it meant, but there seemed to be only one explanation that made any sense. I figured if I told Mrs. Bigelow, she could decide for herself whether it meant anything."

"Yes . . ."

"I heard Mrs. Luedeke at a garden club meeting. My boss was speaking that night about plant collecting, and he had asked some of the members to bring in their best specimens.

When everybody was socializing after the speech, I heard Mrs. Luedeke trying to talk a woman into entering her plant in one of the flower show categories. 'I'll handle everything, if you can't be bothered,' that sort of thing."

"I don't understand," I said. "What would that mean?"

"At first I didn't understand either. But then I heard her giving the same speech to somebody else, except this time she said, 'It'd serve Iffy Bigelow right.'"

I still didn't understand, so I said so.

"Well, think about it. Why would anybody go to the trouble of entering someone else's plant for them when they have enough to do entering their own?"

"Friendship?"

Jo dismissed that idea. "Mrs. Luedeke really wanted Iffy Bigelow to lose, enough to enter other people's plants for them. She was trying to influence the outcome of the sweeps."

It was stretching a little thin for me, and my doubt must have shown.

"I thought it was impossible, too," Jo agreed, "but when I heard her go through the same routine with a third person . . ."

Even with the sun on the back of my neck, I shivered. Then I scowled and bit my thumb.

"What? What is it?" Jo asked.

I told her about the car accident involving Iffy, Helen Luedeke and Alice Gifford.

Jo's pale face went pink. "Do you think Mrs. Luedeke might have killed Mrs. Bigelow?" The thought appalled and frightened her.

"No. No, she couldn't have," I reassured her. "Helen was arguing with someone in the niche area at the time of the murder."

Arguing about whether or not she deliberately bumped the wall to jostle Iffy's entry—an alibi and sabotage with one well-placed elbow!

If anything Helen said to the garden club women constituted a conspiracy against Iffy, George would be forced to take the possibility of a hired killer seriously.

I asked Jo the names of the women Helen approached.

"I only knew one—Gloria Miklos," she said, "and only because she hired my company for a day."

At my request, she wrote the name and address on a corner of newspaper from the coffee table between us. When she tore it off and handed it to me, the cat lifted its head and shot me an indignant glare.

"If she's not home, she's probably at State of the Arts."

"That store in Suburban Square?" I'd purchased a non-fogging shaving mirror for the shower there last Christmas. Rip loved it so much I was forced to forgive the store for the exorbitant price.

"That's the one."

I stood up to leave. "Thanks," I said, "for everything." I punctuated my parting word with the piece of newspaper. Jo smiled and held the door for me.

My intention was to turn the lead directly over to George, but Mother talked me out of that. I'm still not sure how.

❈ *Chapter 32* ❈

*F*rom Jo Pescatore's I proceeded to Ludwig to pick up my mother, and we spent the rest of the morning sifting through Iffy's walk-in closet full of expensive clothes. It was a tiring, morbid job, and our conversation consisted of single syllable *ehs*? and *umphs*.

Most everything was of consignment quality; very few items showed any wear or were as out of date as the "lucky" Pendleton tweed. Keeping the majority of things on their hangers, we slipped large green trash bags over them and piled them on the bed.

The discards—shoes, nightgowns, underwear, gardening clothes, an inexplicable lavender sweat suit with paint on one knee and a few sweaters with moth holes—I folded and stacked for the Salvation Army while Mother listed everything for Arthur's tax receipt. He was an accountant, after all.

About noon I ventured out in search of boxes, not an easy task considering the latest recycling frenzy. Fortunately, an Acme grocery store had just finished unloading bananas, and the produce manager had a soft heart. In gratitude I bought our lunch at the store's salad bar.

Back in the Bigelows' kitchen, Mother faced me across

the table and spoke one of the longest sentences of the morning.

"How's the investigation going?" she asked. She extracted a bread stick from its cellophane package and took a bite. "Needs butter," she remarked before returning her attention to me.

"We're eating healthy today. No butter." I still suffered vicarious anxiety over Iffy's death. My mother could stand to lose a few pounds, get a little more exercise. Come to think of it, so could I.

"Don't change the subject, dear."

Trying not to speak with my mouth full, I skipped the effigy incident and related the sweepstakes-tampering idea. "What do you think?" I asked with an artichoke hunk poised in front of my mouth.

Mother nodded vigorously as she chewed. After swallowing, she asserted that Helen Luedeke was certainly capable of any sort of nastiness I'd care to name. "Dreadful woman. Simply dreadful." But that opinion was no surprise. The entire gathering at the niche section and half the Philadelphia homicide department were well aware of it.

"So when do you meet with the co-conspirator?"

"I wouldn't call . . ."

Mother stared at me pointedly. Probably the table manners thing. While I daintily consumed the artichoke heart, I realized that Mother had never once admitted she exaggerated.

"George will talk to her," I said. "That's his job."

"Nonsense. You'll go while I'm at the consignment shop."

I must have groaned, because Mother raised an eyebrow.

"Oh, all right," I conceded. Confirmation from a second source would make Jo's conspiracy theory sound more convincing.

"Good. Glad that's settled. Now pass me the butter."

I bit a bread stick in lieu of my tongue.

* * *

State of the Arts was a broad, triangular showroom spanning a corner of the upscale shopping center known as Suburban Square. On the perfectly climate-controlled, thickly carpeted sales floor merchandise was displayed at waist height on small rectangular tables. Tall items, such as a six-foot brass-and-ebony telescope, were set on carpeted blocks eight inches high. New Age music, that stuff they always name after bodies of water and sunsets, weighed on me like an herbal wrap. "Relax," it insisted. "Allow your imagination to play with the merchandise. Indulge yourself."

In keeping with the atmosphere, a young salesman lounged over his counter and conveyed a patient message. "Take your time," his smile seemed to say. "I'll be here . . . watching you."

I took a leisurely stroll around the store, not expecting to see anything remotely relevant to my life, but trying to imagine who would want the stuff. Shiny socket wrenches of every size nestled in the red plush grooves of a leather case. A globe as large as a beach ball in a cherry wood stand housed crystal decanters and glassware. There were stereo jogging radios and CD players, watches that did everything short of computing your federal tax return, and brass garden tools that would last several lifetimes. A six-inch dart board in cork, red, green, and black was available to help the brain-dead executive make decisions: buy, sell, hire, fire, play golf, put it on hold. Hilarious. And please don't forget the "freezer balls," colored plastic ice cubes guaranteed not to water down your martini.

Over there we've got your essential oil-gauge wiper, your home blood-pressure kit, your bathtub alert so you know when the water level is perfect without actually being in the bathroom. And for the terminally uptight, there's the clock on a rope to remind you how late you are even in the shower.

While I struggled to absorb the idea of a whole shopping center devoted to such overpriced frills, I noticed the salesman drumming a tatoo on the counter with his neat manly nails.

"Is Mrs. Miklos available?" I asked from my position halfway across the room. Since I was the only customer and the music was no threat, naturally he heard me.

"I'll see." He went to see.

In a second a middle-aged woman emerged from the office behind the counter. She extended her hand and introduced herself. I did the same.

Gloria Milkos was pretzel-thin and about that brown. Her tightly pored face shone from moisturizer beneath brittle, black hair set in arched curls that broke around her face like unhealthy surf. She wore a black, short-sleeved silk dress and black high heels. Focal points were her large, evenly capped teeth and the diamond cluster ring on her right hand.

"I have a peculiar question to ask you, Mrs. Miklos." I tried to achieve a casual air by leaning against a table covered with bird feeders.

"Gloria." Astutely, she had discerned that I wasn't there for another fogless shower mirror.

"Thank you, Gloria. Do you mind if I ask you the question and then explain?"

"As you wish." Her thin fingers clasped each other in front of the black silk with the diamond cluster front and center. So relaxed and natural was the stance that she probably had ceased noticing the habit years ago, or perhaps the music had mellowed her into a permanent alpha state.

"Do you remember the night Helen Luedeke spoke to you about entering a plant in the flower show?"

The businesswoman shrugged her left shoulder in a fashion that struck me as European. A miniature scowl creased her suntanned skin.

"It was at your garden club meeting. You had a program about plant collections that night."

"Oh yes. What is it you wish to know?" With perfect proprietor/customer diplomacy she hid any reaction to my strange conversation. Beatrice Crumb should have taken etiquette lessons from this one.

"I'm wondering if you remember exactly what Helen said."

Gloria studied her carpet for a moment then turned her gaze on me. "She said, 'Your rex begonia is really a fabulous specimen, why don't you enter it in the Philadelphia Flower Show.'" Another European shoulder roll.

"Anything else?"

Gloria blinked at a bird feeder. "She said, 'I'll take it down with me if you need me to.'"

"That's all?"

"I think so."

"Are you sure?"

"Yes, I'm sure. Now what is it exactly you need to know? You said you'd explain."

"In a second. Did Mrs. Luedeke happen to say anything about Iffy Bigelow?"

"Who?"

"Winifred Bigelow, flower arranger, grower, won lots of awards."

Eyes the pale green of Jo Pescatore's cat stared at my sleeve for a second before the woman answered. "She did say my begonia was certain to beat somebody."

"Why?"

"Why what?"

"Why do you suppose she said that."

"Probably because I wasn't particularly interested in entering my plant. She was trying to convince me."

I wondered if State of the Arts sold crowbars. Trying to pry something out of this woman must have frustrated Helen Luedeke to distraction.

"So what finally convinced you?"

"Well, she said something about the ribbon being a coup for our club. She also said she'd pay the fee and make all the arrangements."

"Did it win?"

"No."

"Too bad."

"Not really. I forgot Helen was coming by for the plant. I came to work, and of course she couldn't get into my house . . ."

"I see."

"Now you said you'd explain."

I was suddenly reluctant to accuse Helen Luedeke of trying to fix the sweeps. If she was guilty, she moved higher on the list of murder suspects and it became police business. If not, the car accident, the bumping of Iffy's niche entry, and the hort competition scheme could easily be characterized as innocent actions. My accusation of conspiracy, no matter how much I believed it to be true, could be construed as libelous.

I patted Gloria gently on the arm and told her, "The police will be in touch."

"So did she try to rig the sweeps?" Mother asked when I picked her up at the consignment shop. I held her car door and settled her inside before I answered through the opened window.

"In my opinion—yes," I said. "Can I prove it? No."

From the driver's seat I completed my observations. "Gloria Miklos seems so self-absorbed she would make a lousy witness even if she watched the murder first-hand, which she didn't."

Mother grunted.

For most of the drive back to Bigelow's she scowled and pursed her lips. After I parked the Nissan in the driveway near the front walk (let the neighbors think what they would), she said, "Are you going to tell George anyway?"

I got Mother's door and offered her an arm. "Yes. I really think Helen tried to ruin Iffy's chances of winning, probably so she could win herself. And I really think George ought to know. What he'll make of that, we'll just have to wait and see."

Mother nodded reluctant approval.

Half an hour later the remaining personal effects of Iffy Bigelow, deceased, were listed, boxed, and loaded into the back of my car. There aren't many drop-off locations for clothing donations, but one happened to be on the way back to Mother's.

While we were still in Ardmore and before I spoke to George Mills, there was a matter I wanted to clarify. Mother agreed to wait in the car while I made a quick visit to Arthur Bigelow's office.

When I got inside, who briskly emerged from Arthur's inner sanctum but my best friend, Didi!

Naturally, my mouth dropped open; but before I could put my foot in it Didi effused, "Oh, you must be here about the job opening, too. Well, break a leg, dear, if I do say so myself." She dangled a hand on my arm, tilted her blonde head away from Arthur and Cloris, winked, and mouthed, "You don't know me." Which, as usual, was true enough.

"Later," she said, much like a Brit aping a Main Liner for a B-movie audition.

From his doorway Arthur smiled thoughtfully. Cloris's face was vacant, as if her mind had already moved on.

What it all meant would have to wait until later—perhaps until after a steadying vodka on the rocks.

Chapter 33 ❈

*A*rthur was busy watching Didi's departure. I used the moment to reassemble my own thoughts, then I said, "May I speak to you a moment?"

"Of course." Arthur gestured me into his office, and we both sat down.

"Everything all right at the house?" he asked.

"Oh yes. All finished. I hope you won't find the emptiness too upsetting ..."

He waved the thought away and put on that expectant/patient face executives use when they want you to get to the point.

I obliged. "May I ask you something about Jo Pescatore?"

Arthur leaned forward, a serious but puzzled expression replacing the former. "Jo? Our old gardener?"

"That's right."

His chin canted left to emphasize his confusion. "But she hasn't been with us for, for about two years. And she wasn't even with us long. Whatever brought her to your attention?"

"She phoned your house last Friday morning, ostensibly to warn your wife that one of the other garden club women was trying to ruin her chance of winning this year's sweeps. That may or may not be true, but Jo wanted to tell Iffy what she overheard and let Iffy decide."

"That strange message on the machine was Jo? How did you find this out?" Little blotches of eagerness had appeared on Arthur's square, gray jaw. An extra sparkle glowed behind his glasses.

"More or less by accident."

"Go on."

"I began to wonder about Iffy firing Jo. Do you remember anything about that?" Lost in thought, Arthur stroked his cheeks between his thumb and forefinger. "Could Jo have harbored thoughts of revenge, something like that?" I asked.

The accountant shrugged and leaned forward. "The answer is I don't know. Iffy, my wife, wasn't an easy woman to work for. She is, was, quite exacting. I personally didn't see anything wrong with the young woman's work, but gardening is hardly my area of expertise."

He spread his hands. "You expected something more dramatic, didn't you? An argument or something."

"Not if it doesn't exist."

"Of course, I see what you mean. Afraid I can't be much help there. The last I remember was mailing the girl's severance pay. But this other woman, the one who wanted Iffy to lose the sweeps. Who was that, may I ask?"

"What? Oh, Helen Luedeke."

"Can't say I. . ."

"Big chest, pointy elbows . . ." My mind wasn't on Helen Luedeke or even Jo Pescatore anymore.

"Oh, her," Arthur mumbled, while my eyes flew open.

Suddenly my mind was computing at the speed of an IBM PC. Adrenaline sharpened my senses to an almost unbearable clarity.

Watch people, see what their behavior says, my grandmother advised me as a child. Pay close enough attention and you'll hear what a person thinks, see what they feel.

In smaller ways I'd been profiting from that advice for years—doping out petty jealousies or hurt feelings, warning Rip about a secretary who yes-bossed his face and backstabbed every chance she got—but this was big time. Common sense had been tugging at my sleeve, but I'd been ignoring it.

Until now.

I focused my mental computer on the widower across the desk, temporarily storing my fears along with my doubts about whether any flower show prize of any sort was worth murdering someone to win. Jealous deceit, I could believe; malicious sabotage, too. But not murder. For a lot of reasons, Didi was right; spouses made the best suspects.

"You were there," I told Arthur Bigelow.

"I was where?" he responded, tilting his chin inquiringly.

"You went to the flower show Friday morning." My guess carried all the conviction of common sense. A precise man, Arthur would have phoned the airport about his flight and learned that it was delayed. With the extra time he easily could have stopped in at the Civic Center—whether to mollify his irate wife or to kill her I could not say.

Arthur Bigelow remained unnaturally silent, eying me askance. The prolonged moment telegraphed the accuracy of my guess more convincingly than words.

"What makes you say that?"

I went coy on him. "Maybe I saw you."

He smiled ironically and abruptly stood. I flinched, and my heart pounded "Get the hell out of here" in Morse code.

Bigelow folded his arms. "No, you didn't. You'd have spoken up right away."

"Maybe not. Or maybe I just realized what I saw. The trouble is, you can't be sure. I was there, and dozens of people knew it. Somebody may even have taken your picture." The professional photographer in the cherrypicker was a long shot, to be sure, but I felt safer for having made the suggestion.

After a while, Bigelow wagged his head and huffed. Then he said, "Oh hell. Maybe you did see me. What's the difference. I didn't kill my wife."

I relaxed enough to breathe. "So why didn't you admit you were there right away?"

"I preferred having an alibi. Innocence is not always the best defense, you know. Sometimes it's no defense at all. If you'd had as much time to think as I did before the police got to you, you'd have kept quiet, too."

"But if you're innocent . . ."

He had been pacing and now whirled to confront me.

"Listen. I found out my plane would be delayed two hours. And yes, I took the opportunity to stop by the Civic Center before checking in at the airport. Iffy had been disappointed that I wouldn't see one of her biggest events. Very disappointed. I wanted her to know I made an effort."

Disappointed? *Furious* was the word Cloris used. I raised an eyebrow, but Bigelow stared it down.

I told him, "The police know about the departure time."

"Who cares? They can't prove I wasn't at the airport."

"And you can't prove you were."

"Innocent until proven guilty. And I'm not guilty."

I thought about the guard at the only open gate, the one who turned up his nose about my muffler, the one who Mother embarrassed with a dollar tip. Perhaps he could testify that Arthur was there. Heaven knows, I couldn't.

"How did you get in?" I asked. "Did you have a pass?"

"No. Iffy needed all the passes, and I'd given my ticket away after I made my reservations for California."

"So what did you do?"

Arthur laughed shortly at the recollection. "I explained my predicament to a lady carrying some plants from her car. She thought it was wonderful that I wanted to see my wife's entry, so she handed me a big bushy plant. She convinced the guard I'd be leaving as soon as I finished helping her."

Two possible witnesses. George and I were going to have a lot to discuss.

"So did you get to see Iffy?" Perhaps her husband had

been the person she spied across the room during the clivia inspection. If so, maybe someone other than Iffy noticed him.

Arthur flopped down into his swivel chair. "No. For some reason she wasn't at her niche when I got there. All I saw was your mother and that Luedeke woman arguing like fishwives. I couldn't even get close enough to see Iffy's entry before I had to leave."

"That's too bad."

"Yes, it was too bad. We might have had a better farewell." Was he alluding to an argument? A post-argument cold shoulder? Or had the Bigelows merely parted as old couples do—the careless good-bye from another room, the "See you tonight," verbal kiss-off?

I nodded as if I understood, but mostly I needed to get away—to think, to breathe.

Arthur Bigelow lunged toward me across the desk, placing his face within fifteen inches of mine. I held tight on the chair arms, and blinked.

"So don't you see?"

I blinked some more.

Arthur hammered home his point. "Sneaking over to the Civic Center without telling anyone I was going, hiding behind a plant to get in, leaving before I spoke to my wife or anybody—how would that look to the police?"

I pressed my lips tight and waited. Arthur drew back, then rubbed under his glasses and across his face with a dry, hard hand. A moment stretched.

Finally, I offered the obvious comment. "You thought the police would harass you."

"You're damn right I did. And I still do." He looked at me with contempt, as if I were a process server who just nailed him at his own front door. "But it's too late now, isn't it."

I reminded myself that he was a murder suspect, that I didn't want him worried about me.

''Maybe I won't tell them.''

Arthur sighed and told me point-blank, ''You're Cynthia Struve's daughter, aren't you?'' Open, If-I-know-it, everybody-knows-it, Cynthia. The first thing you learn about my mother.

His painfully accurate assessment seemed to invite an apology, but I resisted. Recent days had reschooled me on my mother's virtues. Too bad if her, make that *our*, honesty inconvenienced Arthur Bigelow.

When I got back to my car, Mother's head lolled against the seat and her nasal buzz added to the nearby drone of three o'clock traffic.

I let her sleep another five minutes, until I was calm enough to drive.

❋ *Chapter 34* ❋

My interview with Arthur Bigelow, also Didi's appearance in his office, had obscured the effigy scare that started the day. Consequently, a pleasant surprise greeted me when I got home from dropping off Mother.

Five assorted Bryn Derwyn students, supervised by Jacob the maintenance whiz, attacked the leaf mess on our front lawn with dubious enthusiasm. Since spring vacation began after school tomorrow, evidently Bryn Derwyn's weekly detention had been moved back to Thursday.

Jacob sent me a smile as I approached him at the curved brick walk to the front door. At least I know his eyes smiled; the thickness of his black mustache nearly obscured his lips. Around his bald dome a short-clipped equally black fringe added to his always immaculate appearance. A small, muscular man, he could pass himself off as anything from an executive to a fitness coach, or possibly a haberdasher.

Yet through Rip I knew of the flip side to his fussiness—the hell-raising, thoroughly irresponsible side that struck a rapport with the students even as it confined him to the salary ceiling of his Bryn Derwyn job. "Never see a dime of my raises as it is," he once confided. There were two ex-Mrs. Jacob Greens and three little Greens under the age of four.

He held open a huge brown paper leaf bag while a serious girl about Garry's age with thick glasses and lavender bows on her braids deposited a clump of leaves and jammed them down with her foot. The girl wore jeans with plaid cuffs, red buckled shoes, and white socks. I wondered what on earth she had done to earn a detention.

Then I remembered about my own sweet daughter cursing out her science experiment.

Jacob winked. "Anything else you want done while we're here?"

"Barney needs a bath."

Jacob snorted. He tries not to, but he invariably cringes away from Barney's big muddy paws.

"How come I'm so lucky?" I asked, pointing my chin toward the busy kids.

"School's still in good shape from the Open House. Detention squad needed something to do. Rip sent us over here."

"The sheets?" I asked, tactfully trying to find out whether the effigy had been removed before the students saw it.

Jacob stuck his own small foot in the leaf bag to improve on what the thick-lensed girl had begun. She was several feet away scratching at the ground like a chicken with a rake.

"Rip told me about the, uh, sheet. He took care of it before he went in to school."

I breathed with relief. "I'll be out to help in a few minutes," I said. It was already four and twilight would arrive before they finished unless they picked up the pace or borrowed a magic wand.

First I took an aspirin with a glass of cranberry juice, washed my face in the kitchen sink, and dried off with a paper towel. Then I flopped in the corner of the sofa by the phone and dialed Didi's house.

"I can't come to the phone right now," her voice told me, "so wait for the beep . . ."

"Didi, this is Gin. Call me *immediately*," I said. "I need to tell you how crazy you are."

After I hung up, I realized that I wouldn't return a call to anyone who sounded like that, so I punched her number again.

When the time came, without preamble I said, "Honestly, Dee, this is important. Please call me!"

Much better.

Then I left messages for George at both his work number and his home. His wife sounded as solid and distant as the Rock of Gibraltar. Despite the temptation, I refrained from blurting everything I had learned to her. The person with the stressful job can at least act toward solving the problems; but the spouse worries impotently. Rip doesn't tell me half of what happens during his day for exactly that reason.

"Please ask George to call me as soon as possible. It's very important," I said, hoping my message was enough but not too much.

During my travel time I had re-examined the revelation that frightened me so in Arthur Bigelow's office, the suspicion that the flower show was less the cause of Iffy's death than an auspicious opportunity.

Helen Luedeke might have been a vicious competitor, even underhanded, but I no longer believed her demented enough to hire a killer to eliminate her main rival. None of the things I knew she did—the car accident, bumping the wall near Iffy's niche, convincing friends to enter their plants in categories that Iffy might otherwise have won—none of those actions would have been necessary if Helen knew Iffy would soon be dead.

Even Beatrice Crumb slipped down a notch on my suspect list. Didi had asked, "Why now?" and the question remained sound. A few years ago the woman had a huge grievance; but when we talked, she admitted that Iffy saved her from wasting more time on a floundering business. "Next time I made sure I had better sources, deeper pockets," she told me, and I felt she had spoken the painful truth. Unless some other, more recent incident between the two women came to light, I could think of no reason for the nursery owner to exact her revenge at this late date.

Yet Arthur received a delivery from the Tuckahoe Nursery just before Julia's breakdown, so I could not rule out Beatrice Crumb entirely.

Howie Hancock was still a possibility, much as I hated to think so. Iffy's recent, irresponsible remarks had precipitated two serious losses—Tom; and with the loss of Tom, at least some potential business prospects.

"Ginger, haven't you forgotten something?" Howie had sung across the funeral home's parking lot, and obligingly I gave him my home address—too late to throw paint on my car but just in time to place an effigy on our lawn.

In my clarified state of mind, I discounted Alice Gifford entirely, but not her husband, the professor. Losing a child is a tragedy some endure better than others. Grief may have left the poor man so vulnerable that the suspicious injury to his wife may have caused him to snap.

Yet no suspect looked quite so logical as Iffy's husband. Didi was right. Now that I knew he had been on the premises during the murder, he moved to the top of the list. Until I could tell George about Arthur, I wouldn't be able to sit still.

I flipped on the outside telephone bell, pulled on a sweatshirt, and went out to expend my nervous energy on the front yard.

When I joined the detention squad, the tallest boy near the front pines muttered a sly remark that prompted self-conscious giggles, probably at my expense. I quickly glanced at the thick-lensed, lavender-bowed girl to see if she seemed offended. She gave me a neutral stare before bending to scoop an armful of leaves.

Jacob returned from carrying a full bag to the school's pickup. Perish the thought of unsightly trash blighting the

Barnes' yard at party time. The kids, four boys and the girl, stopped snickering as soon as their taskmaster was close enough to hear. Perhaps it was perversity on my part, but I grabbed a new paper bag and went to work near the jokester.

The cool sunshine of the day was fading to gray, and the humidity from last night's rain began to settle to the ground in the cooling air. With just over an hour until dark, I raked vigorously just to get warm.

The jokester wore a gray Penn Crew sweatshirt with cutoff sleeves and perfectly fitting jeans spoiled by a smear of red paint down the right leg. The boy's wavy, dark brown hair belonged parted and tamed for a yearbook portrait but presently hung artfully over his left eye. The eyes were an interesting pale green/hazel combination with dark lashes to contrast his candlewax-clear skin. He was beautiful rather than handsome, and it was easy to imagine him courting detention just to reconfirm his masculinity.

Then I heard his name.

"Miles," Jacob shouted. "Help Dotty with that bag." Miles Pendergrass, the troublesome senior.

When he returned from carrying Dotty's leaf bag to the truck, I struck up a conversation.

"Nice jeans," I said. Exorbitant designer jeans, as a matter of fact, equivalent in value to about five bags of groceries.

"They're old."

"Too bad about the paint, though. How'd it happen?"

Miles Pendergrass, spoiled grandson of some wealthy benefactor, curser of lacrosse coaches, inventor of lewd jokes about headmasters' wives, looked me straight in the eye and said, "Art class," without a flinch.

"Too bad," I lamented. "You like art?"

The youth tamped a clump of leaves into my bag. "Oh yeah," he said. "Art's my favorite subject."

Still joking at my expense. Dumb, dumb, dumb.

You see, when Miles Pendergrass carried the leaf bag to the driveway, I happened to notice that the red paint on his jeans perfectly matched the blotches on my Nissan.

All in all an eventful day. And it wasn't quite over.

❈ *Chapter 35* ❈

Side by side at the plank table, our kids were so engrossed in my dinner revelation that Garry accidentally ate some peas. Rip appeared far less impressed, so I spoke louder.

"Bryn Derwyn students wear *uniforms*," I insisted, punctuating the dinner table with my fist. "Miles Pendergrass couldn't have worn designer jeans to art class, *if he even takes* art."

Knowing full well what his students wore to class, Rip refused to react to my discovery. He flaked off a bit of grilled halibut and speared it with his fork.

"Relaxed dress code?" he suggested, the reward for selling lots of yearbook ads or winning a soccer championship. So sometimes, on rare occasions, the students did wear jeans to class.

"The paint matched," I complained.

"Look," Rip said, waving expansively with his fork. "Even if you're right, we couldn't prosecute the kid for vandalizing your car—assuming that's what you'd want to do—without positive proof that the paints are the same. That means a lab test, and that means convincing the police you have a case." He waved the next thought away. "Forget the break-in at the school—there's no evidence there at all. So it's the car or nothing. And if you push this thing to the legal limit and find out Miles slopped up his jeans in art class, or in his neighbor's garage—anywhere but our driveway—the damage to the school would be incalculable. Face it, Gin, it just isn't worth the risk." He rested his fork and his case.

After I reinflated my lungs, I tried to wheedle a concession. "Come on. Admit you believe he did it as much as I do."

Rip shrugged and resumed eating fish.

"You'll watch him?" I asked.

"I am watching him."

"You'll keep your ear to the ground?"

"I have been all week. Nobody's talking. Miles's father comes home soon, and I'm counting on the old man to keep him in check until graduation."

Despite what he said, Rip didn't look hopeful. Miles's well-off parents were the largest contributors toward the boy's behavior, rarely correcting the impression that he was privileged while starving him for quality attention. Buying him designer jeans and other teenage luxuries, but regularly leaving him to go on extended vacations.

While Chelsea and Garry delivered plates to the kitchen, I scraped and Rip loaded the dishwasher. After our kids disappeared, Rip stretched tall and yawned, giving me a guilty pang. Talking business at the dinner table was usually taboo. I'd just thrown another straw on the camel's back.

"Have time for a glass of wine?" I asked. In the evening Rip habitually read school stuff or wrote letters and memos on a portable computer.

He put his arm across my shoulders. "Sure," he agreed. "If we're not going to get a vacation, the least we can do is have a quiet evening."

While I debated whether to feel more sorry or pleased, the phone rang. I answered it in the kitchen.

My mother, sputtering and sniffing in an effort not to sob. "Mom," I said, "What is it?"

"Oh, Ginger," she said. "Whatever shall I do? I'm sure

Arthur thinks I took Iffy's sable, and I didn't. You know I didn't. It wasn't even there today. Did you see it?''

I realized I hadn't thought about the sable at all because it hadn't been in the upstairs closet. Nor had it been in the downstairs coat closet, because Mother and I removed Iffy's belongings from there, too.

"What did Arthur say?" I asked.

"He said it was all well and good to consign Iffy's every-day clothing, but the sable was much too valuable to sell like that and could I possibly get it back?

"I told him we hadn't done anything with it, but I don't think he believed me. Oh, Gin. What am I going to do?"

"Just relax, Mom. I'll call Arthur and suggest he check with his relatives before calling the police. The house was full of people yesterday, anyone could have walked off with it."

"That's right!" Mother eagerly agreed. "Oh, thank you, Gin. Whatever would I do without you?"

Manage beautifully, I'm sure, by delegating to someone else.

I hung up and looked around for Rip. He was carrying his briefcase toward the cubbyhole we consider his home office.

So much for a quiet evening. I placed my call to Arthur Bigelow.

"Whatever made you think of the sable tonight?" I asked after cooler-than-usual preliminaries.

Rather defensively Arthur said, "My daughter-in-law Carol called to thank me for the things your mother helped her find. She happened to mention it."

"She's happy with everything?"

"Oh yes," he said, too irritable to realize I had helped him bypass Carol's obvious greed.

"So the coat isn't with your son and daughter-in-law. I don't suppose Aunt Lila . . .?

"No," Arthur quickly replied. "I helped her close her suitcase."

"Then I think you better call the police. Julia can't possibly have it either." I didn't need to remind him that his niece left on a gurney.

"If I don't, I'm sure you will," Arthur sniped, referring to my intention to report his presence at the flower show. More than ever I couldn't wait to turn the whole witches' brew over to George Masterson Mills.

When my phone rang right after I finished with Arthur, my pulse did an anticipatory jig.

"I got the job," Didi enthused into my ear.

Since I'd been expecting George's voice, I needed a moment to adjust. "What job?" I asked.

"You are speaking to Arthur Bigelow's new secretary," my friend said with all the pomposity and care of a beer distributor who had been celebrating with one of her products.

My skin felt cold and slick. "Didi, please say you're kidding."

Silence. Then, "I thought you'd be as thrilled as I am. More thrilled, since it's your murder."

Didi has never acknowledged danger. Rock-climbing, para-skiing and white-water rafting all sounded like swell vacations to her. She claimed not to read newspapers because they depress her, but I think the truth is she doesn't believe them. My chances of talking her out of this adventure, as she surely thought of it, were slim to nonexistent. Especially since she had been drinking. However, I had to try.

I spoke slowly, with great emphasis. "Arthur Bigelow may have killed his wife, Didi. He was at the flower show Friday morning at exactly the right time."

"Okay, so good. I'll be able to check him out. No problem."

"Really, Didi. This isn't a good idea."

"Course it is. They do it all the time on TV. And anyhow—what could happen in an office?"

"Please don't—" She spared herself the rest of my argument by hanging up.

My palms were so sweaty I had to wipe them on a dish towel. I needed the calming touch of my husband. Rip had been able to afford the evening off before, he could afford to take off now. I poured a couple glasses of burgundy.

Somebody knocked on the front door. By sheer luck I managed to place the wine on the kitchen counter without splashing anything. Then I flipped on the outdoor light and peeked through the curtain.

George, looking harried. He stepped inside and stood expectantly on the oval rug inside the door. He reminded me of Barney when he'd been waiting a long time to be let out.

"Who is it?" my husband called from his cubicle.

"It's for me," I called back. "As you were."

I handed George Rip's glass of wine, guided him into the privacy of the living room and gestured him onto the sofa facing the fireplace. I pulled my legs under me on the rocking chair and sipped my wine. George hadn't bothered to remove his coat. He set his wine on the coffee table and laced his fingers together between his knees. I noticed his tan raincoat had brown leather buckles on the cuff tabs, a larger one to match on the belt. Dapper.

"My wife said you called. Said it sounded urgent."

"You get dinner?" I asked.

"Yeah, yeah. A sandwich. Now what's this all about?"

I took a deep breath. "Did you know that Arthur Bigelow was at the flower show at the time of his wife's death?"

George's black eyes lit with excitement, but not with surprise. "Yeah, we thought so. But how'd you find out?"

"I sort of guessed, and he sort of admitted I was right."

"What? When was this?"

"This afternoon in his office."

"Shit. Do you realize . . .?" He broke off and stared at something internal. Then he asked, "He give you anything we can verify?"

I told him about the woman who helped Arthur get past the guard and suggested he might find her on the list of people who brought new horticulture entries in Friday morning.

George glared and grumbled, "Mm-hm," through his teeth.

Before he could test his four-letter vocabulary, I told him about the photographer in the cherrypicker. George nodded and clenched his hands in and out, in and out, while his eyes narrowed at me.

"I know it's a long shot, but . . ."

"What else?" he said when I paused to sip my wine.

I pretended to think. "Well, I happened to meet a former employee of Iffy Bigelow who phoned her the morning of her death . . ."

"Oh?"

"Yes. She wanted to warn Iffy that Helen Luedeke was possibly—probably—sort of arranging for Iffy to lose the sweepstakes. It was beginning to work, too. But I don't think that has anything to do with Iffy's death, do you? I mean Helen still has that alibi, that argument with my mother, and you already said you didn't think it was very likely that she hired a killer . . ."

George glared.

"So I finally agree with you, but I thought you ought to know about the sweeps thing. I mean, you're the professional."

"Thank you. Anything else?" he hissed through his teeth. His mustache scarcely moved.

"Well, Iffy's sable coat is missing."

"What has that . . .?"

"I just wanted you to know. Arthur's going to call. At

least I think he is. The coat was probably stolen the day of the funeral.''

It took so much restraint for George to say, ''Is that it?'' without imploding that I decided not to mention Didi.

''Yes,'' I lied. ''That's about it.''

❈ *Chapter 36* ❈

Caulking the bathtub would have to wait, but it had waited several months already. Tonight was the party for the fundraising committee, and it would be all I could handle to pick up the house, move furniture, get out dishes, buy mixers, disposable cups, lemons, limes, soda, napkins and ice cubes, set up the bar, find something to wear . . . and so on.

Patrice, the sturdy young woman who cleaned at Bryn Derwyn, loved us to entertain for the school. Not because it was any sort of break to whisk the Barnes residence into presentable shape in four hours or less, but because I was available for conversation while she did it. Cleaning empty classrooms is lonely work.

"Sarah's goin' in for a gall bladder operation," she offered suggestively as she lifted the vacuum cleaner out of the hall closet. I took it to be a quiz, so I scanned my mental catalog of Patrice's relatives to come up with the proper response. Was Sarah the sister with four children and nary a husband or the aunt with arthritis who gambled for a living?

"Who will take care of her children?" I asked.

Patrice threw me a hard stare.

Baby-sitter. Sarah was Patrice's baby-sitter. "I mean who will take care of *your* children?"

Big difference. This was a problem she should have discussed with Jacob, her immediate supervisor, but he always became impatient with her verbal wanderings.

Patrice is afraid of Rip, for no reason in particular, so she always told me what she wanted him to know. The tactic has become transparent to me mainly because so many people use it. Must be a lot of shyness going around.

"Don't know." Patrice wagged her head and plugged in the vacuum. "Mavis ain't good for much of nothin' since her last man left, and Auntie Pam needs all her time to study those racing forms of hers. Anyhow she says she can't do with Chantal and Buddy, what with her arthritis and all."

"Would you like me to find out if you can put Chantal and Buddy in Bryn Derwyn's day care until Sarah's better?"

"Well, I don't know. Let me think on that." Meaning she needed to know what it would cost. So I would ask Rip; Rip would ask Jacob, the day care people, and the accountant; Rip would summarize to Jacob and Jacob would summarize to Patrice. I was confident they would find some way to help her.

In the interest of efficiency, both hers and mine, I decided to run errands. Among other things I had Rip's early paycheck to deposit, thanks to spring vacation, which unfortunately meant very little to the Barnes family just now.

As usual, Rip had forgotten to endorse his check, so I added a stop at the school to my itinerary.

Someone had eschewed the visitors' slots and parked smack in front of the school's entrance. I clucked my irritation as I walked around the sleek black car to get to the door.

The dent in the right rear fender brought me up short. It looked very much like the dark car that had slowed in front of the school the night of the break-in.

A step inside the lobby answered several questions and raised a few fresh ones.

Sitting like a bundle of cashmere beached on the lobby

sofa was Iffy Bigelow's nemesis, Helen Luedeke. Today the Grande Dame of Niches wore a twilight blue wool dress and jacket. Her elbows were clasped to her side the way I prepare my Thanksgiving turkey for its stint in the microwave. Behind glasses her hard raisin eyes stared blankly into the middle distance.

Helen Luedeke. Sitting in the Bryn Derwyn lobby looking miffed that nobody had come to kiss her shoes. Why?

Just then Candace McQuinn, Bryn Derwyn's Director of Development, stepped out of the main office, caught me eying Helen and rushed to make introductions. Forced to notice and, therefore, recognize me, Helen suffered Candace's amenities with slightly less patience than she had possessed a moment before.

In response, the bridge of Candace's attractively straight, patrician nose creased, and the center portion of her light brown eyebrows dented. The resulting expression wasn't quite patronizing—Candace was far too experienced for that—but the professional kid gloves were quite obviously in place.

"Mrs. Luedeke will be touring Bryn Derwyn along with the head of her foundation. She especially wanted to see us for herself because she has a grandson here." Her voice had a smile in it that begged me to be nice.

I extended my hand to squeeze Helen's jeweled digits; I can switch into Gracious Hostess Mode in the blink of an eye.

"Oh yes. That must be Miles Pendergrass," I said. I remembered that when Rip originally listed all the possible student vandals, he mentioned that the school had applied for a grant from Miles's grandmother's foundation.

The small surprise was that the grandmother happened to be Helen Luedeke. Small surprise because, despite Philadelphia's size, there just aren't that many wealthy families who are interested in being socially prominent, at least not in the style of the old, old money. And of those who espouse that particular upper-class lifestyle, most manage to remain down-to-earth, genuinely nice people. Only a few choose to affect Helen Luedeke's pain-in-the-ass snobbery. Modern consciousness and economics have made such an attitude increasingly difficult to sustain.

But knowing the way Fate loves its little jokes, I should have guessed that Rip's foundation's founder would be someone like Helen Luedeke.

Aware that he would be dealing with the cowcatcher in person today, my accusations against Helen Luedeke's grandson at dinner last night must really have made Rip squirm.

"Rip available?" I asked Candace, waving the gray pay envelope to show that I'd only need him for a second.

"On his way," she assured both me and the cowcatcher.

Of course, last night Helen Luedeke was no more the cowcatcher to Rip than she was Miles's grandmother to me. Neither of us had expected her name to mean anything to the other, so neither of us had mentioned it. At least now I understood his impatience with my paint discovery.

Plus, he was also right. The school's insurance company and ours would have to swallow the damages, all in the interest of the greater goal.

Yet I was certain Helen Luedeke's dented car had cruised the school just before the break-in last Saturday night. Unless it was Miles himself, it had to have been his grandmother looking for him. The young man's anger about being thrown off the lacrosse team was public knowledge; and if Helen knew her grandson at all, she probably suspected he would attempt some sort of revenge.

I'm not an educator. An educator might say that you can't avoid a few sour apples when you're making cider. Me, I'd say that if Miles Pendergrass were ever to become a responsible adult, he needed to take responsibility for his behavior—real soon.

The question was—who would make him? The way things

stood, Miles and his arrogant, underhanded grandmother were both going to get away with their dirty tricks—on Miles's part the smashed hall lights, the broken classroom window, and the paint on my car; his aunt's deliberate attempt to damage Iffy's niche arrangement, her efforts to rig the sweeps, and the questionable car accident that injured Alice Gifford. I'm sorry to admit the prospect of their impunity ignited something nasty in me.

Candace prompted, "Miles's parents are in Africa for a few weeks, so he's been living with his grandmother."

I oozed sympathy. "I bet it's been difficult keeping up with a teenager, especially considering your involvement with the flower show." The raisin eyes regarded me with slightly more interest, and Candace beamed with satisfaction.

"Yes," Helen agreed cautiously.

"Mrs. Luedeke is quite well known for her niche arrangements," I told Candace. "Actually she's quite skillful in all areas of flower show competition. She almost won the overall sweepstakes."

Candace emitted an eager, "Oh?"

"Yes, I was speaking with Alice Gifford just the other day, and she mentioned what a fierce competitor Mrs. Luedeke is. Quite formidable, I understand."

"Really?" Candace asked, warming to her part in the discussion even if Helen was not.

I turned toward the woman. "Of course, between you and me, I doubt if Alice posed much of a threat, her first year back and all."

Helen compressed her lips. The raisins eyed me steadily.

Candace clutched one hand with the other, puzzled that my cordial remarks seemed to be creating tension in her guest. Could a rescue possibly be in order? From her boss's wife?

"Too bad about the dent in your car, though," I pressed

on. "Don't those things always happen at the worst times? You must really have been rattled."

"Yes," Helen responded weakly. Reading her mind was impossible. And unnecessary. If the car accident had been unintentional, nothing I said constituted an accusation. If not, her guilt would certainly hear me loud and clear.

"I believe I ran into a garden club friend of yours this week, too. Gloria Miklos? You know, State of the Arts. Interesting gift ideas. She was sorry she wasn't home when you went to pick up that plant, but we agreed it was awfully nice of you to offer to enter it . . ."

Helen Luedeke stood up and shifted the shoulder strap of her purse. We had all glimpsed a man bustling toward us from the Admissions Office where I'd noticed him using the phone. The foundation head, if I'm any judge of dark suits and conservative neckwear.

"Ready for the tour?" Candace said brightly, stepping back from me on Helen's cue.

Rip emerged from the main office.

I smiled and moved to intercept him while addressing Candace over my shoulder.

"Don't forget to show Mrs. Luedeke where the new art room will be," I suggested cheerfully, contemplating whether or not to mention that it was her grandson's favorite class.

A glance at Rip abruptly brought me to my senses. He added a we'll-talk-later glare and hastily signed his check on a handy display case.

Helen blinked toward me with either disbelief or confusion, then in response to Rip's shepherding arm turned to follow Candace and the stuffed suit.

I watched them go, the Needing and the Needed.

For someone who had just scored about four bull's-eyes in a row, I didn't feel very pleased.

Actually, I felt ready for a bath.

❀ *Chapter 37* ❀

When I returned home from my party errands, the house was immaculate. Patrice had set a large, white paper package in the middle of the entrance floor. Howie's flower arrangement. Maybe this party would come together after all.

Twenty-six guests were expected, and with Candace, Rip, and me that made twenty-nine—few enough that we wouldn't have to eat in shifts like when the faculty comes. Move the sofa against the wall, add a few folding chairs and tray tables, use the plank table as a buffet. The usual. I threw an off-white tablecloth in the dryer a few minutes and put it in place to finish unwrinkling. Then I unveiled Howie's creation.

Birds-of-paradise and poppies formed a dramatic wedge filled in with something navy blue clustered on a delicate stem. The whole arrangement was framed by huge, shiny leaves. All by itself, Howie's thank-you gift elevated the ambience of our country/casual room into the range of cocktails with the necktie and earring bunch. He must have been very pleased with Iffy's plants.

Then I noticed the little bunch of business cards among the wrappings, the one with the mauve rose that I promised to display. No fool, Howie wasn't putting forth his best foot just to show his gratitude.

When fundraising is involved, it doesn't do to appear either too cheap or too extravagant. Rip and I had erred on the cheap side a few times too many, so for tonight Rip commissioned Candace to find us a new caterer. Buffets by Betty got the call.

Betty arrived at four, gasped with dismay at my narrow kitchen, giggled, touched my arm and said, "A bit like the aisle of a railway train, i'n it?"

She looked like a Betty, too, one who liked to cook—round face, dimples, brown curls, apron. Her daughter was a younger version, and her job seemed to be carrying things. But by the time I was dressed in my peach dress with the silver belt, the daughter was gone. Guess who would be carrying things now? I went back and changed shoes, making a mental note to find out why Candace hadn't hired a server.

Rip rushed in at quarter after six, checked the bar (the corner of the kitchen counter nearest the living room), put on a fresh shirt and was ready to greet guests at six-thirty.

I delivered sandwiches to the kids in the TV room, then hovered by the front door doing my best to prevent Barney from poking people's backsides with his nose as they came in. Candace doled out the name tags she had prepared, and Rip fixed everybody's first drinks. By ten of seven we had a party going on.

When I stuck my nose in the kitchen, Betty handed me a silver platter covered with parsley and tiny pie shells. Voila, her hands seemed to say just before they smoothed down her apron.

I sampled one of her creations when I got to the hallway. The pastry exploded when I bit it and rained shredded stuff down the front of my dress. I dusted off, a bonus for Barney, then grabbed a pile of paper napkins before heading into the lurch.

A very tall man with a patterned red bow tie intercepted

my first foray with long, dainty fingers. The little doll of a woman earnestly listening to him waved me away with a no-thanks head shake that made her dangling earrings gleam. "Nuff du bidden bray," said the man, his mouth full of food. The woman tilted her head and blinked.

My next group consisted of three ladies, the first one saying, ". . . social services, you know, and I had a woman come in today about child support." Her listeners mumbled supportive mm-hmms. "Except she'd been artificially inseminated."

The woman on my left choked trying to laugh, and the remains of her hors d'oeuvre disintegrated between her fingers and rained on the rug. We both bent to clean up and bumped heads on the way down. Returning her self-conscious smile, I moved along.

The next cluster was comprised of four men, and I watched enviously as one by one they tilted back and popped the messy little foodstuffs in their mouths whole. As I departed, I heard the word "handicap" and took a wild guess that they weren't talking about wheelchair access.

Over by the bar Rip answered a man in charcoal pinstripes, who obviously hadn't stopped home after tying up the week at his brokerage firm. I recognized him as Rip's chosen chairman for the fundraising committee gathered here tonight.

"I think we have a reasonable chance of getting something from the Luedeke Foundation," Rip said as he snagged one of the pastries off the tray. "Probably not their max of a hundred thousand dollars, but we might realistically expect fifty." I gulped.

Rip continued. "They usually like to see what recipients do with the first grant before they offer more."

Pinstripes ignored my platter but Rip slipped two more hors d'oeuvres onto a napkin and winked at me. I moved on before he noticed my discomfort, secretly praying that my remarks to Helen Luedeke hadn't already rendered him a liar.

Fifty thou! What had I done? In the future I vowed to be nothing but sweetness and light, the very clone of Candace. Smile, smile, smile.

The next tidbit by Betty was a tray of toast triangles adorned with endive and a cluster of radish roses. Upon the toast were thin strips of filet mignon with a dollop of sauce topped by a teeny sprig of dill. Betty handed me the tray with a sigh and crumbled her apron in her fists.

After the last experience, I thought it best to try one alone in the hallway again. The toast was very crisp. When it broke in half, it plastered me in the nose with sauce. Half the wedge bounced off my chest while the other nestled in the palm of my hand. The strip of beef dangled from my lips.

Was it just me, or did Betty specialize in booby traps? I decided to conduct an informal survey, sort of a personal self-help seminar on how to eat exploding hors d'oeuvres.

Naturally, the doll-woman was a nibbler. She would still be approaching the dill sprig when my tray was empty.

Another woman with a heart-shaped face, a chin-length blonde bob with bangs, and chocolate brown eyes gestured with her toast. "You know you could take that wallpaper to my man in New York and his people could weave you a carpet to match . . ."

I moved on. "Isn't it depressing listening to all those couples complain about each other all day?" a nebbish in a flowered sweater asked a woman in a pink suit. The marriage counselor stared at her questioner with disbelief and lingered only a moment longer, long enough to watch the other woman eat Betty's booby-trapped roast beef first, as if it were the icing from an Oreo. I do-si-doed with her as she headed for the bar.

The tall man with the red bow tie dispatched his toast wedge with a double chomp, chomp. Dusting off his long fingers, he told his new companion, a skeptical woman with green eyes, he thought sterilization was the answer to the deer overpopulation in Lower Merion. "What do you think?" he prompted.

His companion said she thought it would be tricky getting the deer to authorize the operation.

Sitting along the wall where I'd pushed the sofa and coffee table, three women huddled close, the better to hear each other over the noise. I thought one of them said, "Bigelow," so I eased over.

It was a gossipfest all right, and they weren't too concerned about eavesdroppers because I stood in front of the coffee table and they didn't give me a glance.

"He's Stanley's accountant, and Stanley says the company's solid as a rock. They've been in business for years, and you know how competitive things are around here. He's got to be doing well."

"I don't know," a prematurely gray woman in white cashmere disagreed. "My husband used to sell him a new Cadillac every year, and he hasn't bought one in three years now."

"Maybe he's tired of Cadillacs."

"Uh-uh. My bet is he's broke."

"Excuse me," I said, insinuating myself into their circle. "Are you by any chance talking about Arthur Bigelow?"

The thin, dark-haired one in a severe sleeveless shift blinked up at me. "Of course," she slapped her knee. "If anyone would know, you would. You knew his wife."

"Well, I . . ."

"Tragic. Tragic, circumstances. Must have been awful," said Cashmere with enthusiasm.

I set the tray on the coffee table and slid a chair over.

Cashmere's cheeks were pink, and the other two had leaned closer. By my perception these were the spouses of Rip's fundraisers, rather than the big guns themselves. "We were just wondering whether Arthur Bigelow was someone the committee should approach about the new gym. Later, of course." After a decent interval, say when Iffy's estate was settled; Bryn Derwyn's present campaign would continue for two years.

"I thought it might give him an interest now that . . . you know."

"She certainly does know. She was there." Unfortunately, they'd spelled my name right in the newspaper.

"But, you see, we couldn't decide whether he could, whether he would . . ."

Sleeveless interrupted. "Whether he would be in a financial position to help." She'd been through this before; she knew the euphemisms.

I had begun to squirm, whether it was from my own effrontery or their conversation I couldn't tell. But I wanted no more. I stood. Shaking my head with regret, I told them I doubted that Arthur Bigelow would be interested in contributing to our capital campaign, adding to myself, "Especially if he goes to jail for murdering his wife."

Leaving them to nosh on the destructibles, I excused myself and wended my way to the bar. Supplied with a plastic cup of my favorite cheap wine, I leaned against the kitchen wall out of Betty's way and considered what bothered me about my last encounter.

Gossipy and inappropriate as it was, the women's conversation had been an attempt to contribute toward the stated purpose of the evening. All things considered, their hearts really had been in the right place. So why was I feeling so . . . so uncomfortable?

In a minute I had it. Since my meeting with Arthur Bigelow, I had been concentrating on "opportunity," Arthur's access to his wife the morning of her death. Just as he feared, his incriminating, defensive behavior had convinced me he was guilty.

It was time to confront the critical problem of motive,

something I had not yet addressed. The debate over whether Arthur Bigelow had money or not related to that question.

Okay. What reason did Arthur have for killing Iffy? What would it take to provoke an upstanding, dignified man to extreme violence?

A financial reversal such as Cashmere suggested might have done it. Iffy may have made impossible financial demands, or she may somehow have precipitated the reversal herself.

Speculation was pointless. I needed to know what the gossips wanted to know—was Arthur Bigelow solvent or not?

Much as I hated to admit it, Didi probably knew the answer. She had just spent the day learning Cloris's job and certainly gained some sense of Arthur's financial condition. I would have to swallow my pride and call her.

Betty bustled by me, grasping the edges of a huge, laden platter as if it were a life preserver. Her round cheeks puffed and a sheen of perspiration coated her forehead and dampened her curls. Steaming rice in a gargantuan bowl also waited to be delivered to the plank table. I sunk in a serving spoon and followed in Betty's footsteps. Dinner was served. Didi would have to wait.

The stir-fried chicken and vegetables were tasty, the rice not bad, the salad an interesting assortment of greens, apples, and raisins with a poppy-seed dressing; plus the rolls were soft and warm. Chairman Pinstripes folded himself onto the floor and ate with his plate held in the air. Simultaneously, he conducted a conversation with Bow Tie, who perched above him on the sofa arm. Everybody else followed suit like a flock of roosting chickens.

Taking my empty plate into the kitchen, I found Betty up to her elbows in suds washing her equipment. She looked around at the clutter and told me, "Put 'em anywhere, luv." Clearly, Betty had no time to relieve the guests of their used plates, even if she had the intention, which appeared unlikely.

I found Candace and tugged her sleeve. She broke off flirting with a wavy-haired father of six.

"We could use a little help here," I suggested tactfully.

"Help?" Bryn Derwyn's young Director of Development swiveled her patrician nose the rest of the way toward me and widened her hazel eyes with genuine surprise.

"Yes, Candace. Rip will want to speak before these people have to go home, and he can't do that until the dinner plates are picked up."

She glanced around the room with alarm. "Won't the caterer take care of that?"

"That depends. Did you hire a server and a cook, or just a cook?" Never mind a bartender.

"But it's a buffet. People serve themselves from a buffet." So there was the hole in her thinking.

She looked around again. "I'm sorry," she said. "You always . . . I guess I never realized . . ."

Bryn Derwyn doesn't pay well enough to entice anybody with credentials that are exactly right. Candace's last job had been campaigning for a politician who lost the election. I probably shouldn't have turned over the catering choice without a little preliminary discussion, but I guess I figured she couldn't do worse than my own previous selection—a company that showed up three hours after the party started. Rip and I had our heads together calculating how many pizzas to order for sixty guests when the tardy caterers finally knocked on the door.

"Never mind," I said. "Just help me clean up so Rip can catch these people before they start to yawn."

So it was another half hour, nine p.m., before I could slip away to the study to phone Didi. The coffee urn and dessert (tiny cakes and tarts from a bakery) were in place next to Howie's bouquet. Most everybody who wanted them had helped themselves and returned to their roost, and now Rip stood in the doorway to the hall asking for their attention.

"I know some of you delayed going on vacation to come

here tonight, and I want you to know how grateful we at Bryn Derwyn are that your commitment to our capital campaign is so great. It wasn't a piña colada on the beach, but we did our best . . ."

I slipped past Betty, who looked as wilted as a grandmother who just did Thanksgiving for the whole clan by herself. She wiped her brow with a dishwater wrist then resumed scraping a pot in slow motion.

Even with Rip's study door closed, I could hear his classroom-volume voice.

"As you know, due to unusual circumstances, very unusual circumstances, we had to stop construction on our new gym . . ."

"Didi," I said softly when she answered. "Do you have a minute?"

"Just a minute, chum."

"You have company?"

"Sure do. Just let me go to another phone."

Good grief. At nine p.m. on a Friday night. I vaguely remembered having a whimsical sex life like that—before our kids could walk.

"There. Now I can talk. He's half asleep anyway."

Asleep? I didn't want to ask. "Listen. I was wondering how it went at the office."

"Knew you'd come around." She deserved to gloat, so I let her.

"So how'd it go?" I asked humbly.

"Fine. No big deal. Arthur's happy as hell to have me. He should be, too, since Cloris goes back to Cincinnati tomorrow."

"What we're trying to accomplish for the school is two-fold—finishing the new gym will open up many athletic opportunities . . ."

"Tomorrow?"

"Yeah, we had a lot to go over in a hurry, but I think I

can do it. Arthur says he'll help me learn . . . but you didn't call to ask about that.''

''No, I didn't. What I was wondering, that is, the question came up . . . Did you get a feeling for whether the company is in financial trouble?''

''Back in a jiff, Norm. Just hold that thought,'' she shouted. ''What do you mean, like is Arthur broke?''

''Exactly.''

''. . . *turn the old auditorium/gymnasium into a much-needed drama center . . .*'' I listened to Rip while Didi considered her answer.

''Well, he's paying me generously—I may be able to afford that roof in this lifetime. And the company checkbook has a decent balance. There weren't any huge bills sitting around; Cloris showed me the accounts payable. It looked as if lots of people owe him money, but they were paying him regularly, too. I don't know what to say. The place seems a lot better off than the Beverage Barn.''

I felt guilty about scolding her for taking the job, but even guiltier about pumping her for information the first day she'd worked there. What if Arthur smelled a rat?

''Did he have any idea we were friends? Any suspicions about you at all?''

''Nah.'' It was pointless to press the issue. Didi was intrepid, trusting, impulsive, stubborn . . .

''So how long do you plan to stay?''

''Jeez, I don't know. The pension wasn't so good . . .''

End of conversation. Didi wanted to get back to Norm and whatever he had on his mind.

'' 'Night, Didi. Sorry to bother you.''

''No problem.''

I fervently hoped not.

❈ *Chapter 38* ❈

Rip and I tumbled into bed about eleven-thirty.

Earlier, Chelsea and Garry fell asleep watching TV, and I had guided them to their rooms for the duration.

Betty stayed mopping and wiping until about eleven, when Rip assured her we could deal with the rest in the morning. Then he tipped her generously and helped her carry her equipment to her car.

We fiddled around replacing furniture and finishing nightcaps until the buzz of being on duty fizzled and we couldn't keep our eyes open.

After tonight, committee members would pair up with Rip to solicit the potential donors who were in any way connected to the school—parents, alumni (a limited number of these because the school was so young), grandparents, step-parents, foundations related to any of the above. Each other and whoever else they could think of, to be exact.

"So what did you think?" I finally asked when we were settled in bed.

"Good. Good start. Thanks for your help." And he was out.

I shut my eyes to a vision of Iffy Bigelow's broken body lying on the cement floor of the Tastee Freeze storage area. It was the most vivid and horrible the memory had been all week, and I resented it haunting me when I was so exhausted. But that's the way it is with apparitions. I tossed a full fifteen minutes before succumbing to a not particularly restful sleep.

The morning alarm might as well have been an ax murderer with his arm raised over my head. Seven a.m. Chelsea had been invited canoeing for the day and needed a ride to her ride. I intended to do the heroic thing and let Rip sleep, so I swatted the clock and sat clasping my knees until my heart settled down.

While scrambling eggs for Chelsea and me, fragments of my nightmares began to emerge from my subconscious. At first they were vague and unformed disturbances, like glimpses through a dark veil. Then the shapes began to take form, widening my eyes suddenly as I spooned eggs onto Chelsea's plate. Her head swung to look, and her hand tucked her hair behind her ear. Her favorite swan earrings swung to and fro as if trying to break free, and all at once I had it.

I set the hot frying pan right on the table. "Excuse me," I told my open-mouthed daughter. "I've got to make a phone call."

"Mom, it's only seven-thirty!"

I knew that, but I didn't care.

The phone in Rip's study offered the warm, masculine closeness I associated with him, plus some privacy.

My mother answered on the third ring. In a minute she was alert enough to give me the exclusive attention she always reserved for me. I never appreciated it more. My questions would most likely distress her, and I needed three thoughtful answers before her emotions interfered.

She gave them to me, then I asked another.

"Could that have been what Iffy needed to talk to you about? A decision she could only discuss with you?"

"I suppose that's possible. It would make sense, wouldn't it? Oh dear," and she was crying.

I told her it would be all right, that she shouldn't worry; but I could have saved my breath. Worrying is what mothers do best.

Next I phoned Didi. "Umph," she said into the phone. From somewhere beside her I heard a growl.

"Didi, it's me. Wake up. I've got an important question. A critical question."

"What?" She was one hundred percent awake, as awake as anyone ever gets. Thank heavens.

"When is Cloris Huber leaving for Cincinnati?"

"Today."

"No. I mean exactly when. Do you know?"

"Sure. I saw her plane ticket. Let me think."

I strangled the phone cord with my left hand, and finally she answered. "Eight-forty a.m., U.S. Air. Why?"

"A. M.?"

"Yeah, why?"

"Thanks, Didi."

I hung up and punched George Masterson Mills's home number from memory. The phone rang four times before he picked up.

"You awake?" I asked.

"Who is this?"

"It's Gin. Gin Struve." In my agitation I had reverted to my elementary school name, my name when I'd helped George out of a jam.

"Yes. I'm listening. No, wait a minute." He went to pick up another phone and I heard his wife hang up in the bedroom.

"Okay. Shoot."

"Cloris Huber killed Iffy Bigelow," I said. My heart was hammering to get out of my chest.

"You're sure?"

"You're damn right I'm sure. We've got to hurry. She's leaving this morning—eight-forty on U.S. Air."

"Okay, okay. Slow down. Give me a minute on this. You have evidence?"

Evidence. Proof. "Not exactly. But she did it, George. You've got to believe me." Then I told him the bare bones of it. When I finished I could hear him thinking.

"Not enough there, girl. Give us a little time, we can get some proof together now that we know what to look for, but we can't bring her in on just that."

"No. No, you can't wait. What if she doesn't stay in Cincinnati? What if she never goes to Cincinnati at all? She could disappear, George. She could get away."

"I don't like it either, but sometimes that's the chance we have to take. We can't arrest people we'll only have to let go. The case has to be airtight before we can move."

"She's guilty."

"I'm convinced, Gin. I really am. But there's nothing I can do. Even if I had proof, shit, it's ten to eight. There's no time, and no way to hold her."

Wild-eyed, my mind bucked and kicked like a stallion aiming to break down its stall.

"The sable," I shouted at him. "She's got Iffy's sable with her, George. A thousand dollars says it's in her suitcase."

"How do you know this?" His deep voice snapped with urgency. I almost had him.

But not quite. So I said, "I saw her take it, George." It was inside a trash bag at the time, but I could admit that later. After Cloris Huber was in custody.

"Gospel?" George asked.

"Absolutely. It just didn't click until now."

George groaned, a pitiful sound coming from a full-grown cop.

"Okay," he caved in. "Meet me at the curb check-in for U.S. Air."

"Me?"

"Yeah, you, Watson. And step on it."

"But why . . .? Oh." During Iffy's funeral Cloris remained at the Bigelow house, and George had been excluded from the reception. Of the two of us, I was the only one who knew what Cloris Huber looked like.

❈ *Chapter 39* ❈

"Wake up your father," I told Chelsea. Then I said I was going to the airport to point someone out to the police.

Chelsea exclaimed one of those teenage things like, "Awesome," or "Radical." I didn't listen carefully, I was too busy getting myself out the door.

Just as I put the Nissan in reverse, the passenger door opened and Barney jumped in. His leash was attached, and Chelsea was on the other end.

"Protection," she said. Luckily I noticed her eagerness in time to thank her—before I blurted the "Get him out of here" that automatically came to mind. She tossed in the end of the leash and shut the door. At my last glimpse before turning onto the street, she was shivering in her bathrobe and waving good-bye.

"Protection," I snorted as I negotiated the circuitous route out of our neighborhood toward an eastbound expressway entrance. "From an Irish setter."

Still, I was touched by Chelsea's gesture—more than I cared to admit. I was jittery as hell, my mind scattering in panic, so what did my daughter do but send me off with eagerness and a useless dog? If I'd had the time, I'd have cried.

To my surprise, Barney served a purpose, more or less. Another living being hopping around the car reminded me to pay attention to the road.

Traffic was light until about Belmont, when some Saturday workers or early risers caught up with each other on their way into the city.

Still, the way was pretty clear. The whole trip from the suburbs through the city down to the airport departure area took an amazing thirty-five minutes. My hands were stiff on the wheel and my armpits clammy, but I was there, intact. Scared, but functioning.

No short-term parking happened to be opposite the U.S. Air check-in area, so I stopped between a cab and a tall blue van both unloading some paying customers. George yanked my car door open before I even realized he was there.

"Let's go," he ordered.

"But . . ." I cast a concerned glance toward Barney, who paced the back seat with agitation borrowed from me.

George followed my eyes and shouted, "Why on earth . . .?"

I opened my mouth, but nothing came out.

"Oh hell, let's go." He flexed his shoulders inside what was for him casual attire, a buttoned-down yellow oxford topped with a red Shetland wool crew neck. His pants were black, his running shoes red, black, and gray. Somewhere he probably had a tie that matched everything perfectly.

"At least they won't tow you," he said as we trotted up to the automatic doors. A small sign read NO PETS ALLOWED.

Here at ground level was a long wall of check-in locations all for U.S. Air, according to the banner and the raised letters mounted on the wall. Waiting their turn at the desks, a hundred adults and children threaded through a maze of chrome poles and black tape like a crowded day at Disney World. Luggage lay in heaps along the innermost tape. A woman with a clipboard wearing a casual uniform shouted, "Anyone here going to Bermuda?" A few people tried to pick up luggage and raise their hands at the same time. Cloris Huber was nowhere to be seen.

"She's on the eight-forty flight to Cincinnati," I reminded George. He was already skirting the crowd to the left, aiming for the escalator and stairs up to the boarding piers. A glance at the row of overhead monitors beside the escalator confirmed that Flight 121 for Cincinnati was on time and leaving from Gate B8.

"Ten minutes," George told me, taking the moving escalator steps two at a time. I put my shoulder bag strap over my head, the better to grab railings and murderers, and hurried after him.

"Can you delay the plane?" I asked as we trotted across twenty paces of carpet before angling off onto Pier B.

"Maybe, if there's time."

On the left at the beginning of the pier an empty booth was labeled CITY OF PHILADELPHIA INFORMATION. Manned entirely by a yellow telephone, there was no one to ask about a plump, frizzy-haired woman with glasses. A penny saved and another earned. Perhaps the security guards would be more useful.

As he jogged, George reached into his pocket for identification. At the nearest of the two security checkpoints twenty yards along Pier B he flashed his badge and kept going.

I considered running along behind him, but since nobody was in line for either metal detector I threw my shoulder bag onto the first x-ray conveyor, slipped though the archway without setting anything off, then broke into a sprint yelling, "I'm with him," back over my shoulder. One of the guards called out, "Hey, your purse!" and tried to catch up to me for a short distance. I ignored her, and she dropped back.

Philadelphia International Airport is laid out like a scrabble game of lengthy rectangles growing from the center starting point. The boarding piers have glass exterior walls, waiting rooms left and right, and miles of noise-muffling charcoal gray carpet. Gate B8 was to the right a hundred yards down the way.

When I got there I saw George's red sweater in the middle of a crowd of people all trying to speak to the flight attendant at the desk. Boarding had already begun.

I scanned the group for Cloris. No luck.

Catching my breath, I eased along the railing that kept people from tumbling into the sloped, L-shaped boarding ramp. When I reached the end of the rail, I could see what had been obscured by the angle and a wall of telephones—the final passenger check before the cloistered jetway onto the plane. Cloris was just around the turn of the ramp, third in line for showing her ticket.

"George!" I shouted, and Arthur Bigelow's former secretary wheeled to look at me. "George, she's here."

Cloris's face went red and her mouth dropped open. I thought for a second she didn't plan to move, that George need only leap over the nearest rail then grab her arm to detain her. Stupid, wishful thinking.

Cloris Huber flung her gray overcoat on the floor, pushed two children and their mother aside, and barreled up the ramp. We reached the end of the rail together. I grabbed for anything my hands would hold, but she straight-armed me across the collarbone. I lost my balance, landed on my hip. Before George could extricate himself from the crowd and their belongings, he caught his foot in a luggage strap and stumbled. I could hear him curse as I began to run.

For her flight home Cloris wore a festive dress in red, green, and yellow paisley with a lace collar. Her hair was fluffy enough to stuff a pillow. She was going to be ever so easy to spot making her getaway.

Also she had to be out of shape from that desk job. Or so I hoped. Hundred yard dashes were not normal fare for me either.

But her motivation was great. She ran fast and furious,

arms pumping, hair flouncing, feet kicking along at an astonishingly efficient speed.

George passed me just as we came abreast of the security stations, where a female guard stepped in front of me and snarled, "Here's your purse, lady. You shouldn't ought to have left it. We ain't allowed . . ."

"Thanks," I said, grabbing the shoulder strap in my fist and pressing on by.

At the right turn into the main corridor just past the City of Philadelphia information telephone was a snack bar dotted with elbow-high tables for eating standing up. Cloris cut the corner through the handful of patrons, putting her a couple more seconds ahead of George, whose size prevented him from running that particular gauntlet.

When I turned the corner myself, I nearly collided with him. Hands on hips, he stood glaring down the long mud-colored hallway between Piers B and C. Also in that direction, according to the sign overhead, would be MAC, United, and Wings, then Delta, Northwest, and TWA.

Cloris was nowhere in sight.

"Check the women's room," George told me. "I'll check the men's."

The facilities in question lay diagonally across from the snack bar. If Cloris was nearly as breathless as I, she'd have ducked out of sight somewhere to recover. The women's room seemed most likely, but the men's room was a possibility, too.

My assigned room was divided by a central row of white porcelain sinks with sensors to turn them on when you passed your hands under the faucets. An older woman stood staring into one, apparently wondering where the handles were. Stalls on either side of the sinks sported shiny chrome doors. I peeked under all of them for Cloris's feet or a glimpse of paisley, but no luck.

I rushed back to the hallway and George. "You take the left," he said. "I'll take the right."

"Do we have to check every place? What if she just kept running?"

George threw me a hard stare. "She's no athlete, Gin. And we can't afford to backtrack."

Just then it occurred to me to wonder why George was alone, why legions of men in blue weren't swarming the place. Only one explanation fit: He was breaking the rules, literally trusting me with his career. My chest tightened, realizing how much depended on my calculations.

We had damn well better catch Cloris Huber.

The corridor remained undisturbed by running women. There were people with hand luggage to get by and a golf cart warbling that two-note warning used by European police cars. But no Cloris.

While George stuck his head in the doorway of a restaurant full of round oak tables, I hurried in and out of a dimly lighted arcade. There were two basketball games about the size of tall pinball machines in the back left corner, but their slanted black walls could not have hidden someone of Cloris's size.

Next on my side was a travel service desk, with the common barrier/window arrangement of a bank. The service person listened earnestly to a short woman who waved her hands in frustration. Nothing and no one could be concealed there.

George's opposite side consisted of a thirty-foot expanse of mirrored wall.

For me, an oriental-style store was next, with red silk kimonos hanging in a circular window. The store looked interesting, but it was too long and narrow and the merchandise too well-spaced for anyone to hide successfully.

Just past two yellow, unmarked, card-operated doors, George came to an open cluster of chairs and an escalator up to a private traveler's club. On the triangular wall of the escalator hung an attractive LIBATIONS sign sporting an eight-inch wooden olive soaking in a two-foot-wide martini glass.

The sign advertised a large and dim bar in the recess under the travel club. George would have to explore both quite carefully, so he motioned for me to continue. "I'll catch up with you."

I nodded and wished him luck.

Beyond the kimono store was a florist's glass greenhouse with everything inside clearly visible. For a hiding place I much preferred the card and book store just beyond. Blue lettering on white signs that resembled computer printouts labeled the travel, children's, and fiction sections. Another sign simply said BOOKS, BOOKS, BOOKS. I stepped into the travel section and Cloris Huber jumped from behind an Elmore Leonard display and bolted down the hall.

"George!" I shouted my loudest while keeping Cloris in sight. If I caught up to her without him, what would I do? Sit on her? What?

Nobody in the broad hallway wore a red sweater. No doubt George was upstairs describing Cloris to the receptionist inside the club. I stepped back four paces and shouted again. Then I turned on all the speed at my disposal. Next thing I knew I was face-down on the floor. My shoelace. I'd tripped on my stupid shoelace.

Cloris continued to run, stretching the distance between us.

I tied my shoe in record time, hopped to my feet, and glanced down the corridor.

Out of sight, just like a squirrel keeping me on the other side of the tree. This lady certainly seemed to know her airport.

I held my pace to a fast trot. Cloris knew approximately where I'd last seen her and might have doubled back just to fool me. Because of George's proximity, I doubted it, but anything was possible.

Just past a gray plywood wall where a future store would be, a side aisle offered a set of steps down to who knows where. I spent valuable seconds discovering that Cloris wasn't there.

So far as I could see, that is. Unfortunately, there were some nooks and crannies I didn't have time to check.

Actually, there were hiding places everywhere I was sure I missed, multiplying my concern with every step forward.

On the main aisle neither Cloris nor George were visible. I gave the long expanse of a Midway ticket area across the way a brisk walk-through, but it was fruitless. Then I checked behind a metal travel insurance machine and hurried on.

Running again, I paused to peek into a sports shop selling junk imprinted with the logos of each major Philadelphia team. I spent some precious breath shrieking George's name behind me one last time, but it was no good. A few lethargic travelers gawked at me, then quickly lost interest—just a daffy dame shouting for her husband, worried that he'd miss their plane.

I was beyond where George had checked, so I scurried side to side trying not to overlook possible hiding places anywhere along the wide walkway.

Pink neon signs on a shop to the right read PAPERBACKS and NEWSPAPERS. It looked familiar, and then I remembered stopping there the last time I flew. The clerk told me they didn't sell gum at the airport anymore. She had been surly and lazy enough for it to have been her idea, too.

Some distance behind me I was relieved to glimpse a spot of red—George racing down the steps from the club. By now I was a fair distance beyond him, outside a Colonial Buffet restaurant with square walnut tables. I had already glanced through its yellow, mullioned windows for Cloris Huber without success.

In the middle of the hall I jumped and waved my arms high to signal George. He waved back and began to sprint.

Meanwhile I checked another rest room. Then together George and I examined the last few businesses on the aisle— a barbershop just before CarToonTown on the corner and the Half-Shell raw bar across from that. The idea of oysters soured my mouth, but it may have been the taste of panic.

While we both paused for breath, George's eyes met mine briefly. Very briefly, for neither of us wanted to telegraph our fear.

"Let's go," he said and pointed toward another wide hallway carpeted in brick-colored tweed. Angling off to our left, it spanned the five-lane roadway used to drop off departing passengers.

I took another deep breath and rushed after him up the slope onto the lengthy bridge.

❀ *Chapter 40* ❀

Jogging side by side, George and I covered about thirty yards of the wide carpeted bridge over the departures road. On either side of us tall floor-to-ceiling windows were interrupted by little free-standing billboards advertising CD rates, car rental companies, and hotels. We passed a long row of newspaper dispensers and a rack of luggage carts marked $1.00.

George came to an abrupt stop at a bench beside a set of stairs. He put his hands on his hips and bent from the waist to ease his breathing. The stairs led down to the roadway; somebody had to check them. I cocked my head, and George nodded.

"I'm going into the garage," he told me. "Join me as soon as you can." Straight ahead, the parking facility constituted the main reason for the bridge.

I nodded again, unable to say more.

Cloris probably didn't have a car, or why fly to Cincinnati? But the parking garage would be an ideal place to elude pursuers. George had given me the far easier task of checking whatever lay between us and its pedestrian entrance.

There wasn't much to check. At the bottom of the stairs spread an easy view of the drop-off spots along the sidewalk. It became clear immediately that Cloris wasn't at any of them. Briefly stepping out into the road to check the Nissan, I could see a cop scratching Barney's head through my half-opened window.

I hurried back up to the bridge two steps at a time and glanced around for another exit.

Toward the garage entrance an overhead sign said GROUND TRANSPORTATION, and pointed to more stairs. But closer on my right was an alcove I nearly missed because I wasn't expecting it. An unobtrusive sign stated it accessed the TRAIN TO PHILADELPHIA.

The elevator in the center would take too long, and three yellow canvas rectangles shut off the escalator on the right.

I hurried to the glass-enclosed stairway on the left.

Halfway down to ground level I saw something paisley disappear around a cement corner on the platform below.

My first impulse was to run for George, but there wasn't time. I would have to take my chances without him.

For the benefit of my quivering knees, I reminded myself that Cloris couldn't possibly be carrying a gun. Not with today's airport security.

But after a few more steps, I decided to take out insurance. I retreated up the stairs, rummaging in my shoulder bag as I went. If I had to restrain a murderer, I didn't want it to be all day.

Facing away from the parking garage where I hoped George would see it, I ruined a whole tube of "Poppy Red" lipstick writing a great big GEO and an arrow pointing toward the stairs. My message didn't contrast too well with the reddish tweed carpet, but it would have to do.

An elderly man strolling by with his thumbs hooked behind his back scowled at me; I scowled back.

Then grabbing my purse strap in my fist, I scurried back down those cement stairs as fast as I could and cautiously opened the door.

The raised cement platform had only one track on either

side. Both were set into a strip of dark gray stones, which lay on top of some finer, liver-colored gravel.

The long platform offered very little concealment, just two rows of foot and a half wide posts, and the broad stairwell column. Cloris certainly trusted that she had lost us, because there was nowhere to go. Unless, of course, a train arrived.

None appeared imminent, however, because the platform seemed totally empty. For a second I even distrusted spotting Cloris from the stairs.

My shoes were quiet on the cement as I carefully approached the first pair of posts. While they weren't especially wide, they were wide enough to conceal a woman. I wondered if Cloris's squirrel instincts were working and whether I'd be quick enough to catch her.

The closer I got, the less I felt she was there. Some instinct told me to turn the other way.

At the far side of the near post, just as I began to turn the corner, Cloris came forward from the back of the stairwell. She headed for the door, intending to return to the bridge.

I stormed her like a banshee, screaming and swinging my purse at her head. She had partially opened the door, and I kicked it out of her grasp. She uttered an ''ugh'' and a couple of squeaks, elbowed me in the stomach, and ducked under my upraised arm.

Then she ran along the platform, going outside the left row of posts. I headed down the middle, trying to save space if she turned the corner. There just weren't that many things for her to do.

The final post was a problem. She used it as a foil, starting first one way then the other, trying to get me to commit to a direction like a base runner committed to stealing second.

I got my hand on a sleeve, but Cloris jerked her arm so hard one of my fingernails tore. My proximity must have scared her though, because she gave up the cat-and-mouse game and resorted to straightforward flight.

Racing toward the door she had the added choice of the stairwell as an even bigger barrier. There, if I guessed wrong, she could bolt for the stairs and I wouldn't have the time to prevent her escape.

Tackling her outright would be impossible. She was too big, for one thing, and the platform too narrow. I saw us plunging off the edge together and landing six feet below in a broken heap.

So I used the only other resource available—my purse. Running parallel to Cloris to secure an angle, I pitched it ahead of her legs about mid-calf level. In two tangled steps she was down with a sickening crack. She shrieked with pain and began to breathe in lusty gulps. Her glasses skittered across the cement.

I hurried forward to throw my body across her back. But she rolled to face me and moaned, "My knee."

Eluding me either by train or foot were now clearly out of the question. I had her.

"The police are coming," I said. "They'll get you a doctor."

Without glasses her eyes looked vulnerable and undressed, like something private you'd rather not see. I avoided them as she rocked on her shoulder and caressed her knee with one hand. The leg was canted under her strangely, but I didn't dare straighten it.

Sorry as I was about her injury, I felt an enormous relief that she was immobilized and I wouldn't have to chase after her anymore. My lungs burned, and my body throbbed. I retrieved her glasses and folded them beside her. Then I sat down next to her head and put my forehead on my knees.

We still had the platform to ourselves, and with the bridge overhead and the tracks down below, the still cool air and the sound of cars across the bunker, the spot felt like a large private room or maybe an empty sports stadium after the contest was over.

After a while I was able to speak, but it took a while longer to formulate the question.

"I'm curious," I finally said. "How did you find her?"

Cloris rolled her head to watch my face. "My mother?"

I nodded.

"Easy." She paused for breath. "She stayed with her Aunt Lila until she had me."

"In Cincinnati," I said. My mother had told me the same thing earlier that morning.

Cloris nodded once. "Lila put me with foster parents. I found her through them and my mother through her."

I could imagine sour old Lila's glee when Cloris sought her out, could hear her launching into her "After all I did for Iffy, look how ungrateful she's been" routine.

"Was Lila nice to you?" I meant recently, but Cloris misunderstood.

"Oh yeah. She was a darling. Placed me in a nice safe foster home with rats and roaches and a man turned out to have hands like anvils."

I was stunned. "The man beat you?"

"I wasn't pretty enough for anything else."

I felt my blood pressure rise and my stomach churn.

"What about the woman?"

A wry smile. "Every day from when I could talk to when I left she told me how glad she was I wasn't hers."

"But you got out of it, made something of yourself."

Cloris laughed humorlessly. "When I turned thirty, I thought to myself, 'What the hell do I have? An efficiency apartment and two pairs of shoes?' Mostly I was sick to death of being alone. So I decided to find my real mother. Winifred Bigelow. Lucky me." She intended to laugh again, but her lips were trembling too much.

Cloris closed her eyes then, and her breathing became ragged from pain.

"What was it you wanted from Iffy Bigelow?" I asked. "Money?"

The eyes flew open and glared at me a second. Then Cloris let her head rock back while she winced over something internal.

But then the physical pain took over, twisted her mouth into a grimace and screwed her eyes tight enough for a few tears to spill out.

"Were you blackmailing your mother? Did she refuse to pay?"

The head rolled side to side. "Not money. I never wanted money."

"What then?"

The glassy eyes solicited my sympathy. "Acknowledgement. That's all. I wanted her to admit she was my mother— she owed me that."

I nodded, trying to imagine the need for verification bending the course of a whole life. When Iffy gave up her illegitimate infant, the rejection was impersonal, an attempt to salvage two young lives.

Iffy's rejection of the adult daughter was another matter entirely. It constituted a fatal mistake.

"So many letters. She named me Florence, so that's how I signed them. Every couple months. Whenever I got the nerve."

"Asking her to acknowledge you?"

"Yes. She answered exactly once. 'I can't,' she said as if that was the end of it. Five years of writing to her, and all she said was, 'I can't.'" Cloris's body twisted with pain.

"So you came to Philadelphia."

"After I saved enough to move."

"How did you get the job with Arthur?"

"I wanted to know everything about my mother's life, where the money came from—everything, everything she kept from me. So I took my resume to Arthur's office, made it sound real good. Most of it was true. They put it on file. A few months later he called me."

I began to wonder if George would ever find us. Cloris's face was unnaturally white, and her arm felt cold. I was shivering once in a while myself. Lying on cement after so much exertion was surely worse. I looked around for something to cover Cloris with, but there was nothing, not even an old newspaper. Instead I put my purse under her head and smoothed her fuzzy hair out of the brush burns on her face.

"At the flower show—was that the first time you confronted your mother in person?"

She laughed that ironic laugh again, as if the joke was on her. "I told her in a note a couple days before that I was Florence. Thought that would be easier on her, easier than just blurting it out. It wasn't." She shut her eyes.

I guess to an outsider the theory made sense—present Iffy with flesh-and-blood reality when she was in her favorite element, when she should be feeling expansive, generous. How was Cloris to know that it was probably the worst possible time to approach her, a woman fighting for recognition, even prestige, in her chosen social arena. Before I met Temple Bodell and Beatrice Crumb, Howie Hancock and Jo Pescatore, Helen Luedeke and Alice Gifford—before I met Iffy Bigelow, I'd have made the same error in judgment.

Just then somebody came through the door to the platform, bumping a huge suitcase against it. A kid, maybe twenty. Tall, scrawny, bad complexion.

"Hey, over here," I shouted, not intending to leave Cloris's side. "We need help." He waddled over with his heavy valise and gawked down at us.

"Sure, lady. What can I do?"

I said we were expecting a policeman to come soon. Then I described George and asked the kid to check the bridge and the garage, too, if he could spare the time. Otherwise, would he please get us another cop?

"Sure thing, watch my case for me, will ya?" He dropped it heavily next to Cloris and loped up the stairs two at a time.

The suitcase was so old it appeared to be cardboard, with a scuffed green surface and fake leather corners like a desk blotter. The belongings inside couldn't have been very valuable but certainly meant something to the boy. Yet he entrusted them to me in a heartbeat.

I thought again of my stolen bracelet and the luxury of trust and all the other emotional comforts Cloris Huber had been denied.

We remained silent a while, waiting; but finally I told her, "I think your mother meant exactly what she said, that she wasn't *capable* of acknowledging you."

Cloris looked at me with a pathetic sort of anxiety that could have been mistaken for mild interest if I hadn't known better.

"She may have wished it were otherwise," I continued, "because she contacted my mother, most likely to talk about you, but she never managed broach the subject."

I was thinking aloud now, but certainly not to a disinterested audience. Cloris had all but stopped breathing, the way a kid does during a bedtime story, as if she were afraid I would close the book and turn out the light.

"I think your mother purposely flaunted her high standards so nobody would suspect she was just as human as anybody else. The scandalous Iffy Macleish from Ludwig became the flawless Mrs. Winifred Bigelow of Bryn Mawr.

"Unfortunately, climbing up on her pedestal involved stepping on a lot of heads. A lot of those people were waiting for her to fall." Beatrice Crumb and Howie Hancock, for two handy examples. "I don't think her ego could have taken that."

A few travelers had gathered for a train. One woman approached us, so I told her help was already on the way. Then a man asked outright what was wrong, so I gave him the same speech. Either the few others who were around heard my answer, or didn't care to become involved. The result was the same—we were still down on the fifty-yard line waiting for the stretcher while the spectators were busy leaving the stands.

I kept silent for a while, and Cloris closed her eyes again. Now and then she grimaced with pain, but mostly she rested.

I continued to think about Iffy, to imagine the morning of her death. She probably looked up from the inspection table and saw Cloris. Hoping to avoid an embarrassing confrontation, she probably rushed into the PHS Members' Lounge where Cloris was not permitted. Her daughter followed anyway, and they began to argue. Hiding nearby, Julia overheard Iffy shout "No" a few times before she ran for the sanctuary of the women's room. Somehow Cloris either maneuvered Iffy into the nearby storage area to finish their discussion, or to secure privacy Iffy herself insisted on going there.

The train pulled in with whooshes and thumps. The conductor who stepped out looked at us, and I waved him off. Then the half dozen people with luggage boarded, the conductor shouted something, and off they went.

"I guess you didn't think it would go quite so wrong," I said aloud.

Cloris opened her eyes, but she wasn't listening to anything out of a storybook now. Some street-smarts were evident, the same I'm-going-to-survive expression I caught along with her elbow in my stomach.

"Nobody can prove I was there," she said.

"There'll be something," I disagreed. Someone other than Julia might remember the beginning of their argument. Julia herself might come around. The redheaded photographer might even have a shot of Iffy and Cloris together. It was unlikely, but it was possible. There would be something. There had to be.

"It was you, wasn't it?" she asked me.

I didn't answer, just watched my hands as if I'd never seen them before.

Cloris sighed and rolled her head away. "The shamrock?"

I shrugged. The St. Patrick's Day plant had been a hint, as had her use of the word "pass" instead of "ticket" the first afternoon we met in Arthur's office.

Also, Cloris had avoided Iffy's Aunt Lila at the Bigelow house after the funeral. Originally, I figured her reason had been the same as mine: the woman was an insufferable bore. But after speaking to my mother, I realized Cloris hadn't wanted to be recognized by the source of her information about her mother.

Probably I should have been suspicious when no one answered my call to Arthur's office right after the body was discovered, but I hadn't been. I only recognized those clues in hindsight. And, of course, who except Julia could say whose presence at Bigelow's frightened her into a trauma?

The main reason I put things together was too embarrassing to admit. I didn't say it to Cloris, and I certainly didn't tell George when he and his wife came to dinner Sunday night. That stupid I'm not.

It was the shape of their nostrils, actually, Iffy's and her daughter's. I'd seen Iffy from her feet up when Mother opened the curtain and gave me a view of her body. "Twin keyholes" I remembered describing them to myself. Later that afternoon, I saw Cloris from below when she was up on the file cabinet watering a hanging plant. Something about viewing her from that angle bothered me, but at the time I thought it was because I'd just seen Iffy's corpse.

Only when I noticed Chelsea's swan earrings and began thinking for the second time how her earlobes were cookie-cutter duplicates of my own, did I start thinking about heredity and the tiny details that only a geneticist or a mother would ever notice.

My mother confirmed that Iffy had carried her child to term and that it had been a girl. She also told me Iffy lived with her aunt in Cincinnati during the pregnancy then allowed her aunt to place her daughter in a foster home.

Just like me, Cloris must have been thinking through her own version of what happened, because she started talking to the ceiling or maybe to herself.

"All she had to say was, 'Yes, I'm your mother,' one time. Just once." She turned toward me. There was vicious bitterness in her eyes along with the tears. "But it was never going to happen."

She stared at the underside of the bridge a few seconds longer, then turned away.

A couple minutes later George and the trusting, pimply-faced kid burst through the stairwell door.

❈ *Chapter 41* ❈

*B*efore leaving the airport I did something irresponsible and good. I charged four tickets to Florida for the next day. I could paint the inside of the clothes dryer until the motor quit. Plus the Nissan and I got by. Life is short.

At home I did my best to express how touched and grateful I was for the way Chelsea sent me off to the dangers of the airport. I didn't mention the exorbitant parking ticket I got, just that Barney kept the car from being towed. I hoped by the time she moved out on her own I found a pair of earrings with Irish setters on them. By then maybe she would understand what they meant, and maybe I would be adult enough to follow her example.

My grandmother insisted you should let people thank you if they feel they must. Refusing was impolite, possibly even unkind.

I kept reminding myself of that while Rip, Mother, and I had dinner with Arthur Bigelow at L'Auberge. The evening was meant to thank me for the return of Iffy's sable, which turned up in Cloris's luggage just as I predicted. (George was credited with apprehending Iffy's murderer, but evidently Arthur entered professionals in the accounting column marked PAID.)

He tried, he really tried to be a jovial host, but Didi had

only been in his employ a week and hadn't yet metaphorically loosened his tie. Five weeks later she invited him to stop at Pizza Hut after work, but he couldn't go because he was expected at a cocktail party. She quit that Friday and went to work on a roofer whose divorce had just become final. Six weeks on the job was a record for her anyway.

Julia recovered remarkably under the highly personal care of Dr. Willoby McDonald. They became engaged just before Cloris's trial.

Mother had saved a tapestry clutch purse of Iffy's for her, and the young woman grasped it throughout the ordeal as if it were the memory of Iffy herself. We sat together when she wasn't on the stand, and I peeked inside the purse once when she took out a tissue. There were keys and makeup and dry cleaner receipts and other scraps of paper that might have been notes about carpet sizes and caterers for all I knew. It reminded me to recommend Howie for the wedding flowers, and I think he got the job.

In a sense, Cloris's conviction accomplished the acknowledgement she craved. The front page of the *Philadelphia Inquirer* spelled out her mother's name for any subscriber who cared to read about it. Also, the TV news at six and eleven made their relationship clear long in advance of the expert testimony. I doubt that the context did much for Cloris's emotional health, but perhaps in time the prison therapist would help repair the damage.

In May Miles Pendergrass got tossed out of school for fighting, much to the relief of all his teachers. The family initiated a lawsuit, but that was inexplicably dropped. Regardless, Rip arranged for tutoring and a special homebound exam schedule so Miles could receive a diploma and proceed to attend whatever college would still take him. Last I heard he had three choices, all meat-and-potatoes places that would do him a world of good.

Later in the year Bryn Derwyn received a check from the Luedeke Foundation in the amount of $50,000. Rip was ecstatic, and I was relieved. My calculations, which I kept to myself, went something like this: After my insinuations about her, Helen giving the school nothing or $100,000 would have constituted either defiance, an admission of guilt, or gratitude for helping Miles. Most likely, giving the normal $50,000 meant absolutely nothing.

"We must be doing something right," Rip beamed over his celebratory brandy.

I drank to that. People in Rip's line of work need their illusions.

In prison, they call her the Sculptress for the strange
figurines she carves—symbols of the day she hacked
her mother and sister to pieces and reassembled them
in a blood-drenched jigsaw. Sullen, menacing,
grotesquely fat, Olive Martin is burned-out journalist
Rosalind Leigh's only hope of getting a new book
published.

But as she interviews Olive in her cell, Roz finds flaws
in the Sculptress's confession. Is she really guilty as
she insists? Drawn into Olive's world of obsessional lies
and love, nothing can stop Roz's pursuit of the chilling,
convoluted truth. Not the tidy suburbanites who'd
rather forget the murders, not a volatile ex-policeman
and her own erotic response to him, not an attack on
her life.

MINETTE WALTERS
THE SCULPTRESS

"Creepy but compulsive...The assured British
stylist doesn't let up on her sensitive probing of
two tortured souls...Hard to put down."
—*The New York Times Book Review*

The Edwina Crusoe Mysteries by MARY KITTREDGE

THE SARAH DEANE MYSTERIES BY

(❧) **J. S. BORTHWICK** (❧)

FROM ST. MARTIN'S PAPERBACKS
—COLLECT THEM ALL!

BODIES OF WATER
_____ 92603-0 $4.50 U.S./$5.50 Can.

THE CASE OF THE HOOK-BILLED KITES
_____ 92604-9 $4.50 U.S./$5.50 Can.

THE DOWN EAST MURDERS
_____ 92606-5 $4.50 U.S./$5.50 Can.

THE STUDENT BODY
_____ 92605-7 $4.50 U.S./$5.50 Can.

THE BRIDLED GROOM
_____ 95505-7 $4.99 U.S./$5.99 Can.